Girl Next Door

Girl Next Door

A Novel

Rachel Meredith

HARPER ● PERENNIAL

NEW YORK • LONDON • TORONTO • SYDNEY • NEW DELHI • AUCKLAND

HARPER ● PERENNIAL

Without limiting the exclusive rights of any author, contributor or the publisher of this publication, any unauthorized use of this publication to train generative artificial intelligence (AI) technologies is expressly prohibited. HarperCollins also exercise their rights under Article 4(3) of the Digital Single Market Directive 2019/790 and expressly reserve this publication from the text and data mining exception.

This is a work of fiction. Names, characters, places, and incidents are products of the author's imagination or are used fictitiously and are not to be construed as real. Any resemblance to actual events, locales, organizations, or persons, living or dead, is entirely coincidental.

GIRL NEXT DOOR. Copyright © 2025 by Rachel Meredith. All rights reserved. Printed in the United States of America. No part of this book may be used or reproduced in any manner whatsoever without written permission except in the case of brief quotations embodied in critical articles and reviews. For information, address HarperCollins Publishers, 195 Broadway, New York, NY 10007. In Europe, HarperCollins Publishers, Macken House, 39/40 Mayor Street Upper, Dublin 1, D01 C9W8, Ireland.

HarperCollins books may be purchased for educational, business, or sales promotional use. For information, please email the Special Markets Department at SPsales@harpercollins.com.

harpercollins.com

FIRST EDITION

Designed by Jamie Lynn Kerner

Library of Congress Cataloging-in-Publication Data has been applied for.

ISBN 978-0-06-343854-5 (pbk.)

25 26 27 28 29 LBC 5 4 3 2 1

Girl Next Door

1

When MC managed to find a spot on the overcrowded subway platform, she made sure nothing about her was disturbing anyone's personal space. Not her messenger bag, not her posture, not even her hair, a blond mess she'd partially wrangled into a topknot. Satisfied, she took out her book.

She was rereading a Rebecca Sloane novel, a self-soothing ritual she performed after breakups. This latest split had been typical—undramatic, blameless, and not MC's choice—so it called for the typical remedy. In this case, the passion and suffering of a Byzantine empress and her handmaiden. Their love was doomed, but it was beautiful and epic and, around the halfway mark, steamy. Though she was twenty-six and theoretically beyond getting excited by fingers brushing a wrist, MC blushed as a train arrived and she was carried by the human tide into the air-conditioned car.

She gripped the pole that ran above the seats. A napping woman in a shawl opened one eye to stare at her, like she knew.

"The next station is . . . Prospect Park."

MC's phone buzzed.

How are you still basically at home?

The train lurched into the tunnel and she lost service. Joe had summoned her to his office with zero notice, zero context, and a lot of all-caps messages about how he was freaking out. And no, he couldn't discuss why, just come, please and thank you.

She'd text him back in a minute.

She looked down at her book again. The empress was getting ready for a ceremony with some priests, and her handmaiden was getting handsy. It was classic Rebecca Sloane: Two women from the distant past were consumed by lust for each other, then cursed by society to either suffer or perish, or suffer and then perish. This was her most hopeful work, in that the lovers got to eke out a secret affair with the blessing of the gay emperor. In the epilogue, the handmaiden died of pneumonia on the Black Sea. Still.

MC knew Sloane's stories were old-fashioned, but they appealed to her on some primal level, for reasons she didn't understand, and didn't want to.

Trundling over the Manhattan Bridge, she pulled out her phone.

Train trouble, sorry!

Ughhhh

Just tell me what's going on?

Joe didn't reply. She figured he was in the middle of a conflict with a writer or minor television celebrity. Painful emails with someone's lawyer needed to be exchanged. He'd been increasingly stressed about work over the past year, calling her late at night or early in the morning to discuss contract details and pitches he was on the fence about. MC was a freelance writer herself, though she mostly worked in advertising these days, so she was a safe and knowledgeable sounding board. Also, highly available. Most importantly, they'd been inseparable since middle school and trusted each other in the way of old married couples—not that either of them knew any of those.

She got off at Canal Street and walked with her hands in her pockets, enjoying the late-afternoon breeze. It was early September. The warmth of summer lingered even as New York's businesslike pace left no doubt that fall had arrived. The scent of cinnamon drifted from a cart selling roasted nuts. Jackhammers pierced the hum of traffic. MC had grown up in a quiet Long Island suburb but adjusted to the sensory assault of the city in college; now she kind of liked it. It helped that when she graduated, she didn't immediately aspire to the office caste. For the past five years, she'd had the luxury of traveling during off-hours, experiencing the grind when it was a little less grinding. Freelance work had been her only option at the time, but now she was glad she'd ended up in it. She made her own schedule, sort of, and she was her own boss, more or less. She knew she wouldn't feel quite so serene if she weren't in good health or had to take care of someone. But for the moment, she was comfortable: an established professional with almost a dozen brands paying her to throw sentences together. And though she'd come to the city with the usual dream of being a real writer—a journalist, to be exact—the mildness of her ambition had at least spared her from the insanities of the media class. Which she had enough second-hand contact with anyway, thanks to Joe.

She arrived at the cast-iron building on Broadway where Jawbreaker kept its offices. The ground floor was home to a certain fast-fashion European clothing store where she'd bought too many things, including the black slim-fit men's T-shirt she was currently wearing. She took a door off to the side and stood in an elevator bank with several sharply dressed people in clear-framed glasses.

An elevator arrived, and they all shuffled in. MC remembered her first time riding to the fifth floor. It'd come as no surprise that her best friend was capable of ruling the world, or at least the arts-and-culture beat at the highbrow gossip hub of cubicle drones and young literary types everywhere. Being kept by his side on the way up had been a thrill and a relief.

"Mischa Celeste," Sheena called out from her desk, phone tucked against her shoulder. She liked to elongate MC's full name in a singsong voice, accentuating its absurdity, which never failed to delight Jerome, who sat across from her. He leaned back in his ergonomic chair as far as it would go, then tempted fate with another inch or two.

"New assignment?" he said.

"Does dealing with Joe count as an assignment?"

Jerome steepled his fingers. "He's been locked in his office all day."

"Any sense of what's going on?"

"I assumed a variation on the usual drama." He glanced over at Joe's door. "But the paranoid part of me is wondering if there's something else."

MC was about to ask for theories when a man in a matte-black tracksuit walked up to her.

"The woman of the hour," he said, his voice smooth.

It took MC a second to realize she was staring into the icy blue eyes of Seth Flanagan. She'd met Jawbreaker's founder on several occasions over the last few years, mostly at their infamous holiday parties, but was pretty sure he didn't know her name.

Yet here he was, smiling at her.

"Um," she said, convinced he'd confused her with someone else and not sure how to explain it politely.

"Looking forward to Monday," he said.

And then he continued on to one of the glass conference rooms.

She turned back to Jerome and whispered, "What was that?"

Jerome looked stunned. "No idea."

Sheena uncrossed her legs—clad in the usual fishnet stockings—and leaned toward them. "He and Joe had a long-ass meeting this morning." She raised an eyebrow.

"About what?" MC asked.

"You," Sheena said, "would be the only person who's allowed to even attempt to figure that out." She readjusted the phone. "Hi, yes, I'm still here—"

MC took a deep breath, exchanged a final look with Jerome, and walked up to Joe's door.

It flew open before she even had a chance to knock.

"Finally," Joe breathed, waving her in with a frantic hand. As soon as she'd passed the threshold, he drew back to pace behind his desk, his normally perfect curls in disarray. "Close the door behind you."

"Are we in the Matrix right now?" she said, looking over her shoulder. "Are agents coming for us?"

He dropped into his chair and stared at her, the arched lines of his brows high and expectant. He was framed by a wall of shelves stuffed with edgy collections from writers MC had never heard of, corkboards plastered with dimly lit pictures of him with journalists, poets, and podcasters. "Actually, yeah, kind of."

She blinked.

"Sit," he said, his catlike hazel eyes more shadowed than usual. "You're making me nervous."

"I'm making *you* nervous?" She settled into the big leather chair across from his desk. "I hear you had a long meeting with Seth Flanagan."

Joe winced but said nothing.

"I guess that's not nearly as weird as him calling me 'the woman of the hour' just now."

His gaze fell to her lap, where she was still loosely holding the book. "Is that Rebecca Sloane?"

"You mean the high-water mark of eighties historical fiction?" She palmed the paperback. "Why yes."

"Not over Lisa dumping you yet?"

"Getting there."

"Well, I've got something that'll make you forget about her for the rest of your life." He picked up a book from his desk. "You haven't read this. I know, because if you had, you'd be losing your shit."

The cover was highlighter pink, with a cutesy illustration of two women on either side of a picket fence, oh-so-close to kissing. *Girl Next Door*, by S. K. Smith. According to the banner at the top, it was a *New York Times* bestseller.

MC was confused. "Is that a romance novel?"

"Technically, it's a rom-com." Joe's eyes were sparkling now, his exhausted slump replaced by a giddy, spring-loaded perch. "And the only thing crazier than its fan base is the fact that no one has any idea who the author is. I called every publishing boy I've ever slept with to check." He grinned. "S. K. Smith is a bona fide mystery—no bio, no interviews, no nothing."

"Okay . . ."

"Are you ready for me to blow your mind?"

"Not really?"

He took a breath.

"This," he said, pointing at the blonde on the cover, "is you."

And who is that? she almost asked, her eyes moving over to the dark-haired girl on the other side of the fence.

But she already knew.

2

Joe signaled to the bartender. "Whiskey on the rocks and a vodka soda."

MC was too disoriented for a drink. They'd left the Jawbreaker office and migrated to a poorly lit bar where even the draft beer was overpriced. Visually, though, it fit the profile of the archetypal literary dive she'd fantasized about as a teenager: vintage metal signs hung askew, broken sconces, unoccupied booths in red velvet. It was early evening, so the atmosphere was placid. At least there was that.

MC wasn't sure what Joe had been expecting when he'd presented her with the revelation that her childhood neighbor had secretly written a smash-hit rom-com cribbed directly from their senior year of high school, in which she and MC were not distant acquaintances, as they had been in real life, but madly in love. It probably wasn't her staring into space and trying to recall the only moment of potential significance that had ever passed between them.

Despite having lived forty feet apart for fifteen years, MC and Nora Pike were never friends. Nora didn't have friends. She'd been an oddball since elementary school, abrupt and prickly in conversation, when she was willing to talk at all. The only time she and MC had spent together was when they were on the literary magazine. MC had been elected editor in chief after her comic takedown of *The Old Man and the Sea* in English 12; Nora had been tasked with using her layout software skills on the sorry-looking printout the club issued at the end of every year. The teacher who served as the advisor had promised her extra credit.

But even as they'd spent long hours together, arranging terrible poems and stories alongside terrible art and photography, their dynamic remained distant. Sometimes they might have shared a smile or a semi-triumphant moment. Other than that, it was all business.

Then the magazine's reading night had rolled around.

The event had drawn a crowd. Even Nora was in a decent mood. She'd gone from being a reluctant presence at their bimonthly meetings to an unofficial co-editor with MC by spring, delivering an actual publication that put the much-better-funded yearbook to shame. Performances of student writing were met with cheering and applause—especially an anonymous poem that MC had been cajoled into presenting in lieu of the real author.

"On the Look You Give (Before Turning Away)" had come in just before the end of the year. Nora, who served as the submissions gatekeeper on account of her excellent organizational skills, refused to reveal the author's identity. It was the only thing from *Explorations* that'd been passed around the school at large, its short, precise verses perfectly capturing the speaker's overwhelming desire for a person who couldn't or wouldn't acknowledge what was between them.

The after-party was bigger than the reading, a culmination of all the parties that'd been hosted at MC's house that year, which had become their default hangout spot after her mom had moved out the previous summer and her dad had become a lot more permissive, or at least a lot less involved. It didn't hurt that her older brother, Conrad, had decided to drop out of Harvard in March and had little to do but work at the grocery store and look the other way whenever they wanted to buy alcohol. MC had figured his sudden return had something to do with their parents' impending divorce. But he refused to discuss it, at least with her.

Around midnight, when the party was in full swing, MC had decided to head to the basement for another case of beer. She needed a last swig of courage. A moment to gather herself before taking command of a situation she'd been agonizing over for two years: her longstanding crush on fellow *Explorations* member Gabby Ramirez, whose tendency to earnestly compliment MC while making intense eye contact had fostered something like love.

Unfortunately, MC didn't quite get to the beer. Or her confession. Because when she made it to the foot of the basement stairs, she saw Gabby was already making out with someone else on the old suede couch.

And that someone was Conrad.

MC had fled to the shadows of an elm tree in their yard. She could still hear her friends' drunken antics, but the high of the night was gone for her. In its place was a sense that she'd been a fool not to see this coming. Her brother might've been a dropout, but he was an Ivy League dropout, and the glory of his time at Green Hills High hadn't faded.

"Your adoring fans," Nora said flatly, "are wondering where you are."

MC had noticed her walking out the back door, arms folded, but hoped they wouldn't interact. She wasn't in the mood to be seen, especially by the person least likely to show sympathy.

Nora was about the same height as MC, with choppy, shoulder-length black hair permanently pulled up in a ponytail.

That she'd made the effort to maintain bangs was one of senior year's big surprises. She was in all black, as usual, with a thick application of eyeliner.

MC sighed. "They're your fans too."

Nora had gone through a minor social transformation over the spring, her good taste earning respect from even the harshest critics in the club. Not that she seemed to care.

"I'm going home," she said.

"Already?"

"It's boring in there."

MC toed a tree root. "Can I ask you something?"

"I don't know, can you?"

MC was used to Nora's rudeness by that point and skipped over it. "Did my brother write that poem? The anonymous one." He wasn't a student anymore, but he was only a year out. And after he'd become the supplier of their parties, he'd basically turned into an honorary member of the club; maybe he'd bribed Nora into putting the poem in as an overture to Gabby.

"Nope."

MC blew out a breath. She was relieved, even if it didn't change anything.

"Did you like it?" Nora added, her tone slightly less assured.

"Are you kidding? It's the best piece in the magazine. No offense to everyone else."

"You seemed pretty nervous when you had to read it tonight."

MC laughed. "I guess I'm not too smooth when it comes to that sort of thing."

"What sort of thing?"

"Uh, reciting sensual poetry?"

"I thought you did a good job." It wasn't just Nora's tone that'd changed. It was her whole expression. Her posture wasn't so confrontational, her green eyes wide in the moonlight. But as she took a breath—maybe to say something more—a shattering sound came from inside the house. MC seized on it, because an inexplicable panic had begun to rise in her chest.

"Shit," she said, "hope that's not my dad's pottery."

"Yeah," Nora replied, snapping back from whatever had possessed her, "good luck with that."

And then she walked toward the picket fence between their houses without another word.

MC hadn't thought much about their exchange at the time. She'd been too preoccupied with Conrad and Gabby, whose kiss blossomed into a full-blown relationship over the summer. The only way she could distract herself from the romance filling her house was with the prospect of breaking away. She and Joe were headed to the city for college in the fall, a turning point they readied themselves for by acquiring piercings, overpriced haircuts, and an encyclopedic knowledge of gay bars across the five boroughs. Whenever the subject of Nora Pike had come up again in later years, which wasn't often, their conversation under the elm tree had flickered in MC's mind. But she'd refused to linger on it. Too confusing. And anyway, life in the city had been just what MC had hoped—an existence free of her brother's shadow.

"Still among the living?" Joe said.

The bartender had brought over their drinks.

"Theoretically." MC pressed the cold tumbler to her forehead. Had Nora really written that poem about *her*? It still didn't feel possible. But there were more immediate concerns: "Do you think anyone else from Green Hills has read this?"

Joe had put the book on the bar between them. She'd avoided looking at it, like it might burn her eyes, but now she couldn't help staring at the swooping font, the pastel palette, the cartoon protagonists. The flap copy was damning: *Back in high school, Nicole Penny had it bad for Michaela Carson. But Michaela was too hopelessly obsessed with Abby Rodriguez—her brother's hot new squeeze—to notice.* She'd panic-scrolled reviews back at Joe's office. The novel was "charming, stylish, and dazzling," yet somehow also "refreshingly down to earth." Nicole, the main character, was "whip-smart and not afraid to show it," while Michaela was "next-level clueless in the most adorable way." MC had been shocked that anyone would refer to a romance between teenagers as "unabashedly sexy," but then Joe had explained that only the first couple of chapters took place during high school, while the rest detailed a ten-years-later reconnection between Michaela, a bestselling novelist, and Nicole, a curmudgeonly librarian with a heart of gold.

None of it should've mattered. MC didn't care if Nora Pike had made it big. Even if she'd done it by twisting the quiet agony of MC's senior year into a cute little romp.

Joe tucked the book under his arm, plucked up his vodka soda, and guided them toward a booth.

"Gabby would be the likeliest to have bought something like this," he said. "But if she'd read it, she would've told Conrad, who would've told you."

"Or maybe she did read it," MC muttered, "and now she thinks I was *hopelessly obsessed* with her the whole time she and my brother were falling in love and would prefer never to speak to me again."

"To be fair, you were hopelessly obsessed."

"I was hopeless. Not obsessed."

"You sure about that?"

"She's my sister-in-law!"

"You gave a weird toast at their wedding."

MC put her face in her hands. "Is this actually happening?"

"The fact that you're in a rom-com? Or that you got written as the Oblivious But Sexy Love Interest?"

"Both." She sipped her whiskey and wished it was a beer. "What'd you get written as?"

"The Envious Asshole."

"Envious of who?"

"You."

"That makes no sense."

He shrugged. "She has you as the most popular girl in high school."

Puja Singh, class clown and homecoming queen, had been the most popular girl in their high school. Or Trish Tanner-Cruz, who was now working in the White House. Friendly, unassuming MC Calloway?

No.

"And you're one hundred percent sure it's us?" she said.

"I don't think you need me to review the names."

"What does she call *Explorations*?"

"*Discoveries*."

"Green Hills?"

"White Springs." Joe leaned back. "But the book isn't the story here. It's Nora. And if there's anyone who can tell Nora's story, it's you."

He'd already made this suggestion, back at the office. She'd already swiftly shut it down.

"I know this feels weird as hell," he said. "But it's the opportunity of a lifetime. Everyone wants to know who S. K. Smith is. What she looks like, what she cares about, what she cooks for dinner."

"I have no idea what Nora cooks for dinner. And I'm not outing her."

"Why not?"

"Because it's totally immoral."

"What're you going to say if Gabby or Conrad actually do read it?"

"I don't know. That it's made up?"

"They're not going to believe you."

"Because something with a cartoon on the cover is so incredibly realistic?"

"No, because it makes so much sense."

MC stared.

"Maybe you weren't cheerleading captain or valedictorian, but everyone really liked you." He smirked. "Even the grumpy girls in black."

"Joe," she groaned.

"Then you graduated and disappeared."

"I still visit."

"For, like, three hours on Thanksgiving and Christmas."

"You don't go back either." But that was because Joe's parents didn't live there anymore.

"I'm just saying, to Conrad and Gabby—and probably a bunch of other people—there's missing context about why you've kept your distance. This provides it."

"Appears to provide it." She sucked down her drink. She didn't like to think about how the chilliness between her and her brother was rooted in a moment of teenage jealousy. But she and Joe both knew there were other reasons she'd let things go by the wayside over the years, and they were more complicated than her best friend seemed to want to acknowledge just then.

"Even if I'm not happy about this book, I'm not going to write an exposé in revenge."

"Don't think of it as an exposé. Think of it as a multilayered meta mindfuck."

She gave him a sour look. "Is that how you pitched it to Seth Flanagan?"

He had the grace to blush. "I mean, the idea wasn't exactly formed when I spoke to him."

"Then why'd you speak to him at all? Why didn't you come to me first?"

He shifted in his seat a little. "That was my original plan."

"But?"

"Our editorial meeting was already on the books for this morning. And I had nothing to throw out there, so . . ." He played with his napkin. "I should've talked to you. But I've been getting a lot of heat lately."

"What kind of heat?"

"Clicks are down. Everyone's nervous. We need a big story." He cleared his throat. "I need a big story."

MC sighed.

"Look, this morning I woke up with an insane hangover at this guy's house, freaking out about the meeting. And when I went to take an anxiety poop, I started flipping through this book next to the toilet, which I assume was left there by his lesbian lioness of a roommate, and it just felt like . . . godsend."

"You could've at least texted me."

"I know. But I wanted to figure out how to sell you on it."

"Sell me?"

"I knew this would freak you out. It would freak anyone out. And of course you'd feel disoriented."

"Disturbed." MC took a sip of Joe's drink. "Deeply."

"But also, it's a major opportunity for both of us—"

"For you."

"—and I think it'd be a big mistake to dismiss it before we've looked into its potential."

"New idea." She pressed her fingers to her temples. "What if you just told Nora you figured her out, and you want to do a profile on her?"

He shook his head. "This is Jawbreaker. The second we let it slip that we've figured her out, her team goes to the *New York Times* or *The Cut*. Our opportunity is killed. And then I am killed, by Seth Flanagan."

"What exactly did you promise him?"

Joe took a breath. "An official pitch to the A-team. Me and you. On Monday."

MC closed her eyes.

"Everyone is going to be so excited, MC! We can pull this off."

"I haven't spoken to Nora since high school."

"So?"

"Conrad and Gabby invited her to their wedding, and she didn't come, even though it happened in our yard, which is literally outside her kitchen window. What makes you think she'll so much as pick up the phone if I call?"

"I don't expect you to call."

She frowned. Then it dawned on her.

Joe expected her to engage with the multilayered meta mindfuck by entering it.

She had to laugh. "No."

"Text your brother. Tell him you want to get in some quality time together this weekend, it's been too long, blah blah. Perfect position to lay a sneak attack."

"Nope, nope, nope."

"Nora will open up to you."

"We don't know that."

"Oh yes we do."

"I'm not going to be your secret agent on this." Her chest was burning. She'd drank her whiskey too fast. "Sorry, there's just no way."

"Why not?"

"Because it's wrong! And weird." And the last thing she wanted to do was to spend *quality time* with Conrad.

"This isn't her diary. It's a novel she submitted to an agent, then sold to a publisher, then got paid for."

"I gave you my answer." She took a gulp of water. "If you want to break the scoop or whatever, you'll have to do it yourself."

"Except I have no story. Just a name."

"Maybe that's a sign to find a different story."

"But this book is about *you*. That's why you have to do it."

A long pause stretched between them. MC started to feel guilty, the way she always did when someone expected something of her. She wanted to figure out a solution of some kind, a compromise at the very least—this was her best friend, the person who'd been by her side through everything. He'd even been her first kiss, an impulsive, experimental, and truly awkward meeting of the mouths.

But what he was asking for was too much.

When he spoke again, his voice was quiet. "Also, word on the street is I'm getting fired."

She almost choked on her water. "What?"

"Not right now. At the end of the year." He managed to keep his tone light. "Jerome's girlfriend went to grad school with Seth's. She let it slip that there's a restructuring coming."

MC didn't know whether she was more stunned at the news or the fact that Joe had kept it from her for what sounded like weeks. They'd been friends for long enough that she knew he'd always have some secrets, as she'd have hers.

But this was big.

"Technically it's only a rumor," he said, sounding so cavalier she almost believed he was okay. "But I guess I'm feeling like I need to do something major."

"I'm sorry, Joe. That sounds incredibly stressful."

He shrugged. "It's the business. I just wanted you to know I wouldn't be asking you to chase this otherwise."

She stared at him, the boy who'd walked out in the middle of his British Lit final freshman year of college when she'd texted him, hands shaking, that her dad had died of a sudden heart attack. She hadn't even figured out her summer plans yet. But when she'd confessed that she couldn't handle being back home for three months, where her mom and Conrad would be obsessing over logistics with their usual stoicism, he'd insisted she stay with him in his student housing as long as she needed. Even with an internship at *The New Yorker*, he still found time to cook for her in the dorm kitchen or watch an old movie to pass a Friday night.

"I won't write the article," she said slowly. "But I'll try to get in touch with Nora. See if there's anything there."

Joe crumpled to the table, staring up at her through his curls. "For real?"

"One visit," she warned. "That's it."

He looked like he was about to clap, then sat on his hands and wiggled.

3

All MC wanted was to have the apartment to herself that night, even just for thirty minutes. She needed to shower. To remember that the world was exactly the same as it'd been before Joe had texted her that afternoon, before he'd shown her that stupid book. But when she reached the third floor, she saw the usual deathtrap of fixed-speed bicycles and Pat's longboard.

"What up?" said Pat, standing in the kitchen. He was drinking brine from a jar of dill pickles that belonged to MC.

"Not much," she said.

He flipped his long brown hair out of his eyes. "Want a sip?"

"I'm good."

"Oh my god," said Laura, emerging from their bedroom half-dressed, red hair mussed at the back. "Loved that book."

MC tucked *Girl Next Door* into her bag, even though there was no way anyone would associate her with the blonde bombshell on the cover. "A client recommended it."

"The literary magazine stuff is so cute." Laura grabbed the pickles from Pat and gulped. After she'd exhaled with pleasure, she said, "And the scenes where everyone's all grown up . . . ugh. It's, like, one of the most romantic things I've ever read."

"Trail of rose petals to the bed?" Pat cooed.

"The emotions are just dead-on."

"Wow," he said, winking at MC, "hot."

Laura put the pickles back in the fridge. "It actually is hot. There's this one scene—"

MC coughed and said, "I should go get changed."

"Party night?" Pat said.

"Sleep night. Long day."

She turned and walked as fast as she could down the long, dark hall to her room with its one barred window overlooking what was supposed to be a courtyard but was really just an open-air love motel for feral cats. She wanted to shake off her increasing sense of doom. But when she flopped down on her futon and opened her bag, the twin specters of *Theodora's Concubine* and *Girl Next Door* spilled out to haunt her.

Freshly overwhelmed, she put on her pajamas, pulled up *The Matrix* on her laptop, and lost herself in the green-and-black glow until she passed out.

The next morning, she woke up late, got dressed in a disoriented haze, and went for a walk on Eastern Parkway. The pedestrian path ran alongside the bike lane, a jet of activity that normally absorbed her attention. She'd always been a people watcher. She was a people person, or at least a certain kind of people person, fascinated by the infinite variety of experiences and perspectives out in the world. But today she felt exposed, singled out, though no one gave her so much as a passing glance.

By the time she'd looped back to her apartment, she'd convinced herself to get some work done. Real work, for a normal client. Something to take her mind off what she said she'd do for Joe.

But then she found him standing in her kitchen. In an apron.

"Dear god," she said.

He smiled. "Hope you're hungry."

She sat in one of the threadbare couches crammed like circled wagons in the common room. Pat's bong was on the coffee table, along with some half-melted candles and their fourth roommate Zeke's tarot deck.

"When you said 'mission prep brainstorming sesh,' I assumed it would take place somewhere that is not my gross living room."

Joe's big, sunny one-bedroom was a mere five blocks away, in a much nicer building, on a much nicer street. But last year, when he'd asked her to keep being his roommate, just in a much more luxurious setup, she'd had to turn him down. She couldn't afford any of the places he was looking at with his latest raise from Jawbreaker. He'd offered to split rent unevenly, but they both knew it would get awkward. So they'd started living apart. Joe had been self-conscious about the situation ever since. But it was fine. He was always at her place anyway.

"I was craving more of a scrappy PI vibe than lesbian James Bond," he said, vigorously grating a potato. "Look in my bag, by the way."

"I'm starting to develop a Pavlovian response to your surprises."

"Salivation?"

"Panic attack."

"I'm making you an exquisite hashbrown. Open the bag."

She looked into his black pleather backpack. "Yearbooks? Are you serious?"

"If we're going to pull this off, we need to be prepared."

"I agreed to check things out for you. That's it. No preparation needed."

"First thing to note: Nora doesn't have any social media. The only thing I could find about her online is that she works at the town library."

"Just like in her book," MC grumbled, pouring coffee into a chipped mug. "And let's not forget her heart of gold."

"How much of it did you read?"

"None."

"Really?"

"Really."

"It's not as bad as you think."

She sipped her coffee. "I seem to recall a review that described my character as 'next-level clueless.'"

"I think that's reductionist. Not that I'm trying to defend Nor Dog." He wrapped the shredded potato in a dishcloth and squeezed. "You should just read it."

She grimaced at the yearbooks again. "Pretty sure all we'll find about her in here is, like, one photo."

"Senior quote: 'Two roads diverged in a yellow wood, and I took the one that led to *royalties*.'" Joe turned on the burner and groaned when he looked in the cabinet. "Not a single cast-iron."

"What's wrong with nonstick?"

"That you even need to ask." He lit a cigarette. "Can you look in the lazy Susan, Lazy Susan?"

"The name's Michaela Carson, remember? I'm going to open a window."

After Joe had fried up omelets, hashbrowns, and perfectly crunchy bacon, they sat down at the coffee table and poured mimosas.

MC went for senior year, their main focus, and looked up Nora's portrait.

"Jeez," she said, "I forgot they made all the girls wear a black velvet neckpiece."

Joe leaned over, already smoking another cigarette. "Wow."

"What?"

He smiled. "Nor Dog was actually low-key fine."

"You realize saying things like 'low-key fine' makes us seem even older than we are?"

"I mean, do we think she's high-key hot now?"

"I have no idea."

Nora's choppy black hair stood out among the middle-parted, flat-ironed looks of every other girl on the page, as did an intricate silver chain around her neck. MC tapped the jewelry with her finger.

"Her parents were always traveling for work," she said. "Azerbaijan, Malaysia..."

"So, they were CIA agents."

"International business consultants."

"Same difference." He squinted at her. "Did you ever see inside her house?"

"No."

"It's okay, you can tell me if you guys were secret lovers."

"We weren't."

"I'll be sad you didn't trust me, but also, I'll get over it."

"Joe, we never even kissed."

"But did you want to?"

"Wouldn't have occurred to me."

"Too busy being hopelessly obsessed with someone else, weren't we?" He flipped to Gabby's portrait. *College should be a breeze for you,* she'd written to him in loopy scrawl. *All-nighters aren't hard when you spend the day in a coffin!* MC blinked, then remembered that Gabby had taken to calling him a vampire on account of his general sleeplessness. They'd all had so many inside jokes back then.

It didn't take long to go through the yearbooks. Nora hadn't done any clubs, sports, or activities, except *Explorations*, and even that had only been for a year. She hadn't stood for the National Merit Scholars picture or the National Honor Society picture. She didn't go to dances, pep rallies, or even bake sales, and thus made no appearance in the candids either.

MC, however, was in an embarrassing number of them. Joe, too, with his gelled, Cup Noodles hair and massive flannels. They looked young. Oblivious and hyperaware all at once. MC was stunned by how many vests she'd owned.

"I wish I had a copy of the mag," Joe said. "Do you think Gabby has one?"

"Probably." Gabby had been the most sentimental member of their crew. "Is that poem in Nora's book, by the way?" She hoped she sounded casual. "The anonymous one?"

"No. But there's a reading-night scene."

She sipped her mimosa. "And an after-party scene?"

"That's the big one."

"Meaning?"

"It's when Nicole and Michaela have their first kiss, and then an epic fight, and end up going their separate ways."

She stiffened. "What do they fight about?"

"Are you sure none of this happened?"

"For the hundredth time, none of this happened." At least, not the way Nora had written it.

Joe pursed his lips. "Basically, they're getting into it when 'Abby' walks in on them. Michaela gets flustered, which makes Nicole—who has the usual trust issues—feel shitty."

"And what does Michaela say about all this?"

"She admits that she's still really into Abby."

"Wow. Flattering."

"You said none of it happened."

"There are ... parallels."

"That's what makes this such a fun mess to untangle." He smiled. Then his phone buzzed. "Gotta take this real quick." Ashing his cigarette in the candle, he put the phone to his ear and said, "Oh my god, it's been *forever* ..."

Overwhelmed, MC leaned back and tried to tune Joe out.

Then she realized who he was talking to.

"Joseph Khoury!" she hissed, launching herself from the cushions. "Get back here!"

She chased him down the hall like they were fifteen.

He locked her bedroom door in her face like they were twelve.

"Thanks, Con, I really appreciate you getting back to me so fast," he was saying. "No, she's totally fine."

She wanted to scream, but Laura was walking into the apartment just then, waving at her from the other end of the hall. MC waved back.

"She's just been super absorbed in writing a novel," Joe was saying.

MC seethed in silence.

"I know, right? I thought she'd given up on the writing thing. But she's just been keeping to herself, working away at it, and now she's really close to finishing. The only thing is, it's impossible to focus here. You wouldn't even believe what a coworking space costs. That's why I thought maybe she could crash with you and Gab? Like, just for a few days? She'd never want to impose on you, but I think it'd be super helpful." He lowered his voice. "Also, between you and me, she's kind of going through a rough time. I'm sure she'll tell you more about it."

MC closed her eyes.

"Amazing," he said. "She's going to be thrilled."

The door opened a minute later. Joe was smiling like he'd just gotten laid.

"Thrilled?" she said.

"You will be, when this story launches you into literary stardom."

"I won't be writing a single word. Of an article or a novel."

"A journey of a thousand miles . . ."

She sighed. "Begins in Green Hills, apparently."

4

*G*irl Next Door felt like a cursed relic in MC's messenger bag, giving off an evil pulse. But she could handle that. What she couldn't handle was seeing it displayed at a newsstand she passed in Penn Station, then shouted out in a queer pop culture email blast she subscribed to, after which she was served an ad for it as she tried to scroll the paper.

It was Thursday afternoon, and she'd just managed to catch the LIRR, sweaty from her subway commute yet also freezing in the powerful air-conditioning. Her black T-shirt clung to her skin as the train pulled out.

She reminded herself that *Girl Next Door* was ultimately just an annoyance. Something to be lived with and not considered too deeply, until it inevitably dropped off the bestseller list and faded away. Whatever had come out of Nora Pike's imagination had nothing to do with MC's lived experience. And even if maybe in some ways it did, any insights would've been come upon by chance, and were thankfully locked in time, nine years ago, irrelevant to her present moment.

A few nights with her brother and Gabby, however, could not be compartmentalized. Despite Joe's accusations, she did come home for more than just three hours at a time. But he was right that she stuck to the major holidays and never stayed over.

An hour later, the train whistled. MC winced and uncurled herself. She'd had her knees braced against the seat in front of her for most of the ride, slouched as low as her spine would allow.

"*This station is . . . Green Hills.*"

The doors rolled open. MC walked out. The weather was sunny and warm. She tried to revive herself with it, taking deep breaths as she climbed the stairs to the overpass. For a few moments, she had a bird's-eye view of the beat-up hybrid Gabby had been driving since high school, which was now the family car. A car that, once upon a time, MC had fantasized about getting stuck in with Gabby as an ominous weather event took place outside.

"Hiii!" Gabby called from the open window.

"Hey!" she said, smiling with so much force she wondered if she looked insane. "The Destroyer of Worlds is still with us."

"And still getting fifty miles to the gallon, baby." Gabby got out of the car, wearing an oversize tank top and cutoff jean shorts. She barreled into MC, throwing her arms around MC's neck. "I'm so glad you're visiting."

"Thanks for having me," MC said.

Gabby let go and smiled. She had an easy, good-natured grin with an unwholesome edge to it, a combination that'd given MC butterflies in high school. "I cannot *wait* to read this novel of yours."

"Well," MC said, trying to keep her tone even, "it's anybody's guess whether it'll ever see the light of day."

"Of course it will! Ms. Kim said she's been waiting for you to do this since you graduated."

Their senior year was Ms. Kim's first as an English teacher at Green Hills High. She'd volunteered to be the advisor of *Explorations*, among other roles, and MC assumed her above-and-beyond involvement in student life was why she'd already climbed to the role of principal. At fortyish, she was probably the youngest person to ever hold the title there. She hadn't been afraid to pick an even younger vice principal in Conrad. Though he'd graduated by the time she started, his reputation must've gotten back to her, as she'd poached him only a few months ago from the fancy private school where he'd just gotten some Teacher of the Year award. MC had learned about these developments from her brother's Instagram that summer, where he'd posted a picture of himself with some of his old students, followed by a supposedly goofy but clearly just handsome picture of him in high school, under which he'd written a never-ending caption about his journey in education and the humbling power of return. **Congrats dude,** she'd texted him. Thx, he'd replied.

"Do you still call her Ms. Kim?" MC said, throwing her bag in the footwell and getting in the passenger seat.

"She was like, call me Jae! And I was like, I literally can't." Gabby turned the car on. "We'll probably see her when we pick your brother up. They've been pulling a lot of late hours."

"Classic."

"When he was MIA before, I was like, okay, it's a commute. But now, I don't know. I got my hopes up he'd be home more."

"I'm sure it's just first-week madness."

They drove down Main Street. Green Hills looked the same as ever. Scrubby woods and strip malls, fast food and drugstores. A deli that served pretty good sandwiches. A new bakery that was vegan, gluten-free, and virtually abandoned. The Mexican place had gotten a fresh awning. The Chinese restaurant was still extremely brightly lit. There was one playground—empty—and two churches, also empty.

"So," Gabby said, "how's the city? How's Joe?"

"Both good. Joe says hi."

"I wish he'd come visit too. I miss his weird jokes."

"Maybe he'll be around at some point," MC said, though she sincerely hoped he wouldn't. "How's work been?"

"Predictable. All my teens are living in one big, nonstop anxiety attack."

"Some things never change."

"Every Monday I'm like, why did I go to school for social work?"

MC could've told her it was because she was kind, a good listener, easy to be around. But she worried that would sound too intense. "Are you at least enjoying the telehealth lifestyle?"

"I'm definitely happy to be away from my boss. But it's also kind of lonely."

"Have you thought about office space?"

"Yeah, just seems like such an unnecessary expense with the whole house . . ."

MC wondered if Conrad was paying rent to their mom, who was still out in LA. She'd never had the guts to ask. "I know what you mean," she said quickly. "I feel bad when I buy a cup of coffee."

"Well, I'm glad that economics has forced us back together." Gabby smiled. "Do I get to know what your book's about, by the way?"

MC felt heat rising to her cheeks. "It's, uh . . . I'm kind of at the point where it just feels like the worst thing ever?"

"Don't be silly. I bet it's brilliant."

MC was saved by their arrival at the school, a sprawling one-story building with an asphalt circle up front. The windows were plastered with posters and flyers, and an American flag waved listlessly from its pole over a patch of struggling grass. Gabby had her window down, so MC could hear the metal clips clanging in the breeze, lending the place an air of abandonment. She remembered Joe drunkenly peeing on the pole the night they graduated.

"Does it make you feel weird to come back here?" MC asked.

"A little. But I'm one of those lucky people who didn't hate high school, so."

Conrad was waving at them from a back entrance that connected to the parking lot, his tie and collar loose, wavy blond hair swept back and shining in the late-afternoon sun. Sure enough, Ms. Kim—Principal Kim? Dr. Kim?—was at his side, in a black pencil skirt and a green sweater, her thick-framed glasses enhancing her eyes. Everyone had had a crush on her in high school.

"Yes!" Ms. Kim called, clutching a tablet to her chest. "You're back!"

MC got out of the car and gave her a hug. "I hear you're the boss these days."

"Trying to be." She tapped MC's shoulder. "Wow, you look so *cool*."

MC, blushing with pleasure, pretended to be miffed. "Did I not look cool before?"

"I keep telling her she was kind of ahead of the curve with the big pants," Conrad said.

"Hey, brother," she said, using that stupid voice from *Arrested Development*. She and Conrad had binged two seasons of it when he'd been home for winter break during his freshman year at Harvard. It was the first time they'd really watched something together, laughed at the same jokes. It was probably just a reaction to their parents' dysfunction at the time, their separation the previous summer rapidly turning out to be a prequel to their divorce. But MC still thought of it positively.

"Easy train ride?" he said.

"Yep."

Ms. Kim beamed. "A great novelist in our midst."

"I still need to finish the novel," MC said, feeling a fresh wave of irritation that Conrad had spread this story around, "and it's average at best."

She tried to tell herself this was better than her brother informing everyone that she was *going through a rough time*.

"You should come talk to the students about it," Ms. Kim said. "I feel like it would be inspiring." Her eyes widened. "Actually, do you want to run an *Explorations* meeting tomorrow?"

"Oh, I wouldn't be qualified—"

"You're a professional writer!"

"I'm actually just a freelance copywriter, like for ads?"

"And you're about to finish a novel."

"Jae," Conrad said, "I think she's trying to keep a low profile."

"MC would do such a good job," Gabby said, clapping her hands.

MC rubbed the back of her neck, an awkward reflex that'd been with her since childhood. "I don't know, I haven't done anything like that in nearly a decade."

"I'm going to be honest," Ms. Kim said. "Conrad and I are drowning. A bunch of teachers retired last year, and now we don't have advisors for five clubs. Five!"

MC could feel herself softening.

"Mr. Pryor agreed to cover a few meetings, but he's not, shall we say, the most inspiring? Which of course you didn't hear from me." Ms. Kim winked. "Having you as a guest advisor would be such a great start to the year."

MC stole a look at Conrad, who'd been suspiciously silent during the pitch process.

"Just try it," Gabby suggested. "See how it goes."

Ms. Kim pressed her hands together. "Pretty please?"

"Okay," MC said, defeated. "One meeting." She made herself smile. "I can do that."

"You're a hero," Ms. Kim said, and hugged her again.

After they said goodbye and piled into the car, MC took the back seat out of automatic deference to her brother. He proceeded to not even offer to switch with her. She was annoyed with herself for paving the way for someone whose way was already extremely well paved. And she was even more annoyed at herself for agreeing to do something she absolutely didn't want to do—in addition to the other thing she absolutely didn't want to do.

The ride home was a bunch of small talk. Work was going well for Conrad, but the pace was demanding. Ms. Kim was going to be, in his opinion, the best principal in the history of Green Hills. Gabby had run into Jim McDade at yoga that morning, and was there a friendly way for Conrad to tell his bro that his mat smelled like pee? Also, should they get takeout for dinner?

They arrived at the house a few minutes later. It was a modest ranch without much yard to speak of. The oak trees in the back hung dangerously close to the mossy roof, and a new paint job was in order. Their dad had done all the maintenance himself but hadn't bothered to teach Conrad or MC any of it. That was how the Calloways operated. Everyone had the thing they were good at and stayed in their lane.

Not that the place was falling apart. The lawn was mowed. There were some new raised beds in the front. Someone—almost certainly Gabby—had planted lettuce. The interior had brightened considerably since they'd gotten married on the back patio two years ago. It'd been a small, beautiful, annoying ceremony, featuring Conrad performing an original love song to tears and riotous applause.

Which was not a memory MC was interested in revisiting.

Unfortunately, the second she took her eyes off her own house, they fell on Nora Pike's, a shabby red colonial on the other side of the picket fence.

There was no car in the driveway.

It all came crashing down on her. The purpose of her visit, the sudden escalation of unrelated obligations. The way her reluctance to get down to business felt directly proportional to her sense of impending doom.

She had to get a grip. Check things out and leave. The sooner the better.

"I can pick up the takeout," she blurted. "I actually wanted to grab a few books from the library before tomorrow." If she could just lay eyes on Nora, exchange a few words, she was sure she could shut this whole thing down—prove to Joe that his blockbuster scoop was not theirs to dish. Or at least not hers.

"You should've mentioned," Gabby said. "I feel bad that we drove all the way back here." The high school and the library were down the street from each other.

"I totally forgot." MC held out her hand for the keys. "Could use the driving practice anyway."

"Don't do too many doughnuts on the town green," Conrad said.

Before he turned away, she saw his eyes narrow, like he knew she was up to no good.

5

When MC pulled up in front of the library, there were only a few cars in the parking lot. Sensible sedans, mostly, and a massive, forest-green pickup truck with a mud-spattered dirt bike strapped in the flatbed.

None of them were the ancient silver hatchback MC remembered Nora driving.

It was possible she'd gotten a new car since then. Likely, even. But some part of MC was hoping Nora wasn't there, that she was on vacation. Maybe a sabbatical. Did librarians take sabbaticals? If they did, she could tell Joe she'd done her best, but the story was out of town, and would it really be so bad to go back to the drawing board and plan some new way to save him from the chopping block?

She walked up the stairs to the portico entrance, stuffing her hands in her pockets. There was a sudden, strong wind, which upset the high bun she'd arranged before getting out of the car. She was self-conscious about how she'd look to Nora after all these years—maybe because of *Girl Next Door*, maybe because being back home made her feel self-conscious in general. Whatever the case, her preparation was in vain. As she walked through the double glass doors, she caught a glimpse of her reflection, and it did not inspire confidence.

On the surface, the library, like the town, had an oppressive blandness to it. Linoleum floor in the lobby. Industrial wall-to-wall carpeting in the stacks. A few windows in the back, harsh fluorescents everywhere else. But the librarians—many of whom had been there as long as MC could remember—had also made the place their own. Life-size cardboard cutouts of children's book characters pointed the way to the kids' section. A leaf-strewn display of recommended fall reads brightened the circulation desk. A monumental Lego sculpture of Yoda standing on top of a stack of banned books greeted her in the lobby. The sign beside him said, FEAR IS THE PATH TO THE DARK SIDE.

"MC Calloway, all in black." A librarian appeared before her, decked out in a pink wool sweater so soft it gave her an aura. Her hair was close-cropped and not quite uniformly dyed, but the wise eyes squinting at MC from behind half-moon glasses would not be ridiculed.

"Hey . . . Lois?"

"She remembers my name," Lois deadpanned to one of the other librarians walking past with a cart of books. The other woman, who sported a salt-and-pepper bob, gave MC a pitying smile. Lois flapped a hand against MC's arm. "What brings you back to town?"

"Just visiting my brother."

"The new vice principal, isn't he? Past time the high school got a change in leadership. You know, we recently did an event with the English Department . . ."

Somewhere in the middle of Lois's complaint about the curriculum being by and for "a bunch of old farts," MC finally saw her.

She was sitting at the reference desk. Same choppy black hair, a little longer now, no more bangs. She was curvier than MC remembered, or maybe it was just the snugness of her shirt, a sleeveless top made of some heavily embroidered fabric, like the upholstery on a vintage ottoman. She had mascara on, or maybe her eyelashes had always been that thick. When she saw MC staring, there was a brief moment where her shoulders seemed to draw together, but then it was gone, and she was focused on her screen again.

Too late, MC realized Lois had clocked the whole thing. "Weren't you and Nora in the same class?" she said.

"Yeah." MC swallowed. "We were."

"Come on, you should say hi."

"That's okay," MC said, panicking. "I don't want to bother her."

"Why? All she does is sit around." Lois was already walking back toward the desk. MC felt like she had no choice but to follow.

Which was good. Because this was what she needed to be doing. And anyway, there was nothing to be nervous about. Besides the fact that Nora Pike was a secret bestselling author who'd written a book about them.

"Nora," Lois said, "look who's here."

Nora's eyes flicked up from her screen, her face as blank as ever.

"Hey," Nora said.

"Hey," MC replied.

Nora went back to her computer, typing away, her fingers striking the keys harder than seemed strictly necessary.

"Nora," Lois said, "shouldn't you be asking MC if she needs help finding any books?"

MC wondered for a moment if Lois knew about *Girl Next Door*, or if she was just bored and trying to get the young people to socialize.

"I'm good," MC said quickly. "Just figured I'd stop by and look around for a minute. On my way to pick up takeout."

She could hear Joe screaming at her on some astral plane. But she didn't know what to do. Nora didn't even want to make eye contact with her, let alone catch up. She began to suspect that she and Joe had been wrong about the significance of the correspondence between *Girl Next Door* and their senior year.

"How've you been?" MC said.

"Fine," said Nora. "You?"

"Uh, yeah. Same."

Scintillating.

"Look who it is," said another voice, low and smooth. "What's good, MC?"

MC blinked as a woman emerged from the stacks carrying a pile of books in her long, toned arms. Jen Turner had been in the grade below MC and Nora, and the top-ranked women's tennis player in the county. Now her gangly looks had settled into a tall, serene presence of total confidence, like she could bend MC into a pretzel without so much as grunting.

"Hey, Jen," MC said, "how's it going?"

"Pretty well." Jen beamed, her teeth white and straight, her eyebrows stylishly thick. MC remembered something on Instagram about an injury before a national competition, a personal transformation in the wake of promise stolen. Not caring about sports, MC hadn't paid much attention, except to the part of Jen's journey that involved a rainbow-strewn announcement of her bisexuality.

"Checking out books?" MC said helplessly.

"Yeah, just a few things I've been wanting to read for a while now."

MC glanced at the spines: *Freedom*, *The Power Broker*, the *Ramayana*. "Nice," she said.

But Jen had already turned to Nora. "See you out there?"

Nora cleared her throat. "Yep."

"Good to run into you, MC."

"Same. I mean, likewise." MC's hands, which were still in her pockets, clenched into fists for some reason. "I should head out too," she said, mostly just to Lois. "Didn't realize I'd come in right as you guys were closing."

"Come back tomorrow," Lois said. "I have ideas for your brother."

"Okay. Sounds good. Bye, Nora."

Nora didn't even look up.

MC rushed out of the library, past a sullen teen girl in a brown cardigan who glanced at MC over a copy of the *Financial Times*.

As MC got back in the Destroyer of Worlds, she saw Jen come out and load her books into the cab of the green pickup. Gritting her teeth, she called Joe.

"I'm done," she said.

"What happened?"

"Nothing. Nora's a zombie robot. That's all there is to report."

"I'll ask again. What happened?"

"I went to the library just now and tried to talk to her, but she barely even looked at me."

"Come on, MC, she wrote a novel about you, and now you just *appear*. She's freaking out."

She bit her lip. "I didn't think about it like that."

"Because you're also freaking out. Stick with this a little longer, and she'll talk."

"I don't know. This is so shady. I feel like she's going to know what we're up to."

"How would she know?"

"It's not exactly a secret that you work for Jawbreaker."

"But I'm not there. You are."

"I've written for you before."

"A *handful* of times. And she doesn't have social media, remember? How else would she come across all this information?"

"Word of mouth?"

"She's not friends with anyone."

"She's friends with Jen Turner," MC muttered, watching Nora come out of the library with a purse over her shoulder, walking over to where Jen was waiting. MC reminded herself that none of it mattered. She wasn't jealous or hurt in any way by two people who were, for all intents and purposes, total strangers to her. She wished them well!

"Wait," Joe said, "Jen Turner, the goody-two-shoes tennis chick? How do you know?"

"Because they're all over each other in the parking lot right now."

Which wasn't exactly true. Jen had just slid her arm around Nora's waist for a moment, leaning in to kiss her cheek before opening the passenger door for her. The stupid truck was practically eight feet off the ground.

"Okay," said Joe, "I'm on Jen's Instagram right now, and there is absolutely zero evidence of her being in a relationship with Nora."

"So?"

"So it's either early days or pure fuck buddies. Regardless, it's irrelevant. You're not there to become Nora's girlfriend. You're there to get her to tell you about the last nine years of her life."

MC watched as Jen Turner hung a muscled arm out her window. Bad folk music piped into the night air as she reversed the truck and rolled off toward the street, toward whatever date or special moment they were about to share. Which MC didn't care about, except that it presented an obstacle to her mission.

She told herself Joe was right. It wasn't really an obstacle, it just felt that way. In the end, it was better that Nora was involved with someone else. It made the whole absurd exercise a lot less confusing for MC.

"You have to let it all go, Neo," she said to herself. "Fear, doubt, and disbelief..."

"Sorry, what?"

She sighed. "Never mind."

6

On Friday morning, Conrad discovered that the Destroyer of Worlds had a flat. MC, as the most recent driver, felt responsible, but Gabby assured her the car had been acting odd earlier on Thursday.

Conrad whipped out his phone in a self-important huff, messaging Ms. Kim about catching a ride. MC had planned to accompany him to school, so that she could walk to the library and make another go at conversation with Nora before the *Explorations* meeting that afternoon. But she decided she was in no rush. The last thing she needed was an extra ten minutes of her brother's judgment.

"There's definitely a YouTube video for this," Gabby said, out on the driveway and typing on her phone, hair gleaming in the morning sunshine. She was wearing Conrad's flannel pajama bottoms. MC stood next to her, useless with cars, but ready to do any kind of oil-smudgy stuff when the time came.

It'd been surprisingly easy to go back to hanging out with Gabby. They'd even watched a movie together the night before, like old times. It'd been Gabby's pick: *How to Lose a Guy in Ten Days*. A painful reminder that MC, like Andie Anderson, was on a secret assignment of her own. She'd never been big on rom-coms, but she respected the vicarious form of wish fulfillment, not so different from the escapism she'd sought in the fantasy novels she'd loved as a kid.

Conrad hadn't joined them for the movie. When he'd finished his lo mein, he'd excused himself and absconded to his basement office. That was where, according to Gabby, he spent most nights. They'd had a surprisingly tense exchange about it just before he'd cleared his plate.

"Okay," Gabby said, "we need to jack it up, take off the tire, then put the doughnut on."

MC blinked. "Doughnut?"

"The spare." She pulled it out from under a flap in the trunk. It was surprisingly small. "Aw, so cute." Gabby ended up working the pneumatic lever that raised the undercarriage. And removing the hubcap and the tire. And putting the doughnut on.

Even in the realm of basic automotive repair, MC was incapable. The whole time that she was standing there with her hands in her pockets, she kept glancing over at Nora's house, wondering if she'd see Jen Turner rolling out of the garage in her monster truck. Memories of Jen bouncing tennis balls all over the school grounds came back to her. The flexing hand. The forceful, precise release.

"Yay!" Gabby said, pumping her fist in the air. "We did it!"

"You did it."

"With your moral support." She tossed her hair from her eyes in a well-worn gesture. "I'm going to take our Destroyer to the tire place, but you should stay here and get started on work."

"I was thinking of hitting up the library, actually."

"Weren't you there last night?"

"Tried to go, but it was closed."

"Oh. Well, come back for lunch?"

"Sure."

"And let me give you a ride."

"No need. Wouldn't want to stress the doughnut." MC smiled. "I was thinking of breaking out my old bike anyway."

"Exercise, love that." Gabby rubbed MC's arm. "Honestly, it's so good having you around again."

MC ignored a swell of guilt in her stomach. "Happy to be here."

After they said their goodbyes, MC went into the dark, dank cave of the garage. It was a little unsettling to be reminded of how completely Gabby had shaped MC's taste in women. She was why MC always went for the sweet ones, the ones who made her feel like she was valuable. Her most recent girlfriend, Lisa, had been the epitome of this type: short and freckled and serious about experimental theater. She worked at a coffee shop in MC's neighborhood, and had dropped subtle, then not-so-subtle come-ons anytime MC came in. *Do you work in the area?* Lisa had asked, smiling to herself as she tapped MC's order on her tablet. *Sort of. I'm freelance, so usually I can work anywhere.* Lisa had turned the tablet over to MC like she was about to tell a joke. *You should work here sometimes.*

Half an hour later, MC finished clearing the spiderwebs and mysterious egg-like packages deposited all over her old ten-speed. She oiled its chain, achieving the smudged hands she'd been looking for, though the effect was much grosser than she'd expected. She pumped up the crusty-looking tires, then set off, pedaling hard. Her childhood helmet was tight and itchy on her head. Her legs burned from the unfamiliar movements. But it was nice to be getting around on her own, channeling some of her unease into forward motion as she scaled the unimpressive hills that'd given the town its name.

It took her forty minutes to get to the library. She locked

her bike up front with a self-satisfied smile. She didn't need a big, showy truck. She didn't need to be ripped. She was just a regular person, traveling through the world in an eco-friendly, heart-healthy way, nothing to prove. She took off her helmet and smoothed her sweaty hair into a bun, ignoring the fact that her T-shirt was soaked.

When she walked into the library, she felt like she'd arrived directly from an unplanned visit to a water park. But she fit right in. The Green Hills library, like all public libraries, was a sanctuary for out-of-sorts individuals, especially on a weekday morning. She headed for the study wing, noting a man at the computers who was guzzling something chunky from a Styrofoam cup, a grim old woman in a reading nook surrounded by back issues of *Men's Health*—the teen who'd been reading the *Financial Times* the night before was, presumably, in school—and a guy in his twenties who'd set up an entire hard drive and gaming rig complete with blinking lights near the circulation desk.

Passing the reference section, MC nodded at Nora. Nora spared a quick look at MC's waterlogged body before flashing the world's shortest, fakest smile.

MC decided not to linger on it. She picked a table deep in the nonfiction section. From that vantage point, she'd still be able to keep an eye on Nora, and hopefully plan some excuse to approach her without seeming creepy.

She sat and opened her laptop. Checked her emails and did a little real work, perfecting some paragraphs about the value of data-driven supply chain logistics in today's fast-paced business environment. Before she knew it, a few hours had passed.

She needed to get a move on.

She gritted her teeth. She was well aware she should've

actually read *Girl Next Door* before embarking on this mission. But it still seemed too treacherous. Like it would give her an outsize or false sense of how Nora felt about her, or the type of person Nora was. Mostly she'd just been scared to hear a stranger—that's what Nora was to her now, more or less—waxing poetic about her own deepest desires. Her greatest fears. Her parents' divorce, as Joe had reminded her. She'd never thought Nora was paying the slightest attention to any of that. Maybe she hadn't been. But even an imagined version of herself was too disturbing to confront.

No time to fix that gap in research now. Even thinking about it dimmed her resolve. She'd never been great at pushing herself to get what she wanted. The risk of suffering was too palpable. Besides, she'd always been able to find contentment with something that was close enough—not a career as a hotshot writer, but a relatively stable setup as a freelance copywriter. Not the star of a sweeping and desperate romance, but the even-keeled girlfriend whose thoughtful insistence on not getting too deep would one day, she hoped, result in a partnership that didn't end in plate-shattering divorce. It was boring. But the nice thing about being boring was that it was safe. Typically.

She decided that overthinking was getting her nowhere. She would go up to Nora and say something insightful. Probably about the weather.

She made her approach.

"Wanna know something crazy?" she blurted.

Nora looked up from her computer. She was wearing glasses. MC was transported back to senior year, when Nora would break out big circular wire frames on long stretches of layout work. Once, MC had asked if she could try them on, and Nora had obliged, skeptical. *Well*, MC had asked, *do I look smarter?*

Nora had snorted. *You look like you need a new prescription.* And she'd slipped the glasses off MC's face more gently than MC had expected, her fingertips brushing MC's temples.

"I'm running an *Explorations* meeting," MC said. "This afternoon."

Nora pursed her lips. "Good for you."

"Ms. Kim's the principal now. They don't have an advisor for the magazine, so she asked if I'd sub in. Just for today."

"Best of luck."

Nora went back to typing, hammering the keys harder than ever.

MC cleared her throat. "It's making me think about the old days, you know?"

Nora stared at her.

"I mean, it's made me wonder how've you been."

Before Nora could reply, the only other youngish person MC had observed working at the library cut in front of MC and shouted at Nora with her hands in the air.

"Darryl is motherfucking 'sick'!" she said. "Meaning he's a motherfucking liar."

"Language," Lois drawled, walking by with a cart of books.

"I have eight million psychotic moms RSVP'd to story hour tomorrow," the woman fumed. She seemed to be in her forties, with bright red lipstick and a large sweater featuring a punk rock Smokey Bear looking baked.

Nora blinked. "So find someone else to wear the costume."

"Who? No one's going to touch that ratty old sack of shit."

"Ask if Darryl has any friends."

"Friends who'll roll in here on a Saturday morning to entertain a horde of spoiled toddlers?"

"Say it's his responsibility to find a replacement."

"He's an unpaid intern."

"If you're asking me to do it, Maureen, the answer is no. It's annoying enough just to be the one reading the book."

Maureen curled her right hand, then lifted it to her face and studied her bejeweled manicure. "I guess we'll just have story hour without Winnie."

"I could do it," MC said.

Nora's eyes widened. "There's really no need—"

But Maureen was already giving MC an up-and-down. "Who are you?"

"MC," she said, "like Master of Ceremonies." She stuck out a hand, then regretted it, feeling overly formal. "Nora and I went to high school together. I'm here for the weekend, visiting my brother, but I don't have any real plans."

Maureen frowned. "And you're willing to wear a Winnie-the-Pooh costume on a Saturday morning for a bunch of screaming children?"

MC shrugged. "I like kids."

Maureen's eyebrows lifted. "See you tomorrow at ten."

MC smiled and went back to her desk.

As she typed, she felt Nora staring at her. Finally.

7

"This is kind of a weird question," MC said to Gabby around a mouthful of chicken salad, "but do you ever talk to Nora Pike?"

"Not really." Gabby poked her fork around a complex bean dish she'd tossed in a mixing bowl. They were sitting at the kitchen island. "I mean, we acknowledge each other if we're taking out the trash at the same time. But other than that, you know how she is."

"I thought maybe she'd softened up over the years."

"If she has, she hasn't bothered to let us know. Why do you ask?"

"I saw her today. At the library."

"Did you guys reminisce?"

"No. She barely spoke to me."

Gabby smiled. "She's probably still into you."

"Into me?" MC's heart started hammering in her chest.

"Come on, we all saw how she looked at you in those *Explorations* meetings."

MC wasn't sure what Gabby was talking about. Any eye contact with Nora had usually involved glaring of some sort. "Somehow I missed that."

Gabby seemed shocked. "Clearly you were the only person on the planet who could get her to participate in a group activity."

"She said Ms. Kim forced her to be there."

"How could Ms. Kim possibly do that?" Gabby was practically wiggling in her seat. "Do you like her or something?"

"What? No—"

"To be fair, you haven't hung out with her in nearly a decade."

"I think she's dating Jen Turner."

"Are you serious?" Gabby laughed. "Okay, this is perfect. Jen Turner is notoriously single, so it's not an official relationship."

"How do you know she's notoriously single?"

"She's the gym teacher at the high school—total player."

MC was surprised.

"More importantly," Gabby said, "this is confirmation that Nora's gay."

"I thought you already knew that."

"I suspected it. But you know how teens can be. Flickers of romantic potential from every gender, no matter where you end up settling in." MC wiped her face with a napkin to hide her expression. It was Gabby's air of romantic potential that'd caused MC so much distress over those years.

It'd started when they were juniors, going out in the woods behind the deli to smoke weed on Fridays while the sun went down. MC didn't smoke, but Joe had been getting into it, and MC had felt obligated to hang around in case he freaked out.

The group consisted of a dozen kids, including Gabby. They huddled around in a clearing lined with initial-scarred trees, passing blunts and forties, Gabby sometimes talking to Joe about whatever they'd botched in chem lab that day. By early winter, she was still showing up without a jacket, and on a particularly cold night, she announced, "I'm going to turn into Jack Nicholson at the end of *The Shining*, fuck!"

People laughed at her impression of his frozen face. But her teeth were chattering.

"Wanna take a turn with this?" MC said, shrugging off her parka.

"But then you'll turn into Jack Nicholson!" Gabby snorted with laughter. "Wow, your coat is massive."

MC blushed. She'd been struggling to figure out how to dress the way she wanted to look, without looking like someone she wasn't ready for people to see.

"I love that it's massive," Gabby added soberly. "Very into the massiveness." She paused. "Here, we can each take an arm."

She pulled the right shoulder of MC's parka down a little farther, then slipped it off and pressed the side of her body tight to MC's, jamming her arm in the free sleeve. MC internally combusted.

But instead of choking up on conversation, as she tended to do when she was with a girl she liked, she was able to come back down to earth. It was Gabby's gift, keeping things calm and light, while also somehow giving off an intense warmheartedness. They'd talked about classes and their parents. TV and stupid things that'd happened that year. MC had started drinking from one of the forties, relaxing even more once she realized everyone had become engrossed in their own private chats. And at some point, Gabby was asking her who she was interested in. Like, *interested* in.

MC took a swig of Olde English. Maybe it was the cold, maybe it was the dark, maybe it was the way Gabby kept pressing a little harder against her side, but she said, "I think I'd feel too nervous to date."

"What? Why?"

There was no way to be clever, MC told herself later, when you were wasted and horny. "I guess I've been starting to wonder if I might be into more than just . . . guys?"

Gabby's eyes widened. Then she threw her head back and cackled. "Oh my god," she said. "Finally. Something cool is happening here." She schooled her face into seriousness. "Who do you have your eye on? I've always wanted to be a wing woman."

"Definitely not drunk enough to discuss that."

Gabby snuggled closer and tapped the forty in MC's lap. "Better get to work, then."

MC had replayed the memory in her mind a thousand times over the rest of that year. She'd embellished, expanded, and, fine, pornographized it until she felt like her whole body was melting whenever Gabby was in the same room with her. Then Gabby had joined *Explorations* the next fall. MC had believed her destiny was on the horizon, at long last, after so long waiting in the wings. She would tell Gabby the truth. The full truth. And then . . .

And then Conrad said Harvard was for assholes and moved back home.

"Well," she said to Gabby, in the kitchen of the house she'd grown up in, the house that was now her brother's and his wife's, "whoever Nora's into, I don't think it's me."

Gabby wore a conspiratorial smile as MC changed the subject.

Twenty minutes later, MC headed out on her bike again, trying to clear her mind before she reached the high school.

Unfortunately, unlike yesterday, when the building had been empty and therefore approachable, the place was now crawling with kids. Freshmen in giant backpacks. Sophomores talking loudly as the buses lined up in the traffic circle. Braces, bad makeup—the details were different, but the spirit was the same. A mass desperation out of which their troubled society continued to reproduce itself.

MC smoothed her hair and walked into the front entrance,

signing in with the security guard and trying to ignore the brief stares coming from gaggles of upperclassmen, who had a sunken common area to themselves near the first hall of lockers past the main office. MC remembered eating lunch—often a candy bar and a Gatorade—in that common area, Joe making fun of the kids in Gardening Club, who wore giant straw hats while tending cinderblock beds in the courtyard just beyond the big windows.

Ms. Kim had told her that *Explorations* would be meeting in their old space, a classroom stuffed with media equipment near the English Department office. MC headed straight for it, ducking her head to avoid being recognized by teachers, custodians, and any of the other dozen staff members she'd been buddies with in the old days. She had always gotten free snacks on the lunch line in the cafeteria, permission for Joe to park his chortling old VW in an empty staff spot senior year, and first dibs on renting laptops from the computer lab.

But she didn't want to engage with that old self. Her sense of Nora's portrayal of her in *Girl Next Door* had started to make her wonder if she'd been depressingly basic in high school, and still was. After all, she hadn't even managed to end up a novelist.

Just a fake one.

"There you are!" said Ms. Kim. She was standing at the door to the English Department with Mr. Pryor, who'd been MC's teacher junior year.

"Welcome back," he said in his smooth baritone. He wore a bow tie and a crisp white shirt. "I think you'll have a nice little group for the meeting this afternoon."

"Great," MC said. Her mouth was chalky. She hadn't prepared for this. Why hadn't she prepared for this? "How've you been, Mr. Pryor?"

"Splendid, splendid. I hear you're finishing a novel."

"I guess I am."

"She's always been so modest," said Ms. Kim. "Come on, MC, let's get you situated."

They went over to the classroom together, and that was when it all became real: the posters of Toni Morrison and Shakespeare on the walls, the low shelves stuffed with beat-up textbooks, the rows of desks with their chairs fused on by metal rods over which Joe had often draped himself in petulant melancholy, him and MC opting for the farthest seats from the chalkboard. Except now there was no chalk. The boards were white. And MC wasn't a teenager who could slink off to the back in her big cargo pants and hoodie.

"I have a meeting with Athletics," Ms. Kim said. MC was reminded, not pleasantly, of Jen Turner. "But I'm going to come back to catch the end of this." She flashed two thumbs up. "Have fun!"

As she rushed out, heels clicking, a few kids started filing in, staring at MC in open contempt followed by immediate dismissal.

MC busied herself with arranging the desks in a circle, like in the old days. The metal legs squeaked and groaned over the linoleum. But the physical task was steadying. Something to pour her nervous energy into. It also gave her an excuse not to acknowledge the students that were growing in number around her.

"Hey," said a gangly boy with tight brown curls. "Want a hand?"

She was so grateful she could've cried, but she tried to sound casual. "Sure." She'd forgotten that there were nice kids out there, who only put on the thinnest front of being cliquey as a gesture of acquiescence to the larger social structure. "I'm making a circle of however many desks we think we'll need."

"I'm Ben," he said.

"MC. Just filling in for today. I used to be a student here."

They worked for a few more minutes as people started to settle in. MC felt a burst of confidence, or maybe resignation to her task, which was now unavoidable. But as she was making her way to a seat at the top of the circle, she saw three kids talking over a book.

"You do realize it's a rom-com about a literary magazine."

"Obviously, that's why I'm reading it."

"I heard it's overrated."

"I heard it's fucking hot."

"Okay," MC blurted, just as the teen reader of the *Financial Times* walked in and took a desk. "Let's get started!"

8

Ms. Kim arrived at the end of the meeting, in time to catch Ben finishing an impassioned recitation of his poem, "The Dump I Did Take."

"The toilet seat I swear I did close, and yet the stench of my lunch arose—"

MC laughed with the students. Over the course of the meeting, she'd leaned back in her chair and crossed her ankles, relaxing. In desperation to avoid any talk of novels, whether it was her fake one or Nora's real one, she'd decided to have everyone introduce themselves with a writing exercise. They were to use rhyme any way they wanted, with twenty minutes to compose something that told a story. She knew there were kids who probably hated poetry in the room. But she remembered how important it was to loosen up at the start of something as pretentious as a literary magazine.

When MC caught Ms. Kim's eye, she waved, and they all clapped after Ben finished his couplets.

"Just so you know," Ms. Kim said, uncrossing her arms and stepping into the room, "not only was MC the editor of *Explorations* back when that role still existed, she was also my best student."

Unfortunately, her praise added a degree of alienation back into the room. The library teen looked especially unimpressed.

"Thanks for giving me a chance today," MC said quickly, and jumped into winding down the meeting before Ms. Kim could say anything else.

After the students had left, the two of them rearranged the desks into rows.

"Looks like that went really well," Ms. Kim said.

MC nodded. "It went okay."

"Sounds like you expected it to be a disaster."

"I just haven't done anything like this in a long time."

"Did you enjoy it?"

"Yeah. I did."

Ms. Kim flashed an impish smile. "Does that mean you'll be back?"

"I hadn't thought about that yet. Should we play it by ear?"

"Whatever you want."

"In case you end up finding someone on staff who can do it."

"I'll take what I can get, when I can get it."

"Noted." MC cleared her throat. "So, how's it been? Running the school. Working with my brother."

"Good, good." Her lashes fluttered for a moment. "He's intense!" She laughed. "I mean, hey, I like that about him."

"Lucky you."

"He told me to say hi to you, by the way. He's still tied up with Athletics." She took a breath before adding, "We spent a lot of time together this summer. I hope you don't mind me saying this, but I got the sense that he misses you."

MC knew it would be rude to laugh. "Really?"

"I think when you're good at so many things, the one thing you're bad at becomes extra overwhelming. If that makes sense."

The observation felt more insightful than MC would've expected from someone who'd only met Conrad that summer.

But Ms. Kim had always had that way about her—a laser focus she carried so lightly it took students by surprise whenever she started unlocking layers of meaning in even the most boring assignments.

"Well," MC said slowly, "thanks for telling me that. I felt like he was annoyed that I invaded his turf or whatever."

"Don't be silly." She winked. "It's your turf too."

They said goodbye. MC reassured her that they'd be in touch about the possibility of her running another meeting. When she left the building, her steps lighter from an obligation having been fulfilled and put behind her, she squinted up at the dark clouds and geared up to bike as quickly as her sore legs could manage.

She winced as she pushed off onto the street, droplets of rain beginning to speckle the asphalt. By the time she was on the main road, thunder was rumbling. If she saw lightning, she'd probably have to get off her bike and find shelter. Somewhere.

A car honked behind her. Worried she was blocking the road, despite the fact that this wasn't physically possible, she veered farther onto the shoulder.

She got honked at again.

Then the car pulled up beside her, a window rolled down.

MC prepared to apologize, though she wasn't sure for what, when she saw it was Nora.

"Need a ride?"

"Oh, hey!" MC sputtered. "I'm good, actually." She felt rain streaming off her nose and chin. "Thanks for the offer, though."

Somewhere in the ether, Joe was screaming.

Nora frowned. "You're good?"

"Little rain never hurt anyone."

Thunder roared.

"From a safety standpoint," Nora said, "I think you should get in the car."

"You know what? I think you're right." She looked down at the bike. "But I don't want to get dirt all over your seats."

"It's fine."

MC hitched a thumb over her shoulder. "I'll just throw my bike in the woods."

"What?"

"It's a piece of junk, no one's gonna steal it."

"You . . . don't need to do that?"

"It's no problem, seriously."

"MC. I really don't care if you put it in the back."

"I'll get it later." With some effort, MC shoved the bike into a bush, wiped her hands on her sodden jeans, and opened the passenger-side door. "Thanks for doing this."

Nora shook her head. "Giving you a ride to the place I was already driving?"

MC cleared her throat. "Yeah."

Nora pulled back into the street. MC dripped onto the upholstery.

"You can take off your helmet," Nora said. "Unless you really like to wear it."

MC laughed, then struggled for a long time to get the warped clasp to come undone. Awkward jokes about how this did not reflect her ability to undo clasps in general popped into her mind. As did the phrase *next-level clueless*.

"I'm still shocked you volunteered to be Pooh," Nora said. Her gaze flicked over to MC for a moment. MC thought she saw a hint of nervousness there, but maybe she was just projecting.

"To be honest," MC said, "I can't believe it either."

"You can change your mind."

"And let down a nice person like Maureen?"

"She'll get over it."

"I'm committed now."

"You just really want to wear a disgusting costume tomorrow morning."

"It's like being a mascot, right? I've always been curious about that."

"Why?"

"I don't know—seems exciting to have fans."

It took a moment for MC to become aware of the possible double meaning. She stared out the windshield.

Nora said, "I don't think you'll feel too exciting as Pooh."

"Uh, Pooh is the definition of exciting."

MC was pleased to see a twitch at the corner of Nora's lips. "Maureen's glad you feel that way."

"I just need to work on my *Oh, bother*."

"You definitely don't need to do that."

Maybe it was the absurdity of the situation, or the intensity of the silence that yawned between them, but when MC took a deep breath, what came out was a glottal, high-pitched *"Piglet."*

Nora was almost smiling now. "Jesus Christ."

"I know. My impressions can be stunning."

"I'm stunned."

"I get that all the time."

Nora managed to get her frown back in place. "Why are you here again?"

"Like, in your car?"

"No, like in Green Hills."

"I'm visiting my brother."

"Then why didn't you leave school together?"

"Because he works super late."

"You're just . . . trying to spend time with him?"

Of course Nora would doubt her explanation. As Joe had reminded her, she'd written a bestselling book about their fake romance, based on their not-fake senior year, and all of a sudden MC just materialized, not simply at home, but at Nora's work.

Twice.

She was going to need to be a little more convincing.

"No," she admitted. "I'm actually trying to finish a novel."

Nora's eyebrows went up. "A novel."

It occurred to MC that Joe's cover for her was almost certainly inspired by Michaela Carson's career in *Girl Next Door*, which MC was pretending not to know about, while talking to the author of that very book, who was already suspicious of her.

"I also just got broken up with," she added.

"Oh."

"Yeah. Happens to me all the time."

"Is there a reason for that?"

"Probably."

"But you're not sure."

"I have my suspicions."

"Should you try to figure that out?"

"It's why I decided to come home for a few days. To reflect."

"How's it going so far?"

"I'd say zero progress."

Nora settled back in her seat a little. "So, what kind of novel is it?"

"Um . . . a bad one?"

"What?"

"A bad novel."

"You're being self-deprecating."

"Kind of. I mean, I gave up on writing fiction in college,

when I got the memo that I wasn't very good at it. And it seemed like such a hard thing to do, emotionally, so I figured maybe I dodged a bullet."

"And then you forgot the memo?"

"Breakups make you do weird things. Plus, I don't know, maybe I finally need to get a few things off my chest."

Nora's expression softened. "I don't know if this is what you mean, but . . . I was really sorry when I heard your dad passed. I wrote you and Conrad a card. Not that my condolences matter."

"No, they do. Thank you."

"He seemed very talented. Not just with the carpentry business, but his gardening, his pottery . . ."

MC smiled, wanting to skip over how uncomfortable the topic made her. "That's the Calloways. Talented, I mean. The gene just skipped me or something."

Nora gave her a serious look. "I think when you've perfected your *Oh, bother*, you'll be singing a different tune."

MC raised an eyebrow. "So, you admit you're excited to see me dress up tomorrow?"

"Excited doesn't even begin to describe it."

And then, for whatever reason, MC felt heat rushing to her cheeks. She cleared her throat. "How come Maureen doesn't read to the kids, by the way?"

"She does. But for special events, they make me do it."

"Why?"

"Because I'm good at it, MC." Nora smirked. "Is that so hard to believe?"

"No. Well, maybe a little."

"Ouch."

"I just mean that you seem . . . I don't know what I mean."

"I do." A muscle leapt in Nora's jaw. "You think I'm an asshole."

"What? No, I don't."

"Everyone does. Or they used to, anyway." She took a breath. "They're not entirely wrong."

"You were always really independent. That can be intimidating to some people, especially teenagers."

"Did I intimidate you?"

"No." MC had no idea why she was blushing. Again. "Fine, maybe a little. But I liked it." Nora shot her a look. "I mean, I liked the things about you that were intimidating. Not the experience of being intimidated by you."

"Really?" Nora checked her mirror and turned onto their street. "I always got the feeling you kind of enjoyed it."

MC swallowed.

Were they *flirting*?

As if Nora was having the same train of thought, she said, "Anyway, that was probably just you being nice."

MC bristled, thinking of *Girl Next Door*. "I wasn't being nice. I genuinely thought you were brave to be yourself at that age."

"Speaking of that age," Nora said, "how was the *Explorations* meeting today?"

MC was relieved to change the subject. She hadn't realized how hurt she'd felt, deep down, about Nora's cookie-cutter portrayal of her. "It was good," she said. "Just like old times, actually." Except for some of the kids fawning over the book Nora had written about them.

"I'm not surprised. You were a natural in that role."

"So were you."

Nora rolled her eyes. Which made MC's heart sink even lower. She had a memory of working on the magazine, just the two of them, a few weeks before reading night. Nora had showed her a printed draft, and when MC saw how elegant it looked, the maturity of the design, she'd found herself saying, *You do know you're amazing, right?*

And Nora had said, *What corny-ass movie did you get that line from?*

Nora pulled up at MC's house. She stared down at the wheel in her hands like it had a nuclear code on it. MC took the opportunity to study Nora's profile a little more closely. Full lips. Strong nose. Long lashes and intense green eyes behind a sweep of wavy black hair. The phrase that popped into MC's mind just then was *unabashedly sexy*.

"Sorry for dumping a lake in your passenger seat," MC said.

"It's fine." Nora finally looked over at MC. "It'll dry."

9

On Saturday morning, it was Conrad's turn to go grocery shopping. Which meant it fell to him to drop MC off at the library for story hour. Not that she'd explained anything to him about her involvement in the event.

"Didn't know you were such a library head," he said, pulling out onto the street. Gabby had picked up the Destroyer of Worlds from the tire place the night before.

"Is that a term?" she said. "Library head?"

"I don't know."

"It's easy to concentrate in the study wing."

He shuddered. "Mom made me do practice SATs there. Forced me to drink coffee, which I'd never had before. She even brought a stopwatch."

MC laughed. "Why did she do that, anyway?"

"Because it's a timed test?"

"No, why did she get so intense about making sure you practiced?"

"I have no idea. Every now and then she felt the need to exert her control over me, I guess."

"I think she just had high expectations of you."

Their mom hadn't so much as checked MC's grades, let alone invested herself in MC's SAT scores. Neither had their dad. Then again, by MC's senior year, Dr. Linda Case-Calloway was out in LA, leaving the whole family in a state of turmoil.

MC never wanted to live through drama like that again. She was pretty sure Conrad didn't either.

"Can I ask you something?" she said.

"Sure."

"I'm not trying to butt in or anything. But are things okay with you and Gabby?"

His shoulders bunched. "What makes you ask?"

"Just offhand comments. Nothing serious."

"Must be serious enough for you to bring it up."

"No. I just think of you guys as smooth sailing most of the time."

"Well, that's because you're constantly projecting a fantasy onto me."

"Excuse me?"

"I'm not perfect, MC."

"I know that," she said defensively. "Like, very well."

"Sorry to be a dick right now, but I'm still trying to figure out why you've gone from mostly avoiding us to crashing with us without any warning." He shot her a look. "And I know what Joe said about your writing or whatever, but as far as I can tell, you don't seem too in the zone with that."

She felt heat rushing to her cheeks. "Well, I haven't been as focused as I'd hoped."

"And why is that? Why are you really here?"

She could've pulled out the same excuse she'd used with Nora, allude to her breakup without going into detail. Joe had even set her up for it with his little aside about the tough time she was having. But she wasn't ready to trust Conrad with anything resembling the truth—even if it was a convenient one. "I'm working on a project, Conrad. Why is that so hard to believe? Do you think you're the only person with goals?"

"I just pointed out how random this visit feels, and I'd rather you be honest with me than sneaking around, watching rom-coms with Gabby, and running *Explorations* meetings with my boss."

"Your 'boss' came to the last thirty seconds of one meeting. And I'm not trying to do any of this stuff. I was asked to do it, pretty intensely."

"Gabby asked you pretty intensely to watch *How to Lose a Guy in Ten Days*?"

"Because she wanted *you* to watch *How to Lose a Guy in Ten Days*, but you were too busy being weird in the basement to realize. God."

"Is she complaining to you about me?"

"She's not complaining. She's just lonely. She probably thinks I understand you and can better illuminate your brilliance for her."

"I'm a vice principal, not a rocket scientist."

"Are you fishing for compliments?"

"I'm trying to tell you that you seem to go out of your way to treat everyone like a human being except for me."

"That's not even true. Also, you're my brother, it's different. We can speak more freely."

"Can we?" He pulled up at the library. "Good luck with the contemporary American *Anna Karenina* or whatever."

"Thanks. And don't worry about groceries or dinner for me. I'll take a train back in a few hours, spare you my projections."

"Whatever you wanna do."

"I have a pretty important in-person meeting on Monday that I should prep for anyway."

She was supposed to keep gathering info until tomorrow afternoon, but this conversation was a crucial reminder that she didn't want to be here, that she'd kept Conrad at a distance because they'd always been terrible at talking to each other. They could do stupid jokes or surface-level back-and-forth. Or bickering, clearly. That was it.

"Right," her brother said. "See you whenever you feel like dropping in again, I guess."

She got out in a huff, hoping he would roll down the window or push the door open and tell her to get back in so they didn't have to leave things on such a sour note. But in true Calloway fashion, he sped off. She remembered her dad dumping her at school one morning just the same way. She'd asked to borrow the car for a weekend camping trip with Joe and Gabby. After he'd said no, the discussion had devolved into her grumpily pointing out that he barely left the couch, so why did he need the car? He hadn't even yelled at her. Just asked her to get out, then drove away.

A crow squawked somewhere in the trees on the far side of the parking lot. She tried to shake off her brother's words. But it was hard. Tears welled in her eyes.

She looked at her phone.

She was late.

"There she is," Lois announced when MC walked in. "Showtime."

"Let's get this over with," Nora said, standing up from her desk and coming around to the lobby. She was wearing tall leather boots and a long black button-down. MC's heart, which was already thudding from her argument with Conrad, began to beat even harder.

Nora frowned. "Are you okay?"

"Totally. Ready for Pooh Power Hour." MC blinked rapidly, all too aware of how obvious it was that she was on the verge of crying. She remembered seeing Nora in a similar state once, her eyes puffy when they'd met to pick up a proof from the print shop on a sunny Friday before school. MC had stopped at Green Hills' lone coffee shop on the way, grabbing hot chocolates for them both and a pastry for herself.

Try this apple turnover, MC had said, lifting a greasy paper bag.

Nora had looked away, her arms crossed. *I hate apples.*

It's more about the cinnamon sugar.

What?

They skimp on the fruit. It's pretty much just for texture.

Nora kept her arms crossed as she leaned over and took a bite.

Wow. MC had laughed. *It's like feeding a tiger at the zoo. Awe, fear, majesty.*

For once, Nora had smiled back. *This,* she said, *tastes like a heart attack.*

The figurative kind, where all the world seizes you with its beauty?

The real kind. As in heart failure caused by lard.

Whatever, more for me. MC had cleared her throat and added, *Everything okay?*

Yeah. Nora paused, like she knew she shouldn't go on but also couldn't stop herself. *Just got a rejection letter from my top-choice school.*

What? That's so dumb of them.

I think I'm the dumb one in this scenario.

I guarantee you're not.

How could you possibly guarantee that?

You're a genius.

Nora gave her a rueful look. *A genius would've made sure to do more than one extracurricular activity. Or, like, get better grades.*

I regret to inform you that geniuses don't do a bunch of extracurriculars.

If only you were in admissions.

I mean, I'd definitely give you a full ride.

Nora had stared at her for a second, then burst out laughing.

"Where's Maureen?" MC asked now, looking away from Nora and rubbing the back of her neck.

"Home sick," Nora said, "with whatever Darryl has." She leaned in and whispered, "Meaning she's a motherfucking liar."

MC smiled.

Nora whisked them toward a door in the back just as the first families were starting to arrive. Among the desks was a cardboard box overflowing with discolored rags.

Nora stared at it and said, "Your big dream is about to come true."

MC forgot her tears in an instant. "My dream smells like pee."

"And corn chips." Nora gave her an up-and-down. "Did you bring a change of clothes?"

MC ran a hand over the front of her perfectly white T-shirt. "No."

"Oh well." Nora walked over to the box and reached in.

A garment sewn with concentric wire hoops went over MC's head, its straps resting on her shoulders. It hung like a lampshade. Next came the main portion of the suit—the bulk of the yellow-brown pile in the box. MC tried to bend over to put it on, but the hoops were prohibitive. She got her legs through, only to get stuck at the torso.

Nora stepped closer. "Stick your arms out in front of you."

MC obeyed, and Nora slid the sleeves on. Then she shimmied the rest of the suit up onto MC's shoulders. MC tried to help by wiggling.

"Stay still," Nora grumbled.

MC straightened as Nora walked behind her and started on the zipper. Which got caught halfway. Nora tugged on it—hard—to no avail.

"The zipper's stuck."

"Maybe it's a sign."

"Too late for those."

"I don't want to get, like, an infection—"

The zipper finally regained its track, enclosing her.

"Okay," Nora said, "shoe covers."

MC heard the growing chatter of children in the lobby.

"Left foot first," Nora said, bending down in front of her. As Nora slipped on the fuzzy covering, MC tried to keep herself steady.

"Right foot," Nora said, and put the other covering on over MC's sneaker.

"Now the shirt." Nora had gotten a little breathless. "Wow, this thing reeks." She unfolded a giant red T-shirt, which had been jaggedly cut off several inches above the waist, and held it up for MC to duck her head into. After that was on, there was only one piece left.

They both looked at the scuffed monstrosity on the windowsill. Half of a black plastic eye was cracked off.

There was no nose.

"There's no nose," MC said.

"I can use a Sharpie to fill it in."

MC swallowed, then put the head on.

She was already sweating. But with the costume complete, her body's attempts to cool itself went into overdrive, drenching her. The pads of the helmetlike contraption on her head made her scalp itch. She was pretty sure she was going to get lice. Or die. Get lice, then die.

"How bad is it in there?" Nora asked. Her voice sounded muffled.

MC tried to move her head, but it wobbled violently, making her dizzy. "I can't really see." The open maw of the creature was covered by a thin black fabric through which MC could make out only the vaguest outlines. A copy machine. Nora's silhouette. "I think there's a chin strap." She reached into the head with her gloved hands, but it was hard to get a decent grip.

"Let me do it," Nora said. Her touch was cool and gentle. Her fingers slid up either side of MC's jaw, searching for the straps. MC cleared her throat, disturbed to find she was getting turned on.

Nora said, "I'm not going to pinch your neck, am I?"

"All clear." But MC clenched her teeth as the clasp clicked into place. "Okay." Nora held MC's hand. "Don't let go of me."

They walked out into the crowd.

"Look who's here!" Lois announced.

And then the sobbing began.

"It's okay!" someone cooed. "It's just a costume!"

"Pick me up!" a child wailed.

"Mommy, what is it?"

MC did a wobbly side-to-side sway, waving to what she hoped were children but could easily have been the middle distance.

"Why does he look so dirty?"

"Where's his nose?"

Lois shouted that it was time to go sit on the carpet.

"Uh-oh!" Nora said, louder than MC had ever heard her speak. "You know what, guys?" The mock sadness in her voice was so ridiculous, MC couldn't imagine it would be effective, but it earned a moment of quiet. "I think Pooh is a little sleepy! Pooh, should I bring you back to your house for a nap?"

MC gasped. "Only if I can have honey in bed..."

The crying resumed.

"Come on, Pooh," Nora said, "you really need some help."

She tugged on MC's hand, leading her back to where the whole mess had started.

As the sounds of distress faded behind them, MC peeled off her gloves and scrambled to undo her chin strap. She took the head off and threw it on the ground, then doubled over. She was unable to clutch her stomach on account of the hoops.

"Do not vomit," Nora said. "If you vomit, I will vomit."

"Not gonna vomit," MC panted. But her head was spinning.

Nora ripped MC's belly shirt over her head, tugged down her sleeves, and unstrapped the wire contraption. "Put your hands on my shoulders," she commanded.

MC was going to pass out.

But before she did, she braced herself on Nora, and Nora yanked the rest of the suit down, bringing a rush of cool air over MC's sweat-soaked body.

"Thank god," MC breathed.

"Now let go of me."

MC didn't want to.

"I have to go read the damn book," Nora said, sliding her hands up MC's hips and squeezing—just for a moment—before laughing and turning away.

10

"Come on," Joe said, breathing vigorously through his nose as he ran along the pedestrian path that circled Prospect Park, "*push!*"

Behind him, MC clenched her sweaty hands into fists as a steep rise came into view. The park was full of hills, but this was by far the biggest. Her heart sank so low it was basically in her stomach. One after another, runners passed her by, sleek and strong in their performance wear.

"When . . . do we . . . stop," she said.

"At the top!"

"I'll . . . meet you." She put her hands on her hips and slowed down, wobbling along like someone had just taken a baseball bat to her legs. She was wearing sweatpants and a sweatshirt that said GREEN HILLS BULLS on the front and NO ONE GRABS THESE HORNS on the back. She'd found it in the guest room closet just before leaving Conrad and Gabby's the night before.

She watched Joe pump his muscular calves, taking the hill like he took every challenge, without pause and at full sprint. He'd had a deeply awkward phase in middle school—it was the reason they'd become friends in the first place—that lingered, subtly, into high school. But as soon as he'd escaped their hometown, the boy who'd once huddled with MC on the bus and doodled comics in which the worst kids they knew suffered public bouts of explosive diarrhea had blossomed. His confidence still startled her sometimes. She couldn't imagine pushing past doubt, choosing to ignore it.

At the summit, she wiped her face inside her sweatshirt. Joe squirted water over his head, pulled her in for a selfie, then checked his smartwatch.

"Okay," he said, stretching his quads. "Now I feel like we can talk."

"About what?"

"The draft."

"You mean my notes." She grimaced. "And here I was thinking you just wanted an elite running partner on this beautiful Sunday morning."

He posted the selfie and put his phone away. "I canceled the meeting tomorrow."

Her mouth fell open. "What? Why?"

"Because we're not ready."

"But—"

"I shouldn't have rushed this. It's too big."

Her heart swelled with hope. "Like, too big to pull off?"

"No. Too big to rush."

Her heart deflated.

"I can tell you think there's no story. But your notes are legit brimming with potential."

"What kind of potential are they legit brimming with, exactly?"

"It's hard to explain. But something deeper than an exposé. Juicier."

"You got that from what? My observation that Nora's still really unfriendly?"

He started doing jumping jacks. "I believe the term you used was *misanthropic*. Which is interesting, because she writes mushy rom-coms. Or at least, she's written one mushy rom-com. Everyone's going to want to know the reason behind that contradiction. And I think, if you went back home again, you could figure it out."

"Hang on, that wasn't the agreement."

"I'm not saying do it right this second—"

"And I'm saying I can't do it, period."

He finally stood still, breathing hard. "I realize this is a huge ask."

"It's not about the size of the ask." She ran her hands through her hair, trying not to think about how she and Conrad had left things. "It's that I don't want to put the spotlight on someone who is clearly trying to avoid it at all costs."

"Then why'd she write a book where she barely changed all our names, including her own?"

"I don't know."

"Makes you wonder if some part of her wants to be figured out."

"It's none of our business either way."

"Maybe it's none of mine, but it's absolutely some of yours."

"Even if there had been something between us—something I missed at the time—Nora has moved on. It's been almost a decade. She's dating Jen Turner! We should leave it in the past."

"But it's not in the past. It's right here in the present, in this wildly successful book that I think you owe it to yourself to actually read."

"I can't. I just can't."

Joe put his hands on his hips and toed the ground. "I wish I could let this go."

"I get it." MC winced. "Your job."

He cleared his throat.

"Is there something else?"

"Huh?"

"Did Seth say anything to you? When you rescheduled?"

"Well . . . kind of."

"What?"

"Ugh, I shouldn't—I mean, if my bullshit isn't your problem, then this really isn't your problem."

"But?"

"I'm freaking out," he said quietly, "because Seth said he'd be *remiss* not to mention that, as far as a potential restructuring goes, there's been talk with the investors about collapsing arts and culture into entertainment. As in, Sheena and Jerome would become redundant too."

MC's stomach twisted. "Oh."

"Yeah."

"Do Sheena and Jerome know that?"

"I'm not sure. They might suspect. And obviously it's not your responsibility to fix any of this," he added in a rush. "It's my responsibility." He sat on a rock. "I just have no idea what the hell I'm going to do." He blew out a breath, shoulders slumping. "It was already so goddamn hard to get this job in the first place."

"It's not over yet. And even if it is, you'll find something else."

"Something salaried?" When he looked up at her, his eyes were dark. "I'm glad that you've made a good situation for yourself with the freelancing. I really am. But my parents didn't spare me from student loans like yours did."

She blushed, feeling a wave of guilt and gratitude that her mom's professorship had come with family tuition benefits.

"But like I said," he muttered, "none of that is your problem. I'm just stressing. About trying to save my own ass, and now the asses of the honorable, wonderful, very hardworking Sheena and Jerome."

She nodded, nibbling her lip. "Maybe there's some way to make this work."

His back straightened a little. "What are you thinking?"

"I don't know yet. But maybe we can still deliver a big story without completely screwing over Nora."

"Okay, I like the sound of that."

"And you said we have time, right?"

"For now."

She rubbed her forehead. "I have a busy six weeks ahead with my other clients. But maybe I tell Conrad"—even saying his name made her clench her teeth—"that I want to come home for my birthday weekend next month."

"MC." Joe bolted to his feet and put his hands on her shoulders. "You would be my fucking hero."

She shrugged. "You've been mine."

"You don't owe me for that."

"I know. But I'd hate to see you give up because I wasn't there to kick your butt."

He smiled. "Speaking of kicking butt, are you ready for our next lap?"

"Uh, no?"

He jogged off. "Torture can be fun!" he said, starting to run backward. "You should try it!"

She followed in a huff. "I'm good!"

"I think you'd like it if you gave it a chance!"

"I'd rather not!"

He stopped. She stopped.

They panted for a moment, facing each other. Then he

jammed his hand into her sweatpants pocket, snatched her phone, and ran away with it, cackling as he went.

"Come back!" she said.

But he was too fast. The phone wasn't up at his ear, but she could see he was furiously typing as his legs ate the pavement.

"What are you doing?" she moaned.

When she finally caught him at the entrance to Grand Army Plaza, he was smiling. She yanked the phone away from him and looked down at the message thread between her and Nora. They'd exchanged numbers after Pooh-gate so Nora could send her some of the photos Lois had taken that day: Nora hand-in-paw with the demon that'd devoured Christopher Robin's childhood and puked it back up over a dozen crying toddlers. Now the latest message was from MC:

> Is it weird that I kind of had fun yesterday?

"Okay," she said, "that was unnecessary."

Joe grinned. "Don't forget out of line."

Then her phone buzzed.

Are you coming out to me as a furry?

Joe huffed a laugh over her shoulder.

"Will you get away from me?" she said.

"Am I not allowed to make a stressful situation the slightest bit fun?"

"I never should've told you about Pooh."

"It was critical info. What are you going to say back?"

He reached for her phone again, and she swatted his hand away.

As they were lightly slap fighting, MC caught sight of a familiar face across the plaza.

"Oh god," she whispered, pulling Joe back toward the bushes at the park entrance.

"What?" He tried to follow her gaze. "Is that—"

"Lisa."

MC's latest ex was sitting on one of the stone benches. Her strawberry blond hair was shimmering in the sun, a loose green scarf around her neck. Beside her was a well-built guy with a halo of reddish curls. For a few moments, as Joe and MC watched them from between the branches, all they did was laugh. Then Lisa put a hand on his neck and kissed him. He kissed her back, trailing a hand over her chest. In broad daylight.

Which she seemed to like.

"Ew," said Joe.

MC couldn't speak. She knew Lisa had been ostensibly done with her for a good month before officially calling it off, but she'd expected a longer mourning period.

"You okay?" Joe said.

She couldn't believe she was sniffling. She didn't do this in public. She didn't do this, period. Except she'd done it in front of Nora just yesterday. And now she was doing it again with Joe.

What was happening to her?

"MC. Look at me."

"Can't," she said softly, even though he was the only person who'd ever seen her break down before.

He held her close. "You are better than that."

"I'm really not."

"Yes, you are." He rubbed her back. "You're smart and funny and loyal."

"I'm a joke."

"Hardly."

"Then why does it always feel like the world is laughing at me?" She wiped her nose with the back of her hand. "Especially Nora freaking Pike."

"For what it's worth, I think her book shows that she also really admired you." Joe leaned back, looking her in the eye. "One thing she definitely got right is that you've always been scared of offending anyone, even when they're slinging shit at you." He squeezed her shoulders. "Maybe you should sling a little back."

"But I don't want to."

"Okay, fine. Keep being a good person or whatever. I'm just saying, you're always doing everything you can to make sure no one experiences any discomfort, while the things that you want are put aside."

"I don't have that many wants."

"That's what you've told yourself."

"Thanks for the TED Talk."

"See, isn't it nice to be a little sarcastic now and then?"

"Enough of Life Coach Joe."

"Think about what I'm saying." He took off running again. "You could at least try being a little more bold!"

This time, though it took all her willpower, she didn't follow.

11

Six weeks after discovering-slash-reaffirming her constitutional inability to run uphill, or run in general, MC stared down at her phone with the distinct sense that all her carefully laid plans had been in vain.

Sorry, can't make the meeting. Work.

That morning, MC had invited Nora to another round of *Explorations, Special Guest Edition*. Ms. Kim had spent the past month raining compliments on MC's initial visit, declaring that she—and the students—would be over the moon if MC did a reprise. The sooner the better. MC had finally agreed, mostly to rope Nora in, imagining that a librarian could easily take a late lunch, or just leave early. It was Halloween, for god's sake.

But if Nora wanted to pretend her high-powered job was preventing her from doing a little community service with MC, that was her choice.

MC would choose to take a cab straight from the train station to the library so she could get a little "work" done before her commitment to Ms. Kim and the illustrious writers of Green Hills High.

She tapped her phone on her knee, staring out the train window as the scenery rushed past: lots filled with sand and gravel, pallets of stone. Vacant storefronts. Excavators.

Backyards overtaken by slimy aboveground pools and children's toys, garbage everywhere. She still hadn't figured out how to give Joe the big story he needed without exposing Nora's identity, but she hoped this quick—and final—visit home would deliver the key.

Especially because their meeting with Seth Flanagan and Jawbreaker's top brass had been rescheduled for that coming Monday.

She texted Conrad.

> Heading in for Explorations, will I see you there?

Then:

> Also, thanks for having me over again.
> Nice to be home for my birthday weekend.

It took him about twenty minutes to reply:

Sure. I'll come find you after the meeting.

She was glad he wasn't raking her over the coals for their spat back in September. On the other hand, the same stiffness remained between them. She told herself an apology wouldn't have fixed that, anyway.

She took *Girl Next Door* out of her backpack and laid it on her lap. For the past six weeks, as fall had arrived in force, she'd dipped in and out of it, still too flummoxed to read it from start to finish. Part of the problem was the confounding factor of her increasingly frequent texts with Nora. Part of it was her research into the larger fandom that surrounded the book.

One minute she'd be scrolling Instagram accounts devoted

to cartoon art of Nicole Penny and Michaela Carson in what MC assumed were critical scenes in the book: Nicole sitting at a desk as Michaela loomed over her, comical red splotches on their cheeks; Michaela wolfing down a slice of pizza as Nicole stared at her with lustful eyes; and, of course, the iconic picket fence, the young lovers on either side, pretending not to see each other, with a sickeningly familiar exchange scribbled just overhead:

You do know you're amazing, right?

What corny-ass movie did you get that line from?

The next minute, Nora's name would pop up on MC's phone:

Did you ever go back and get your bike?

                                                                  I totally forgot! Oof.

Poor bike.

All alone in a bush.

On the side of the road.

                                                                     Is that a poem?

As if I'd ever write poetry.

The blurred lines between Nicole Penny the character, S. K. Smith the famous author, and Nora Pike the reference librarian—to whom MC was sending flirty messages on an almost daily basis now—had created a fixation that manifested in a growing notes document on her computer. While her initial dispatch to Joe had been thin, she'd since indulged in copious speculation, trying to sift reality from fiction. But what she needed to do was figure out what it all meant.

Then there was all the time she was spending online, consuming reviews, think pieces, and breathless sales milestones. Trawling through *GND* fan fiction, *GND* meme accounts, and several hashtags, such as #LaughingThenCryingOverGND, which rounded up videos of readers going through a roller coaster of over-the-top facial expressions while staring into their paperbacks. She'd even discovered a forum of *GND* erotica. *"Your body is a poem,"* Michaela said as she caressed Nicole's thigh. *"Every part of you is a stanza."*

"Oh my god," MC had said aloud to no one.

There were also forums devoted to discussing the identity of S. K. Smith. Theories ranged from this or that established romance writer, eager to nab a queer audience without diluting their brand, to a middle-aged man living in Montana, who'd self-published a number of lesbian romance novels, including one called *The Gals Next Door*. Business names in the book were constantly being cross-referenced to businesses in real life, creating a minor surge in sales for Dellafino's Pizza in suburban New Jersey—Delfino's, in Green Hills—and Dairy Haven twenty-four-hour minimarts on Long Island. Snack Barn, the knockoff, was the true analog.

But nothing could distract MC for long from the portrayal of herself in the book. She'd been prepared for Nora writing her as clueless. Instead, Nora had captured something more subtle: a longstanding desperation to avoid anything that might've given away the fact that she possessed complicated emotions, which was somehow worse. To add insult to injury, Michaela Carson the adult had managed to grow up in ways that MC hadn't even begun to work on. Michaela was more confident, less self-effacing—a person with a sense of direction. And so, over the past six weeks, MC had managed to go from feeling relatively content about her life to embarrassed and, wonder of wonders, kind of grumpy about it.

She got off the train at Green Hills and took a cab straight to the library. For once, she was eager for a confrontation.

When she walked in and saw Lois, she waved and said, "Happy Halloween."

Lois frowned. "Where's your costume?" The librarian was wearing a headband with glittering red horns, a fuzzy red cardigan, and red slacks that had a velvet tail pinned to the backside. MC was trying to figure out how to excuse her lack of holiday spirit when Lois barked, "Mine's in hell."

MC laughed. "You know, I think I forgot mine there the other day."

"Actually, you left it in the supply closet behind the circulation desk."

"You should've seen the emails we got after that," said Maureen, striding over in a giant banana costume, purple lipstick set off by the yellow peel that surrounded her face. "I almost got fired."

"Seriously?" MC said. "I'm so sorry—"

"Don't apologize to her." Lois turned and shook her head at the children's librarian. "You're the one who saw that getup and decided it was the perfect thing for impressionable children."

"I only saw it in pieces," Maureen fired back.

Then she shot MC a look and continued on, her costume waggling obscenely.

"Did I actually almost get her fired?" MC asked. The idea of threatening someone's livelihood, even if it was an accident, and well-intentioned at that, was unbearable.

"No. Helen does want to fire her, though."

"She does?"

"It's taking forever to put the documentation together in case she decides to sue. Nora's in the children's section, by the way."

"Oh, I wasn't . . . I'm just here to get some work done."

"Uh-huh." Lois's eyes were barely discernible, but MC could still detect a sly look.

"Lois, have you ever . . ."—but asking about *Girl Next Door* was a step too far—"had a project you really needed to finish, but had no idea how?"

"My taxes."

Lois walked away without another word.

To make a point of not heading straight over to Nora, MC took her usual spot in the study wing. At the table next to her, three older women were knitting, holiday pins bright and colorful on their sweaters. They were talking in low voices as MC pretended to get to work on some web copy for an aviation client. But after a few minutes, the volume went up.

"Do you know what corn started out as?" one woman yelled. "Maize. The Native Americans grew it to grind it up. They didn't just eat it."

"But what I'm saying is, it's different now—"

"I can't digest it."

"There are new strains."

"It wasn't designed for human consumption."

"There's nothing quite like summer corn," said a third woman.

"Well, *I can't digest it*."

MC shut her laptop and left it on the table, meandering over to the stacks, where she could pretend to look at books while sussing out whatever Nora was up to.

She was in a witch costume. Black hat rumpled as if from regular use, velvet cape draped across her shoulders. Her fingers were laden with rings of heavy metal and gemstones. She'd done some kind of stage makeup as well, darkening her eyes and tracing colored veins at her temples and jaw. She was reading to a group of small children.

MC didn't recognize the book, but the narration was weird. It seemed to be a retelling of "The Ugly Duckling," except at the end, the duckling didn't realize it was a swan. It was just ugly.

As soon as Nora had finished, the kids demanded that she read it again. MC hadn't seen her in action at the Winnie-the-Pooh story hour back in September, due to overwhelming nausea. But now she understood why Nora was the reader of choice.

The kids loved her. They climbed into her lap, put their grubby hands on her velvet-clad shoulders, squealed when she practically shoved them out of her way to get up and dust herself off. They trailed after her, begging her to stay, whining when she told them she had work to do. Her cool demeanor didn't put them off at all. In fact, it delighted them. There was a wicked warmth just beneath it, so strong MC couldn't believe she'd never noticed it before.

When Nora turned a corner at the graphic novels, she bumped into MC, who'd forgotten to move.

"Jesus," Nora said, putting up her hands. "Are you stalking me?"

"What? No." MC cleared her throat, not sure if that was strictly accurate. "Nice costume."

"I thought you had an *Explorations* meeting to get to."

"Yeah. In an hour. Just finishing some work first."

Nora strode off to her desk.

MC wanted to retreat to her table, but she heard Joe's voice in her head, encouraging her to be bold.

"I actually need help finding some books," she said. "If you have a minute."

Nora took off her hat and ran a hand through her hair. "Use the catalogue."

"I'm searching by subject."

"There's a field for keywords."

"Nora!" Lois called from circulation. "Do your job!"

Nora took a breath. "What subject?"

"Uh... the Byzantine Empire."

Nora walked off to the stacks, MC trailing behind her yet again.

"Just some light reading?" Nora said.

"It's research. For my novel."

Nora stole a look at MC over her shoulder. "The novel that's about getting some things off your chest?"

"Right." MC swallowed. "I'm using history as a lens."

"Uh-huh."

"There's this empress—"

"Theodora?"

"Yeah, exactly."

"I should warn you, a bunch of authors have already taken her on."

"Like Rebecca Sloane?"

Nora's pace slowed. "You've read her?"

"I'm writing a response. So to speak." MC gestured wildly with her hands. "Like, trying to do the emotional stuff, and the history, more realistically."

"Why?"

"Because accuracy"—she gave Nora a significant look—"is important."

"Not in fiction." Nora slipped into a row in the back of the study wing.

"Okay," MC said, a little hotly. "That's your opinion."

"I'm aware."

"What do you think of her? Rebecca Sloane?"

Nora was too busy scanning the shelves to look at MC. "I think she's maudlin." She put her finger on a spine. "But her sex scenes are good."

"I only wish they were, like, ten times longer."

MC couldn't believe she'd just said this out loud.

But it got Nora's attention. Her eyes narrowed.

"So," MC said, needing to regain control of the situation, "did you like *Theodora's Concubine*?"

Nora shrugged. "It wasn't as good as *The Vapors at Delphi*."

"Not even close." MC leaned a shoulder against the shelves. "*Vapors* had more of an equal power dynamic between the two women. In all her other stuff, it's too predictable."

"The princess or the general's daughter has the upper hand," Nora said, "but then the tables turn at the midpoint."

"And it's like, well, we know where this is going."

"Right."

"Whereas in *Vapors* they're actually stuck in the same situation, even if their backgrounds are totally different."

For once, MC seemed to have caused Nora to consider her response.

"That row down there is early Byzantine," she said at last.

"Great. Thanks." MC knelt to look at the spines, pulling out the first one and pretending to read the back cover.

"There's also this one," Nora said. "Though it's more of a travelogue—"

The next thing MC knew, there was a sharp pain in the back of her head.

"Oh god," Nora said, dropping down to her knees, "I was trying to pull one and another slipped out."

MC gritted her teeth, staring down at an ancient tome about the Bosphorus strait, splayed open next to her foot. "All good," she wheezed.

"It helps if you . . ."

"What?"

Nora reached out and took MC's head between her hands, massaging the part of MC's skull that was almost certainly shattered.

But after a moment or two, the pain dulled, the hurt lessening as it spread.

"Any better?" Nora asked.

MC relaxed into her touch. "Yeah."

Nora kept rubbing. Her fingers were deft. Experienced.

"I've never heard of this technique," MC said.

"I learned it in BJJ."

"BJJ?"

"Brazilian jiujitsu."

MC deepened her voice and did her best Neo: "You know . . . jiujitsu?"

"Stop trying to hit me," Nora replied, a perfect Morpheus. "And hit me."

MC's heart skipped a beat.

And suddenly Nora's expression softened, made her seem like a teenager again. Like the two of them were just lonely dorks who thought they understood the universe.

Nora must've sensed the slip, because a moment later, her hands were gone and her voice was brisk. "You're fine."

MC wasn't fine. Not even close. She'd already known she was on dangerous ground, emotionally, with Nora. She'd already known that she found Nora attractive.

But in that moment, longing for Nora's touch like it might

complete her, MC realized she had it much, much worse than she thought.

"Everything okay back here?" said Lois, appearing at the start of their row.

"Yeah," MC said quickly, just as Nora said, "I dropped a book on her head."

Lois frowned.

"She did help me find what I was looking for," MC said, casting a quick glance at Nora. "So, thanks for that. And sorry to not be seeing you at *Explorations*."

"What's *Explorations*?" Lois asked.

"Nothing," Nora said, just as MC said, "The literary magazine we did together in high school." She cleared her throat. "There's a meeting today. I'm filling in as the advisor for a little while, to help my brother out. I thought Nora would be a good resource."

Lois looked to Nora. "Why can't you go?"

"Because I work?"

"We're closing early. Go help some teenagers." Lois waved a hand. "And the girl you just gave a concussion."

"I really wouldn't be much use—"

"I think you would," MC said. "The magazine was your baby."

"Take care of your baby," Lois said, then shuffled away.

12

Because leaving the library with Nora Pike would've meant too much uninterrupted time with Nora Pike, MC headed out early, telling her to swing by the meeting whenever.

"And if you really don't want to be there, I get it."

Nora had looked grateful, in a wary way, and MC had realized this meant they probably wouldn't be seeing each other later after all. Maybe it was for the best. Things had gotten too serious in the stacks, even if it'd just been for a moment.

Of course, she was sabotaging yet another opportunity to rescue the sinking ship of her promise to Joe. But she didn't want to think about that.

Then, in the middle of the meeting, as MC was leading the year's first real workshop discussion—Mr. Pryor, apparently, had been turning the group into an extracurricular lecture series on modernist masterpieces of the interwar period—Nora appeared in the doorway.

"Everyone," MC said, "this is Nora, master of the magazine back in the day, which I heard you all want to bring back." She got up and pulled over a desk. "After we finish workshopping, she'll walk us through the layout and printing process."

Nora took the seat, looking ashen. Maybe it was because she'd scrubbed off all her witch makeup. MC was sad to see it gone. Nora's commitment to the holiday had inspired MC to borrow a pirate hat, eyepatch, and fake mustache from Mr. Pryor. Now she felt like she'd missed the memo, as always.

The workshop resumed—a hot debate over whether the main character's epiphany was earned. The emerging consensus was that it was not.

"Why does it have to be earned?" said a girl named Sheila. She had a rough voice and dark nail polish. "Like, can't people just realize shit sometimes?"

"I agree," said a guy across the circle. Patrick. He was dour and solitary, with long skateboarder hair and a nervous foot. "It's not like this is a thriller."

"But it's still a story," MC said. "Readers expect stories to have different rules than reality."

"Hashtag not-all-readers," said Ben, ever the good-natured commentator.

They argued and snarked for another twenty minutes or so. There were a dozen students in attendance, mostly upperclassmen. The only one who didn't speak was the girl MC had seen at the library on her first night back in Green Hills. Her name was Heather. MC had deduced this from the meeting sign-in list by process of elimination.

"Okay," MC said, clapping her hands, "let's move on to the magazine. First off, tell Nora a little bit about why you want to bring back the print edition."

There were the requisite complaints about how annoying it was that everything had to be online, how fake and transient everything felt there.

"A printed magazine is transient too," Nora said. "You can hold it in your hands, but then it gets thrown out. Or stuffed in a box in your mom's attic."

Sheila frowned. "Are you saying we shouldn't do it?"

"I'm saying you should think about what it means to make a record of your lives at this point. Because it won't give you a sense of permanence." Nora's gaze flicked to MC. "And looking back on things later can be embarrassing."

"Whatever I wrote definitely sucked," MC said.

The group laughed, but MC could tell Nora had made them nervous. She'd made MC nervous too. Was her judgment directed at MC's terrible short stories, or her own poem? And if she was talking about her poem, did that mean she was embarrassed about what she'd written about MC back then?

Now?

"The thing is," MC added, taking a chance on her instincts for once, "so what? I think it's brave to put yourself out there, even when you know you'll be a different person down the line." She got a few skeptical looks. "Do you really want to go through life believing that you never had anything to learn?"

"Yes," said Ben.

Everyone laughed again.

"Okay," MC said, "let's move on to design for a second . . ."

MC got Nora to explain their old process of working with the Art Department to solicit illustrations, paintings, and photography. Then Nora named some zines in the library's archive collection that were worth looking at for ideas. After the meeting, MC saw Heather walk over to Sheila and propose checking out the zines together sometime. Sheila seemed surprised by the suggestion, but nodded.

After the students had left, as MC and Nora were rearranging desks, MC said, "Thanks for coming. I really appreciate it."

Nora shrugged. "I mostly did it for Heather."

"Is she a library intern or something?"

"No. She just hangs around a lot."

"I noticed."

"Her parents are screwups."

"So, you guys are . . . friends?"

"Not exactly. But she talks to me. She told me she was into a girl in this club."

"The zines." MC smiled. "You set her up for that."

"My Halloween treat."

"Well, sorry if the rest of the experience was painful."

"I dropped a book on your head. You reminded me how shitty high school was. Now we're even."

MC thought back to being in these meetings together. Nora in the Heather role, but with more confidence. And, in the beginning, more pushback—especially from Joe. Everyone was annoyed by what they saw as her insistence on isolating herself. Whenever she did speak, it was assumed to be a setup for attack.

"I'm sorry people were assholes to you," MC said.

"I don't need you to apologize on their behalf."

"Fine. But I should've stood up for you more."

"I didn't want a knight in shining armor." Nora shoved a desk into place. "I knew what I was doing. I wasn't going to squeeze myself into one of the teen stereotypes available at the time, and I understood there was a price for that."

MC felt a flare of annoyance, thinking of the high school chapters of *Girl Next Door*. "Did you think I was one of the stereotypes?"

Nora's eyes flashed. "Weren't you?"

MC shook her head, pulse racing. "Why do you act like you know everything about me?"

"I don't."

"You do." MC squared off with her. She knew she needed to rein it in, but couldn't seem to help herself. "It's kind of rude."

She'd done it.

She'd said something unfriendly.

For a few moments, Nora seemed at a loss for words.

Then she ripped MC's mustache off.

MC put a hand to the stinging strip of skin above her upper lip. "What was that for?"

"It was crooked," Nora said.

"So?"

"So." She leaned across the desk, her voice low. "It was bothering me." She reached up and carefully put the mustache back on, pressing her palms to MC's cheeks and smoothing the fake fuzz with her thumbs. There was a look in her eyes that made MC's stomach flip. Warmth coursed through her chest, a dam breaking, and her lips parted. She leaned forward, just a little—

"Wow," Conrad said, "the dynamic duo reunites."

Nora and MC reared back from each other.

"How'd it go?" he asked, waltzing into the classroom.

Nora stared at him in disdain. "I have to run." There was a trace of unsteadiness in her voice. If MC hadn't been feeling the same thing, but tenfold, she never would've noticed. "I need about eighty pounds of candy or my house gets egged."

"Kids these days," said Conrad.

"Thanks again for coming to the meeting," MC said hoarsely. "See you around?"

Nora cleared her throat. "Yeah."

After she left, MC and Conrad stood silently, staring at each other, for a solid minute.

"Cool hat, sis."

"Cool camisole, bro."

Trying to shake off the furious blush in her cheeks, she snapped the top of the Superman spandex poking out from his half-buttoned shirt. He'd slicked his blond hair into the Clark Kent curlicue. A pair of fake glasses perched on the edge of his nose. She tried to focus on how annoying he was, as opposed to the way Nora's thumbs had felt as they'd brushed across her mouth. She said, "Is this a literalization of your savior complex?"

"Sure." He flicked the brim of her pirate hat. "You look cute, by the way."

"Don't do that."

"What?"

"Belittle me."

"How could I belittle you when your facial hair's finally come in?" He smirked. "Nor Dog was looking pretty cute too."

"What do you mean by that?"

"Oh, nothing. Just that I finally figured out why you've started coming back home again."

MC's eyes widened. Her mind swirled with images of her brother curiously picking up a copy of *Girl Next Door* left behind in a classroom, reading the back cover, connecting it with Joe's phone call, the fact that he was a magazine editor—

"You have a thing for her, right?"

She laughed breathlessly. "What?"

"I don't know how I didn't put it together when you first got here. All that time at the library, zero interest in catching up with me, though I guess that's typical—"

"Hang on—"

"There was always such an intense vibe between you guys."

"Conrad."

"Come on, am I not allowed to mention something that might be, dare I say it, kind of cool?"

"You—wait, what?"

"Reconnecting with Nora. Getting it right this time."

"What did I get wrong, exactly?"

"Not going for it with her."

"I'm not going for it now."

"If you say so." He shrugged. "Look, I just want you to be happy. Hopefully you realize that."

MC was stunned. "Oh."

They walked out, not speaking. By the time they reached the parking lot, the wind had picked up, threatening to blow MC's hat off. She held it in her hands, feeling silly.

"Sorry to be weird," she said. "I'm not used to talking about girls with you."

"It's your business." He unlocked the Destroyer of Worlds. "Just bums me out that it seems to be a forbidden topic between us."

She ducked into the passenger seat. "I think I'm always embarrassed to tell you how little progress I ever seem to make in that department."

Conrad smiled. "Well, seeing as you're absolutely, definitely not into Nora . . . are you dating anyone?"

She smiled back. "I just got broken up with, actually."

He turned the car on, and they set off. She found it surprisingly easy to tell him about Lisa. How'd they'd met, what their relationship was like. She even described some of Lisa's more memorable immersive theater pieces, in which naked Brooklynites did domestic chores in loft apartments to pulsing EDM.

"And then, just last month, I saw her making out with a hot dude in Grand Army Plaza."

He whistled. "Shit."

"At least Joe was with me."

Conrad got quiet. MC wondered if it was because he was feeling weird about MC's reliance on Joe. But he only cleared his throat and said, "By the way, I invited Jae over for dinner tonight. I know she'd like to see you and catch up a little more."

"Is this your solution to being a workaholic? Polyamory with your work wife and your real one?"

In a shocking first, Conrad blushed. "I think she gets lonely on holidays. Her husband left her two years ago."

"That sucks. But I mean, it's Halloween..."

"Yeah, well, it reminds her of how she'd expected to have kids by now."

"Superman to the rescue."

He shrugged.

"Dinner with Ms. Kim sounds great," she said. "Sorry. I should've just said that off the bat."

"And tomorrow?" He raised an eyebrow. "Are we having a birthday rager or what?"

She sighed. "Technically, Joe got us tickets to a warehouse dance party in Bushwick." Which was true. And at the time, it'd seemed like the perfect excuse to leave Green Hills before anything too complicated could happen.

But now she didn't want to leave.

"Well," Conrad said, "I'll just have to bake you a cake for breakfast, then."

MC smiled.

When they got back to the house, Gabby—decked out in hippie bangles and a beehive hairdo—practically jumped into MC's arms. "I love that this is becoming a thing!"

MC wanted to temper Gabby's excitement, but didn't have it

in her. Maybe it was the fact that Conrad had asked her about her own life for once and listened to her answers, and also wanted to bake her a cake, but she felt like it was probably annoying to always be reminding everyone that she had a foot out the door.

She tossed her bag in the guest room. Which was her own former bedroom, stripped of its Eminem posters and unflattering snapshots from Joe's love affair with Polaroids. Then she hopped in the shower, a little less self-conscious about being back in the house than last time. When she'd gotten dressed and headed into the kitchen, there were already kids ringing the doorbell, chicken and potatoes in the oven, and a small, unusual warmth in her chest.

It felt like she was home.

13

"It's not a Green Hills problem, necessarily," Ms. Kim said. *Jae*, MC reminded herself. "Don't get me wrong, the suburbs were never going to be the cutting edge of education. But the bigger issue, in my opinion, is what people today think high school is supposed to be about."

"The kids or their parents?" said Gabby, spooning more potatoes onto her plate.

"Both. But my focus is the kids, because they're the ones who decide, every day, whether to participate in the experience or not."

MC bit into a perfectly crispy thigh. Conrad had outdone himself with the meal, roasting the chicken over a pile of onions and carrots and baking a crusty loaf of bread to go with it. He'd even shelled out for fancy European butter. Their dad, not just the craftsman but the chef of the family, would've been proud. His handmade ceramic plates had been set out for the occasion.

"We want them to imagine more possibilities," Jae went on. "To think of high school as more than just torture, or a necessary evil on the way to getting into college." MC flashed back to being in her English class senior year, listening to Jae give fiery speeches about Great Works of Literature, everyone spellbound. "Part of that is trying to revive clubs and activities after a decade of focusing on athletics. But a bigger part is changing our classroom culture, which is really hard, given that half of our teachers have been in the building for a long time already."

"I love that idea," said Gabby. "Classes really felt like the thing I missed out on. Even in college, my mind was so wrapped up in this guy." She put a hand on Conrad's back.

MC couldn't help noticing that Conrad leaned away a little, even as he flashed a tight smile.

"MC," said Jae, "how have you been finding the students?"

"They're great. I mean, they're on their phones a lot. But other than that, they remind me of our old crew."

Jae put a few veggies on her fork. "What did you think of high school when you were a student?"

MC stalled, taking a gulp of wine. "I think I mostly just floated through it."

"That's not true," Gabby said.

"Well, working on *Explorations* was definitely the highlight."

"You were also on student council."

"I was just the secretary."

"And weren't you a volunteer Big Sister or whatever?" Conrad said.

"I thought it'd look good on my college applications." MC stared at her bread. "My grades weren't anything to write home about."

Gabby shrugged. "Maybe that was because you took so many classes."

"When I moved back here," Conrad said, "I remember you told me you didn't even have a lunch period because there were too many electives you wanted to take."

"Yeah," MC said. "I forgot about that."

Jae smiled. "Now that you're not a student, I can tell you that there wasn't a teacher on staff who didn't love having you in class."

"You guys are making me blush."

MC looked at Conrad. He was smiling, like he'd won an argument she didn't even know they were having.

"So," Gabby said, "what we're saying is, hopefully your novel is about high school."

Everyone laughed. MC had to force herself to laugh along with them.

Toward the end of the meal, the doorbell ringing hit a fever pitch. Gabby volunteered to wash the dishes while Conrad and Jae manned the door, with MC going between to help dry a plate here, refill the candy bowl there. That feeling of home sparked in her again, and she wasn't sure whether to be wary of it. There was still the slight friction between Gabby and Conrad. The not-slight friction of MC being in Green Hills under false pretenses. Yet she couldn't help enjoying this unexpected break—this new version of being back.

She decided to go big and invite Nora over for dessert. A peace offering after their tense interaction that afternoon, and another chance to see if she could figure out the connection between Nora's various selves.

She went to ask Conrad if he was okay with the invite. But when she got to the mudroom, she saw him sitting shoulder to shoulder with Jae. Not romantically, exactly. Just closer than MC would've expected.

"Hey," she said, and they broke apart in an instant. "Cool if I ask Nora over for dessert?"

Conrad, whose face had looked cloudy at first, broke out in a smile. "Sure."

"I figured since she helped with the *Explorations* meeting today, it could be a way of saying thank you."

"Uh-huh."

"I mean, I'm sure she won't even say yes." She whipped out her phone and left Conrad and Jae alone, trying not to wonder if her brother was veering into dangerous territory.

> Come over for apple pie?
> Unless your house is getting egged.

She flopped down on the guest bed, her chest warm from the heavy food and copious wine.

> Just remembered you hate apples.

And because she couldn't help herself:

> Sorry for making things weird this afternoon.

She wanted to say more, to explain herself. But she figured that might just enhance the weirdness. A minute later, her phone vibrated.

You know I don't mind weird.

MC smiled, thumbs flying.

> Okay, apology rescinded.

Are you drunk right now?

> What?? How do you know?

Just an instinct.

> Based on?

Party persona.

> You only ever came to one of my parties.

One was enough to know you're a chatty drunk.

At least until you get your feelings hurt.

> Are you planning on hurting my feelings?

Yes.

> Ah.

I'm not coming over.

> Because it means interacting with my brother?
>
> Or because it means interacting with me?

Good night MC.

> Noraaaaa.

The thread went dead. Swearing, MC got out of bed, ready to go back out into the kitchen and see if Gabby needed help with any more dishes.

But then she remembered what Joe had said about being bold.

She took her phone back out.

> Do you have any plans tomorrow? It's my birthday.

I do. But happy birthday. Tomorrow.

Crushed, MC lightly banged her head against the wall. She had no idea what she was doing. Texting aside, it was obvious that Nora was still drawing the line at them hanging out alone together, for good reason. She clearly didn't want to tell MC about her runaway bestseller. MC couldn't decide whether this continued withholding was to be expected and therefore excusable, or whether it was unsettling and therefore a major red flag.

Her phone vibrated.

Don't forget to take your mustache off before bed.
Wouldn't want you to have a rash on your big day.
XO

The last two letters hit her like a one-two punch.

MC tried to calm herself. Nora was just making fun of her, as usual. She hadn't even taken the date-bait.

"You okay?" said Gabby, poking her head through the bedroom door.

"What! Yes!"

Gabby narrowed her eyes, but she was smiling. "You're blushing, girl."

"I am?" MC palmed her phone. "You know, I think maybe I had too much wine."

"You're sexting, aren't you?"

More heat flooded MC's cheeks. "No."

"Who's the lucky lady?"

"No one."

"MC, please!" She dropped her voice to a whisper and bounded over to the bed, throwing herself down on her side. "If I have to hear another word about Green Hills High, my whole body will shut down, and I will pass into the grave."

"Same." MC sighed. "But I really am just texting."

"Who?"

"A certain neighbor..."

Gabby clapped her hands. "I am so here for this."

"I mean, there's nothing to be here for at the moment."

"Let me see."

"It's embarrassing. I just tried to invite her over for dessert. Which she said no to."

Gabby pried the phone away. As she read, MC sat on the edge of the bed, arms crossed.

"First of all," said Gabby, "she is one hundred percent flirting with you. And has been for weeks. Second of all, you need to tell me exactly how you made things weird this afternoon."

"I asked her to come to the *Explorations* meeting. Which she did, but seemed to regret."

"Well, duh, I'm sure it was super disorienting for her to see you in your element again. It's been so many years, she's written you off as a romantic possibility—but now you're back, and you're just as sweet and smart as ever."

"You give me way too much credit."

"Why are you always being like that?" She squeezed MC's arm. "You're a total catch."

"Anyone want pie?" Conrad said, sticking his head in. "Or are we satisfied with snack-size candy?"

"Pie!" Gabby said, leaping off the bed. She kissed Conrad on the cheek as she brushed past him.

Conrad turned away before MC could catch his eye.

14

The breakfast cake was from a box, just the way MC liked it, with those edible candy letters on top. They said: YOU ARE OLD!

After Gabby and Conrad had sung her a full-throated rendition of the happy birthday song, which ended with Conrad riffing Mariah Carey–style on the final "you," Gabby said she had a gift for MC.

"We're going to Fall Fest!" she said, clapping her hands. "I will be showering you with candy apples while your brother locks himself in the basement for his usual Saturday you-know-what sesh."

MC nearly choked on her cake. When she got her breath again, she said, "I'm going to have a million cavities after this weekend."

"Mom always said you should've gotten braces." Conrad patted her shoulder. "Now you can have veneers."

"Speaking of Mom," MC said, "do you think she's okay? I got a long voicemail from her this morning. Usually it's just"—MC put on a monotone—"*Wishing you a year of happiness and success.*"

Conrad smirked. "Did she wish you happiness, success, and a new girlfriend or something?"

"No. But she said she misses us?"

"When I told her you were visiting, she was like, 'What? Why? Is she in trouble?' And when I said you were fine, she went dead silent."

"You guys are assholes," Gabby said, somehow managing to sound warmhearted about the declaration. "She's just awkward. And neither of you give her any opening to be emotional."

Conrad picked up a slice of cake in his bare hand and took a bite. "Isn't it her job," he said, still chewing, "to give the opening?"

"In an ideal world. But this isn't an ideal world."

"The therapist has spoken." Conrad put on his thickest Long Island accent. "I need to treat my motha betta."

MC started laughing, until she realized Gabby wasn't.

The first day of November was, as Joe would've put it, iconic. Red, orange, and gold leaves shining in the sun. The faintest hint of smoke on the wind. A nice base layer of crisp decay crackling underfoot as Gabby and MC got in the Destroyer of Worlds that afternoon. MC hadn't been to Fall Fest since she was a kid, but she had strong memories of hot apple cider in paper cups, denim jackets and itchy wool scarves, and toilet paper being cleaned from the branches outside the brick hall where the festival took place. It was a sprawling building at the top of a grassy hill near one of the town's churches, with a high-ceilinged entrance where people voted in elections, shopped for used books during the library's annual fundraiser, and surveyed local jewelry, cutting boards, and ornaments at the craft fair.

MC frowned as Gabby parked in the gravel lot next to the field. "Am I going to see everyone from our childhood right now?"

"Probably."

Gabby—seemingly over the awkward exchange with Conrad that morning—got out and linked elbows with MC, who'd had to borrow her brother's olive-green bomber jacket on account of coming unprepared for the chilly weather. It was too big, but MC had rolled up the sleeves and tried to fill it out with an oversize black hoodie. Otherwise she was in her usual jeans and a ratty pair of white sneakers, Gabby outclassing her in every way with a gray peacoat, flowy skirt, and leather boots.

As expected, they ran into a whole cast of characters from MC's youth: Mrs. Singh, MC's friend Puja's mom, who told MC that Puja was putting her wisecracking to good use as a stand-up comic out in LA; Dan Sommers, who ran the deli where MC and Joe had always gone for onion rings and gummy worms; Clog Man, an elderly gentleman and former professor known for walking very slowly through town in a pair of hand-carved wooden clogs, no socks, even in winter; Claire and Chrissy DeVecchio, twin sisters a year older than MC and Gabby, who'd played, in annual alternation, the damsel in distress and the villain to Conrad's leading man in their school plays; and Jim McDade, a friend of Conrad's and one of Joe's high school crushes, who was already going gray, possibly due to having two kids under three.

"Ugh," Gabby said, "how cute are they?"

One child was carrying and dropping a pumpkin in silent rage. The other was picking his nose.

"I like the matching outfits," MC said.

"Me too. God, I'm so ready to have kids."

MC couldn't even imagine such a feeling, though she'd always pictured a future with a family that included children, who would come about, somehow, fully formed, no pregnancy or babyhood required. "What about Con?" she said.

Gabby smiled, but it looked forced. "He's a little more nervous."

"Guys are like that. Right?"

"Yeah. I guess."

MC tried not to think about the way Conrad and Jae had been shoulder to shoulder in the doorway last night, looking out into the darkness. "He's always been very independent," she said carefully. "I'm sure he's just wondering how kids will affect his lifestyle."

"Wondering?" Gabby laughed. "Sometimes he talks about it like it's going to be the apocalypse."

"The end of one kind of life, the beginning of another . . ."

"See, you could do my job."

"If you and Joe were my only clients."

"Speaking of, are you seeing him tonight? Conrad said you were on the fence."

"Still there. I don't know why I'm not feeling the original plan. Brooklyn dance party. Some drugs. The dream."

"Uh, I know why you're not feeling it."

"You do?"

"Because you're feeling Nora Pike." She looped elbows with MC again. "Also, can we trade places? Minus the drugs."

"Do you want to? I've been trying to think of an excuse to duck out of it all morning."

"I was kind of kidding. It's your freaking birthday!"

"Well, happy birthday," said a familiar voice. "I'm not big on presents, but how about a renewal on your overdue history books?"

Lois had appeared next to them at the pumpkin-painting table, Nora at her side. MC's heart automatically started beating faster at the sight of Nora in her high-collared leather jacket and low-cut black top.

Lois grabbed a speckled ear of corn from the decorative display and pointed it at MC. "They loved sex, those Byzantines."

MC cleared her throat. "So they did."

"The problem with history is, only the most boring stuff makes it to the surface," Lois went on, straightening her fuzzy orange cardigan. "Who cares about the fall of Rome? I'll take the X-rated sequel any day."

"Lois," MC said, "this is Gabby, my sister-in-law. Nora, you guys already know each other. Obviously."

Nora stared coolly at Gabby as Gabby took Lois's hand.

"I think you helped me with a research project a few years ago," Gabby said, beaming. "I was writing my thesis."

"Someone's actually gotta work in that place," Lois said, eyeing Nora.

"Are you guys closed today?" MC asked.

"No. But I got us the day off. Helen knows we love to see the knitwear."

MC looked at Nora and said, "Understandable."

"Actually," said Gabby, an even bigger grin spreading across her face, "this is kind of perfect."

"What's perfect?" Nora said darkly.

"Running into each other." Gabby hugged MC's shoulders. "As you heard, it's my very dear sister-in-law's birthday today, but Conrad and I both have so much work to catch up on. We were feeling terrible about leaving MC on her own, especially when it's going to be a perfect fall night to celebrate . . ."

"I don't need to celebrate," MC said. "I mean, we already celebrated. This is the celebration." She didn't know what Gabby was doing—Nora had already made it clear she didn't want to spend any time with MC that day.

But Gabby was undeterred. "Are you around tonight, Nora? I seem to remember you both being pizza fiends, and I happen to know all MC wants for her big day is a slice from Delfino's."

"I have plans," Nora said.

"What plans?" said Lois.

Nora shot her a look. "Plans."

"I'm sure she can reschedule them," Lois said. "Not good to be alone on your birthday. Nora was alone on hers just a few weeks ago."

Nora pressed her lips together. "Thank you, Lois."

"Oh my god," said Gabby, "a double celebration is in order."

MC remembered a few choice pieces of *Girl Next Door* fan art, including a *Titanic*-esque sketch of grown-up Michaela sprawled out on her side, licking the tip of a pizza slice. She was about to reassure Nora that a night to herself was totally fine—and if Gabby was angling for a ticket to the dance party, she could have it regardless—but then Nora sighed. "Fine," she said. "We can meet there at seven."

"Perfect," Gabby said. "Except Conrad might be working at the school. Is there any chance you guys could take Nora's car?"

MC looked sheepishly at Nora, who rolled her eyes.

After they'd parted ways, MC threw her hands in the air and said, "What was that?"

"Teamwork!" Gabby sang.

"I don't recall participating."

"You laid the foundation. I took things to their natural conclusion."

"Meaning I go to dinner with Nora, and you go out dancing with Joe?"

"Exactly."

MC had to call him. She left Gabby at a tent where a folksy-looking duo were tuning their guitars.

Joe answered on the second ring.

"Holy shit, you're at Fall Fest."

"I thought we agreed to use location-tracking for emergency purposes only."

"Are you drinking a hot cider in your mittens? Are you picking out a stained glass ornament for me? Are you bobbing for apples while Nora waits for the right moment to grab your ass and grind all over it?"

"Oh my god, Joe. None of the above. But let me know if you actually want an ornament."

"Also, happy birthday."

"Thanks. Listen, I told Gabby about the party tonight, and she's very interested. Any chance she could have my ticket and go with you instead?"

"Are you *ditching* me?"

She sighed. "You'll be happy to hear I've made other plans."

"Such as?"

"Going to Delfino's with Nora."

A pause. "That's. My. Girl."

"Try not to get too excited. This is a very forced arrangement."

"Nothing wrong with that."

"You realize how creepy you sound."

"I guess. Anyway, your job is to get her *drunk*."

"Joe."

"Come on, you know what I mean."

"I'm not going to get her drunk." She raked a hand through her hair. "Talking to you right now is actually reminding me how messed up this is."

"Except we are going to make it not messed up by threading the fine needles of our minds through this excellent scoop without destroying anyone's life. Remember?"

"Yeah, once we figure out how to actually do that."

"I have faith."

"In what, exactly?"

"You. And the pagan gods of the autumnal equinox."

She sighed. "I'll keep you posted, okay?"

"Babe, I'll be hanging on your every word."

15

MC took a mirror selfie that night and sent it to Joe. He replied instantly.

Nope.

MC stared down at her black T-shirt and black jeans.

You need to revert to your old style. Set the mood.
                        I think I gave all my flares to Goodwill.
I remember you in cargos.
                        Cargos and what? An old man sweater?
Open flannel shirt.
                        So, Avril Lavigne.
Except authentically butch.

MC sighed and went back to her closet, digging through old boxes of clothing. When Gabby and Conrad had moved in together after college, they'd gone room to room, packing up the remains of MC and Conrad's childhood, trying to make the place their own. MC had helped for about twenty-four hours, mostly by twining together old issues of *Fine Woodworking* and hauling them to the town hall for bulk recycling. She figured her brother had a vision for how he wanted everything, and it didn't include her, so why stick around? After he and Gabby had gotten married, she'd expected them to move out anyway. But whether they were paying rent or not, it must've been a deal compared to the cost of leaving, because they'd stayed ever since.

She sent Joe another selfie.

Perfect.

She put her phone in the pocket of her gray cargo pants and blinked at her reflection. She fit the zip-up sweatshirt and flannel better now. Otherwise, she looked exactly the same. A few lines at the corners of her eyes. A trace of veins on the backs of her hands. It was hard to imagine that nine years had passed.

She shouted to Conrad down in his basement lair and headed out.

Nora was still inside when MC crossed the gate in the picket fence. She realized she'd been half expecting the air to feel different on the other side. To find some pixie dust or enchanted creature that spouted the secret to writing bestselling novels from a nest in one of the window wells along the stone foundation. But it was just another suburban house, curls of red paint casting long shadows in the setting sun, a pile of leaves gathered against the garage.

MC was about to step onto the porch and knock when Nora finally emerged in an army jacket and high-waisted jeans, maroon Doc Martens gleaming. Her hair was down, tucked behind her right ear, which sported a gold earring in the shape of a bowie knife.

"Are your parents living here these days?" MC asked.

"Only on paper."

They walked to her car. "Where are they now?"

"Guatemala. Are you wearing your clothes from high school?"

MC looked down at herself in disbelief that she'd let Joe guide her fashion decisions. "I didn't pack right for the weather. Had to break into the archives."

"You're like a cross between a middle school boy and my electrician."

"I'll save that description for my dating apps."

"It's kind of charming."

MC cleared her throat and ducked into the passenger seat. "So, your parents still travel a lot?"

"More than ever."

"When's the last time you saw them?"

"About ten months ago." Nora turned on the car. "Sometimes they'll go six weeks between emails."

"Do you worry about them?"

"Not really."

"Do you miss them?"

"Not anymore."

As Nora pulled onto the main road, MC wanted to ask more about her parents, why she hadn't decided to get a place of her own after all these years—especially given the advance she'd been paid on her book, plus the royalties she'd seeing by now, neither of which MC could actually mention. But the bigger obstacle to MC's digging was that she didn't want to make Nora uncomfortable. In fact, the whole underlying purpose of this date, of MC's presence in Green Hills, was starting to make her sick.

"Did you actually have other plans tonight?"

Nora shrugged. "I did."

"You should just bail on me."

"We're already on our way."

"But it's not like we have to commit to this. I can just open the door, jump out into the woods, find my bike . . ."

"They weren't important plans."

MC sighed. "I don't know why Gabby got so invested in making this happen."

"Probably because she loves poking her nose in everyone's business."

"Or she just really wanted to hit up this dance party in Brooklyn tonight."

"I thought she was working."

"Joe bought tickets for me and him, for my birthday. But I didn't feel like going, so I offered them to Gabby. I think she felt guilty about taking them."

"Why didn't you feel like going?"

"I don't know. Not my scene, I guess."

"Really?" She shot MC a sly look. "Because I happen to remember a certain performance you and Joe did for the junior year talent show."

"Oh god." MC's stomach twisted. "Please don't remind me."

"Why not? It was incredible."

It was hard for MC to see what was incredible about dancing around to Massive Attack's "Teardrop" in front of their entire school—an earnest and overly serious attempt at modern dance that flew in the face of all MC's preferences for blending in. Joe had confessed to her later that his insistence on participating was actually an attempt to catch the attention of Jim McDade, whose mom ran the dance studio in town where they practiced every day for two months leading up to the show.

"I didn't know you saw that," MC muttered.

"Mr. Marquet asked me to do set design. Plus, I might've seen you practicing your moves in the backyard and gotten intrigued."

MC buried her face in her hands. "This is unbearable."

"Why?"

"We were a laughingstock."

"I wasn't laughing."

"Well, you were the only one."

"I thought it was beautiful." Nora paused. "Maybe the only genuine work of art to come out of our entire high school experience."

MC had to laugh. "Wow."

"If we drink enough beer tonight, will you do a reprise?"

"Not even if I get blackout drunk."

Nora smiled. "That's a shame."

As Nora looked for parking, MC wondered if there was a talent show dance scene in *Girl Next Door*, and how Nora had brought that particular horror to life.

But part of her was flattered Nora had been impressed.

They ended up paying to use the municipal lot.

"Had my first kiss here," Nora said, putting her keys in her pocket and setting a brisk pace. "In the back seat of a woman's van, right next to the dumpster."

"How old were you?"

"Eighteen."

"Was it good?"

"Like my tongue got caught in a vacuum cleaner. Plus, the garbage smell."

Suddenly MC felt hyperaware of the distance between them. "Have you always known you were gay?"

"Ever since I had the hots for Mrs. Eriksson."

MC struggled for a moment to remember their fourth-grade teacher. "Was she the one with the Swedish accent? And the leopard-print leggings?"

"I like a surprise combo." Nora didn't slow down, but MC sensed her changing trajectory slightly, so that she was a little closer to MC. "What about you? When did you know you were queer?"

"It's hard to pinpoint. I wasn't thinking about anyone romantically until high school."

"Late bloomer?"

"Something like that."

"The power of Gabby."

MC winced. "You picked up on that?"

"Uh, yeah." They crossed an alleyway. "Did Conrad know?"

"At the time, I don't think so."

"What about now?"

"We haven't discussed it. Anyway, it was such a long time ago."

Nora raised an eyebrow, but they'd turned the corner. Delfino's was upon them, and MC was eager to get inside. Nora walked off to claim a booth as MC took a spot in line at the counter. The menu was straightforward, just pizza and only three ways to get it: cheese, extra cheese, and pepperoni.

"One large cheese," she said to the guy in front of the ovens. "And what kind of beer do you have?"

"Miller and Miller Lite."

"Let's go with Miller, please."

In her peripheral vision, she saw Jen Turner.

"Wuss eyes."

MC blinked, looking back at the guy in the flour-dusted T-shirt.

"Sorry," she said, "didn't get that."

"Wuss eyes," he said again.

Her throat felt dry. She didn't know why she couldn't understand what the man was saying to her. She peeked over her shoulder and saw Jen striding over to the booth Nora had picked out.

"What size, lady?"

"Oh. Pitcher. Please. Thank you."

He raised his eyebrows, like it was incredible that she managed to remain alive from minute to minute.

Willing her hands to stop shaking, she carried the frothy pitcher to the booth, smiling as broadly as she could manage.

"Hey, Jen," she said.

"MC, we meet again." Jen was in an old varsity jacket and tight pants. She gave MC a look that was very different from the one she'd given her in the library. "Nora told me she had to do a favor for a friend tonight. Didn't realize you were the one who needed the favor."

"It's my birthday. My brother and my sister-in-law were both busy, so . . ."

Jen frowned. "Don't you live in New York?"

"I'm just visiting. For the weekend."

"Even though your family's too busy to hang out with you."

"The trip was a last-minute idea on my part." She toed the grease-streaked floor. "My brother did make me a cake for breakfast."

"Aw," Jen said. "That's sweet."

"MC's not telling the whole truth," Nora said. She was already pouring herself a cup of beer. "She's been coming home to work on a novel."

"What's it about?" Jen said. "Let me guess. A twenty-something suburban girl moves to the big city and walks around having big thoughts about life."

Nora cut in again. "It's actually historical fiction."

"Oh yeah?"

"Set during the Byzantine Empire."

"So, like . . . Rebecca Sloane."

"A response to Rebecca Sloane," MC said, irritated that Jen knew the reference.

"You have your work cut out for you. She's a terrible writer." Jen shrugged. "Well, I'm just picking up a pie for some friends, but you two have fun." She put a hand on Nora's shoulder and squeezed. "Text you later?"

Nora raised her eyebrows and waved her off.

MC saw Jen sneak a backward glance at them as she walked away.

"A favor to a friend," MC said, sitting down across from Nora and filling her plastic cup to the brim.

"I had to say it in a way that wouldn't offend her. We were supposed to hang out tonight."

MC took a long drink. "What are you guys, exactly?"

"Nothing. We just spend time together. Occasionally."

"Looked like more than that back in September."

"Why do you care?"

"I don't. She just doesn't seem like your type."

Nora raised an eyebrow. "I'm really curious to hear what you think my type is."

The pizza came just then, steaming on a cardboard circle, placed on a wire rack at the end of the booth. MC went straight for the paper plates.

"Let's hear it," Nora said, keeping her voice casual as she served herself. "What's my type?"

"I don't know. I have no idea why I said that."

"I mean, for example"—now Nora was grabbing napkins—"would you say that you're my type?"

"Hot," MC exclaimed, putting down her slice. "Too hot." The roof of her mouth was burning.

Nora smiled, like this confirmed something. "So, do you like living in New York?"

MC was still trying to recover from Nora's previous line of questioning. "I like certain things about it."

"Such as?"

"I don't know. All the people."

Nora stared. "You like all eight million people who live in New York."

"Yes, exactly." MC shook her head. "I like the density of people."

"Why?"

"It's just . . . interesting."

Nora's smile deepened.

"What?"

"No," Nora said, "tell me more about these eight million interesting people."

"When you put it like that, I sound vapid."

"Maybe I'm just amazed."

"By what?"

"Your ability to enjoy that. You seem to like being around anyone." She drank her beer. "Even me."

"I feel like most people are pretty cool once you scratch the surface."

"Being around people drives me insane."

"Am I driving you insane right now?"

"No." Nora looked away for a second.

They moved on to their second slices.

"Do you like living in Green Hills?" MC ventured.

"It's fine."

"You strike me as someone who'd want to get out of here. Find somewhere more exciting to live. Or maybe just more remote."

"Remote places don't have much in the way of work for outsiders."

"So, you've thought about leaving?"

"Not seriously. I take care of the house for my parents. They let me live there for free. Until I pay off all my student loans, it's a good situation."

The mention of loans made MC wonder if Nora had written *Girl Next Door* for money—the most obvious explanation. But Nora couldn't have known how successful it would be. And even now, with royalties flowing in, she didn't seem like a big spender.

Maybe the loans were crippling.

Or maybe something else was going on.

"Did you have to go to grad school to become a librarian?" MC asked.

"I did."

"And did you live away from home for that?"

Nora shook her head. "Commuted. Just like for undergrad."

"That's smart. My parents wasted a lot of money putting me through school in the city."

"Well, you're self-sufficient now."

"I live in a small apartment with a bunch of weird roommates. And I don't have health insurance."

"Sounds glamorous."

"Most days, in spite of everything, I feel like I have a plan. Get more freelance gigs, eventually settle down in a contract position. Stumble on a rent-controlled apartment somehow." She slumped a little, thinking about Michaela Carson, queer novelist extraordinaire. "But being home has made me think, you know, maybe I have no idea what I'm doing."

"Because you have no idea what you really want?"

MC blinked. "Yeah. Exactly."

"I feel the same way."

"You do?"

"I tell myself I have to be in Green Hills. To look after my parents' place, and to save money. But sometimes it feels like the real problem is that a part of me doesn't want to leave—like, literally doesn't want to move on, you know?"

MC's voice softened. "Why do you think that is?"

Nora paused.

And just as she was about to answer, MC saw Conrad coming through the door—with Jae right behind him.

"Shit," she said, quickly slipping out from her side of the table and sliding into Nora's, so her back would be to them.

Nora's eyes widened.

"Can I . . ." Panicking, MC scooted closer to Nora, then threw an arm behind Nora's shoulders, on the booth. "Sorry," she whispered, "I just don't want my brother to see me."

Nora's voice turned prickly, but she didn't shy away. "Are you embarrassed to be here together?"

"What? No. He already knew we were going out. I just don't want him to realize I'm seeing him with Ms. Kim."

Nora glanced back over MC's elbow. "Oh."

Nora was wearing perfume, something subtle and citrusy.

"Don't they work together?" Nora whispered, shifting her weight a little toward MC.

"Yeah. But he didn't mention he was seeing her tonight."

Nora pulled MC's hood up. "Let's not have your hair give you away."

"Now what're they doing?"

Nora peered out again, her cheek brushing against the inside of MC's arm. "They're ordering."

"Are they holding hands or anything?"

"I don't think so."

"At least there's that."

"But there's definitely an energy there."

"What kind of energy?"

"You know what kind of energy." Nora slid even closer to MC, their thighs touching. "I feel like one of them is going to notice us."

MC's heart was pounding. Nora's breath was feathering across her cheek. "Hopefully they're just getting takeout."

Nora bit her lip. "She's coming this way."

"Fuck. Does she see us?"

"I don't know."

"It'll be so awkward if she realizes we've been watching them without saying anything . . ."

Nora leaned in closer and laid her palms on MC's cheeks, her touch firmer than it'd been the day before, after the *Explorations* meeting. She tilted MC's face so it was even closer to her own, hiding both of them from Conrad.

"Bathroom," Nora said.

MC's stomach was flipping. "You can't hold it?"

Nora narrowed her eyes. "I mean Ms. Kim just went into the bathroom. As opposed to getting a table."

"Oh. That's good, right?"

"I guess. Except she's going to have a direct view of us when she comes out."

"Should we make a break for it?"

"Your brother will definitely notice that."

"Then what do we do?"

"I don't know."

But as she'd spoken, Nora had slid one of her hands, very slowly, to the back of MC's neck, under her sweatshirt. So when she said, "I think she's coming out," it felt like the easiest thing in the world for MC to close the last inch of distance between them and kiss her.

Nora's lips were soft as they parted, first in surprise, that citrusy perfume making its way to MC's head. But then she seemed to find her confidence, her tongue slipping against MC's, her hair falling across her face as she deepened the kiss. She tasted like beer and pizza and something minty underneath. MC's hand dropped from the table to Nora's hip, her fingers spreading over the generous curve. Nora's posture changed, arching slightly, bringing them even closer. MC knew she should pull away. Check and see if the coast was clear. But she increased her pressure. Curled her arm tighter around Nora's shoulders. Nora made a low, wordless sound in response, practically humming—which seemed to catch her off guard, because a moment later she broke the kiss and said, "Are they gone?"

MC tried to catch her breath as Nora frowned at the front counter.

"They're gone," Nora said. She slid down the bench, away from MC, clearing her throat as she served herself another slice of pizza.

All MC could hear were echoes of that humming sound, but somehow, she forced herself to speak. "Do you want me to go back to the other side?"

Nora poured herself another beer, then offered MC the pitcher. "Up to you."

MC couldn't believe she'd actually let herself get carried away like that. She was there to investigate Nora. Journalistically.

She got up, pulse still racing, and put herself back where she belonged.

But when she took the pitcher, they could both see Nora's hand was shaking.

16

On account of being slow to readjust to the pace of the city after her weekend in Green Hills—or maybe on account of the heart palpitations she was suffering at the prospect of facing Seth Flanagan and the A-team in twenty minutes—MC half skipped, half stumbled across Canal Street, tripping over the curb as her phone vibrated in her sweaty hand.

Conrad was calling.

"Hello?" she said, desperate to distract herself.

"Mom hit me up after you left yesterday. Any plans for Thanksgiving?"

She turned a corner, doing her best to weave through crowds of shoppers and tourists bundled up against the unseasonable cold.

"No plans at the moment," she said. After she and Nora had finished their dinner at Delfino's on Saturday—their conversation slowly relaxing as the fog of their kiss had cleared—MC had been up half the night, thinking, among other things, about whether or not to confront Conrad about what she'd seen. She'd decided she would. Casually. But as soon as she'd gone into the kitchen on Sunday morning, Gabby was already regaling him with tales of the dance party as he hugged her from behind.

MC, apparently, still hadn't found her nerve. "Mom doesn't want us to come to the West Coast," she said, "does she?"

"Nope. She's coming to Green Hills."

"You're kidding."

"Guess she wants to get in on all the quality time we've been spending together."

"Does this mean you're hosting?" Usually, MC met up with Gabby and Conrad for dinner the night before the actual holiday, as the two of them would inevitably be going to Gabby's parents' cozy cape house near the center of town for the official meal. Gabby came from a big, warm family, a contrast to the Calloways that seemed to both excite and irritate her brother the few times he'd bothered to discuss it with MC.

"Yep," he said. "So feel free to invite Joe and Nora and whoever else."

MC cleared her throat. Nora had texted just that morning, but inviting her to Thanksgiving dinner, after the line MC had crossed on Saturday night, would not be wise.

Not that MC was ready to get into any of that with Conrad. "I'm actually on my way to Joe's office now," she said, skirting the issue. "I'll ask him."

"Are you coming back next weekend, by the way?"

"Oh . . . I wasn't planning on it."

"Just figured I'd ask."

"I mean, I'm not sure yet. I have some annual reports I need to work on in person. Finance bros don't take weekends."

"Yeah, sure, I get it."

"But I'll definitely be there for Thanksgiving."

"Great."

"So, um . . . how's your morning?" She wasn't used to keeping in touch with her brother, and she tried not to dwell on how awkward it still was. The important thing was that they were both making an effort.

"Fine," he said, "busy. Just glad we're getting another break in three weeks..."

As they made small talk, MC could almost convince herself that what she'd seen on Saturday was innocent. After all, what had she even seen, really? Two colleagues grabbing a quick bite. Maybe Gabby actually knew about it already, and MC was the one out of the loop, which would be nothing new.

But that was why she'd said yes to his invitation. To clarify things. Get another chance to have some honest talk between them for once, in person, which was only fair. And if that chance came with another opportunity to be in Nora's orbit, so be it.

When MC put her phone back in her pocket, her face was hot despite the cutting wind.

But all that heat transformed on her arrival at the Jawbreaker office, morphing into a burning dread as she approached Joe's door.

"There you are," he said, breathless as he met her halfway and guided her toward the conference rooms. He was wearing a black jacket, his hair carefully coiffed, but his expression was flustered. MC realized she probably should've worn something a little nicer.

"I was hoping we could talk," she said. "Before the meeting?"

"We don't have time."

"I tried to get here sooner, but the subway was screwed up. Look, I was reading over what I sent you, and it occurred to me that maybe we're not as ready as we thought."

"We can figure that out later. Right now, we need to deal with Seth Flanagan."

"You prepped him about how we're going to protect Nora's identity, right? Like, no last name, no geographical details—"

"I told him we're going to deliver the best possible story, and that's what he's waiting to discuss."

"I'm just starting to feel a little panicked."

"MC, I love you, but you're going to have to hold it together until after this meeting."

"Okay," she said, swallowing the lump in her throat.

They walked into one of the glass conference rooms overlooking Broadway.

Seth Flanagan was seated at the head of a long table, flanked by three people with unreadable expressions. As MC understood it, the A-team—referred to in certain circles as the Asshole Team—consisted of Jawbreaker's head of legal and head of strategy, plus someone called the Money Guy. MC had no idea which of these people filled which role, but they all looked to be in their late thirties, and everyone's skin was flawless.

MC stuck close to Joe's side as he pulled up a chair at a respectful distance from their audience.

"Okay, everyone," Seth said, "let's get down to business." He tapped a printout in front of him. "This is, as you know, a major story, and we're all very happy to see you two taking it seriously."

MC blinked. Taking it seriously?

"You're bringing in the psychology," he said, "which I love. S. K. Smith was an outcast by choice, a kid who was totally unsupervised at home—"

"I don't know if she was totally unsupervised," MC said. "I just mentioned that her parents were gone for long periods of time."

Joe gripped her leg under the table.

"Whatever," Seth said. "She was used to being in control from a young age. In her little world, everything was in her power." He pointed at MC. "And she wanted to keep it that way."

MC cleared her throat. "I think we're trying to say something more along the lines of, like, she had an environment in which she could totally embrace her own idiosyncrasies?"

"And that deep need for control," Seth said, raising his voice a little, "made her a perfect fit for rom-com, where conventions and predictability are the point."

She couldn't help herself. "I've actually been reading other rom-coms, and it seems like there's also something about emotional transformation going on there."

Joe, along with the A-team, stared at her.

"The control aspect also explains her insistence on secrecy," Seth said, steepling his fingers. "You could even argue that her book is an act of radical reclamation over her most significant experience of powerlessness."

MC frowned. "Um, this was more toward the end of the doc, but I was trying to suggest that she wasn't so much rewriting high school as she would've wanted it to be as she was revisiting the imagined version of it that offered the best opportunity for self-reflection."

Seth paused. At first MC thought he was considering her point, but then he went on as if she'd said nothing at all. "The main thing we're missing is why she decided not to cover her tracks. Which is crucial."

"What tracks?" MC asked.

"Come on, Michaela Carson, you know what I'm talking about." He smiled. "She barely changed people's names."

"But she added all this stuff from, like, over a decade in the future, which is totally made up."

"If you ask me, it's all part of her publicity long game."

MC almost laughed.

But Joe was nodding along. "She gets to accelerate sales with a mysterious identity," he said, "then whip out the reveal when interest finally ebbs, reviving her audience and maybe even expanding it."

"I guess that's possible," MC said.

A mustachioed man cut in at last: "You don't agree?"

"I don't know," she said. "She just doesn't seem like the type to have a grand plan."

"Based on what?" Seth said flatly.

"She's not even sure what she wants out of her day-to-day. I don't get the sense that she's scheming about her future."

Joe smiled tightly. "Everyone schemes about their future."

"What I mean is," MC said, "she's not scheming about how to be a more successful author in the future."

Seth snorted. "So why did she write the book this way?"

"As you mentioned," Joe said, "we still haven't figured that out yet."

"There has to be a logic." Seth gesticulated wildly. "A goal of some kind."

"Agreed," Joe said.

Blue eyes blazed. "I want you two to find out what that goal was. It's the last piece in this story."

"And if you can uncover it," said Mustache, "I think we'll be ready to go live with this."

MC took a breath. "Joe and I were also talking about some ethical concerns—"

"Which we'll run by legal," Joe said, "once we've finished nailing the article down." He shot her a look. "As you and I discussed."

Seth frowned. "Ethical concerns?"

"About revealing S. K. Smith's identity," MC said. "You know—doxxing her."

Everyone started to chuckle.

"MC," Seth said, "you're working for Jawbreaker. Not the goddamn *New York Times Book Review*."

"Actually," she said carefully, "I'm a freelancer."

Joe whispered in her ear, "This isn't the place."

But wasn't it? MC's hands were clammy, her chest tight. She wasn't sure when she'd started holding her breath. All she knew was that she was afraid to let it go. She could tell them she was off the story. That she was done being their spy-journalist or whatever. And if they threatened to use her research without her permission, she'd threaten right back that she'd go to Nora first, blow up their publication plan.

Except Joe was looking at her like he was drowning. And she knew that whatever mess she made here would be his to clean up. His and Sheena's and Jerome's.

Which reminded her of why she'd wanted more time when she first arrived at Joe's door. Part of her was still hoping that there was a way to pull this off.

To outsmart both Seth Flanagan and S. K. Smith.

"Can I be honest?" she said.

An ergonomic chair squeaked.

Joe's eyes went wide.

Seth's stayed narrow, suspicious. "Honesty," he said, "is our stock-in-trade."

"We need until the end of the year."

The A-team exchanged looks.

"You've had six weeks already," Seth said.

"Well, we need six more. This isn't something that can be rushed."

Mustache said, "What if someone scoops us?"

"That's a risk we'll have to be willing to take," MC said. "Right, Joe?"

"Right." Blinking, he seemed to come back to himself. "MC has been piecing this together by going back home and playing a very subtle game. But if she's suddenly hanging out there all the time, S. K. Smith might realize what she's up to, especially as MC gets closer to the real story behind her writing and publishing *Girl Next Door* the way she did."

Seth pursed his lips.

A long silence stretched across the conference room, pierced by honking and someone outside yelling, *"Will you fucking move?"*

"This article has to release by end of year," Mustache said. "Whether it has your names on it or not. For metrics."

MC swallowed.

"Understood," said Joe.

"But until then, take some more time."

Seth rolled his eyes.

MC and Joe thanked them all, then got up and left, MC snagging a croissant from a side table just before slipping out the door.

"Oh god," Joe breathed. "What a fucking mess."

"It's not. We'll sort this all out."

"I know you want to protect Nora, but these people are vicious."

"You're the one who thinks they're worth working for."

He glared.

"I'm just saying"—she nibbled the croissant—"if we're getting cornered into doing this, let's do it on our own terms."

Which seemed to relax him a little. "Am I hearing some fire from MC Calloway?"

"Something like that." She threw out the rest of the croissant—it was weirdly terrible—and rubbed her temples, a wave of exhaustion rolling over her as they approached Joe's office. "Also, Conrad wants to know if you'd like to join us for Thanksgiving."

"That's nice of him." He went into the office and collapsed in his chair. "But I'm spending the holiday with Tyler." Tyler was Joe's latest boyfriend. They were a month in and going strong. But that was always how the first month went with Joe. "Are you going to make that your big moment?"

"Big moment?"

"To find out why Nora wrote the book the way she did."

MC had planned on telling Joe about Conrad and Jae that morning, and her resolution to confront Conrad about it in person at Thanksgiving. But she suddenly felt protective of her brother's secret, whatever it was. She owed it to him to speak to him first.

If Joe wanted to think her latest trip back to Green Hills was for the sake of their article, she wasn't going to correct him.

"Uh . . . yeah."

"I have a theory, you know."

She sighed. "Care to share?"

"I think it's all about you."

"Like, Michaela Carson?"

"No. Like . . . you."

MC tried not to think about how easy it'd been to kiss Nora on Saturday night, and how important it felt to keep that development—whatever it was—to herself. At least until she had a chance to gauge Nora's next move.

"If it were about me," she said carefully, "the real me, she would've just gotten in touch. Not done . . . all this."

"See, *you* think that."

"I *know* that. She's the most direct person I've ever met."

"Except when it comes to one subject." He got up and squeezed her shoulder. "Do you believe me when I say I'm really sorry for getting you involved?"

"It's all good." She patted his back. "I just need, like, five years off now."

"I mean, same."

When she walked back out, she was hardly surprised to see Sheena was back at her desk, reading the novel of the moment.

"MC," she stage-whispered, face lighting up as she leaned forward. "Joe made us swear not to say anything, but oh—my—god."

MC winced. "I really can't talk about it."

"Of course. Totally. But—"

"I gotta run. Great to see you."

"Wait, you're leaving?"

"Yeah. Sorry."

MC headed for the elevators without even waiting for a response.

When she stepped into the steel box, after the doors slid closed, it was the hardest thing in the world not to scream.

17

Three weeks later, Thanksgiving arrived, crisp and bright, giving way to clouds in the afternoon. A drizzle met MC on the platform at the Green Hills train station, ruining her hair. Not that it'd looked great to begin with. But she'd spent time in front of the bathroom mirror with a mouthful of bobby pins that morning, ignoring the irritated huffing of Pat and Laura as they waited outside the door.

She'd made some tahini chocolate-chip cookies for the occasion, inspired by her chats with Nora, who was apparently pretty adventurous in the kitchen. Their texting had continued at its rapid pace over the course of November, though the flirtatious tone had dimmed a bit. It seemed to be an unspoken agreement between them, a set of guardrails and safe subjects that left MC with a mix of relief and longing. Relief, because her recommitment to the article for Joe was like a lead weight in her chest. And longing, because not a night went by when she wasn't tangled up in her sheets, trying to relive every detail of their kiss in Delfino's.

But they didn't discuss it. Either because Nora was convinced it'd all been a show, a way to remain incognito as MC spied on her brother, or because she was still doing whatever she was doing with Jen, a possibility that made MC feel, for the first time in her life, profoundly jealous.

So they discussed the Byzantine Empire. They discussed the latest antics from Maureen, who was a few F-bombs away from being transferred out of the children's department. They discussed food—Yunnanese cuisine in particular, which Nora was learning to cook by studying YouTube videos—and the TV they watched. Nora was big on reality shows, because they made no secret of being contrived, and therefore compelled her with their unexpected flashes of realness; MC stuck to the over-the-top thrillers with red herrings in every episode.

When they started talking on the phone, they began the slow process of filling each other in about their lives over the last nine years. Nora had apparently gotten more social, picking up acquaintances from library school as well as BJJ. It was through BJJ that she'd reconnected with Jen, who taught intro classes in the evenings, and who Nora refused to go into more detail about; MC nonetheless imagined her wrestling Nora into some kind of steamy make-out session atop a disgusting mat.

Lois came up too. Nora confessed how the librarian had filled in as a parent when Nora's weren't around, pulling her aside for coffee breaks when Nora was just a lowly assistant hiding out in the stacks. She talked about the hard life Lois had led, her messy divorce from a cheating husband when she was in her forties, and the combination of gratitude and bitter regret she felt over the fact that he'd talked her out of having children. MC opened up about her dad, how they'd been in a stagnant place in their relationship when she'd gone to college, and the empty, hanging feeling she was left with when he died—no closure, no change in their family's unspoken policy of keeping things unspoken.

She wondered if she'd be able to turn any of that around with her brother now. But when she saw Conrad wave from behind his wipers, a genuine smile on his face, her stomach twisted.

"Happy Turkey Day," she said, ducking into the Destroyer of Worlds. "I made cookies."

"Nice. So did Nora."

MC froze in the middle of putting her seat belt on, all plans of confronting her brother about his potential affair flying from her mind. "I didn't invite Nora."

"I know. I did. She's coming with her coworker . . . ?"

"Lois."

He pulled out toward the street, pretending to put all his focus into surveying the oncoming traffic. "Jae's coming, too, by the way, and Jim. His kids will be there, and his wife, and Jerry Bickley . . ."

MC tried not to linger on the rapid-fire way Conrad had listed his guests. "Sounds like you went all out," she said hoarsely.

"Dealing with Mom is something I'm only capable of in large groups."

"Did she bring Lance?"

Lance was Dr. Linda Case-Calloway's personal assistant. Also her boyfriend. He was Conrad's age.

"Yep," he said.

MC's heart started pounding triple time.

When they arrived at the house, a fleet of cars were already parked in the driveway. MC pulled down the sunshield and checked the mirror. As suspected, her hair looked like a nest for squirrels. She tried to fix it with a redeployment of the bobby pins, but the humidity and the wind had done their work. She followed her brother into the house.

Gabby swept over in a white off-the-shoulder sweater and floral-print dress, hugging MC. As the air was squeezed out of her lungs, MC spotted Nora in the crowded living room, and their eyes met for a moment.

MC's stomach flipped.

Nora looked down at her beer.

"This is so exciting!" Gabby said. "We haven't hosted in forever."

"Place looks great," MC said. The carpets had been vacuumed and the surfaces tidied. Even the books on the mantel had been dusted. A colorful blanket had been folded over the back of the couch, and new accent pillows had appeared against the armrests. The lights were high and bright, candles burning in corners.

Her mom was already coming over through the crowd. She had a broad, handsome face that she'd passed on to Conrad, along with thick blond hair. It was held back by a tortoiseshell clip, a look she'd been rocking MC's entire life. MC gave her a hug and received a pat on the back.

"Mischa Celeste, you look like a troubled prince of England."

MC had no idea what her mom meant by that, but her attention was already being turned toward Lance, rearing up out of nowhere to reach a hand out to her. "What a wonderful event your brother is putting on," he said.

Who called a family meal an event? She shook his big, soft paw. He was shaped like a barrel, with hairy forearms and a thick brown beard, all of it at odds with his twinkly, boyish eyes. Her mom had officially filed for divorce after it'd come out that she'd had an affair with a colleague, but Lance had arrived on the scene many years after that, a calmer mistake that'd lasted, to everyone's horror, a lot longer.

"Conrad tells me you're working on a novel," her mom said, sipping from a glass of white wine.

MC checked in with her mom on a weekly basis, mostly by text, as if with a sponsor. She thought of Gabby calling her an asshole and wished her mom had picked any other topic to break the ice. "Yep," she said uncomfortably.

"About the Byzantines?"

"Kind of."

"A startling people. Reconciling early Christian belief with Roman pantheism created a profound tension in their conceptions of gender and social hierarchy."

"Totally. How've you been, Mom?"

"Stimulated." She adjusted her half-moon glasses and brushed a piece of lint off her turtleneck. "We're running a study about polyamory."

"Wow."

"Your generation has brought a degree of intellectualism to romance that is, frankly, unprecedented."

MC realized she lacked the mental bandwidth to address her mom's attempt to reconnect right that second. "Sorry, I'll be right back, I'm just going to grab a drink."

She slipped away before her mom could say anything else.

The kitchen smelled like sweet potatoes. The oven was on, making the air even more sweltering than it'd been in the living room. MC went straight for the fridge, tugging at her collar.

"There's no more beer," Nora said behind her.

MC spun around. Nora's sudden proximity made her dizzy. The outfit wasn't helping. She was wearing sheer stockings and a midnight-blue velvet dress that hugged her hips, her hair swept up in a silver clip. MC tried to think about anything other than how soft the velvet would feel under her hands, the slight roughness of the stockings against her palms. Because she'd vowed not to go down that road again. She was here to get to the bottom of whatever her brother was doing with Jae, before it wrecked the great thing he had going with Gabby. And maybe, after that, she might see if she could figure out a way to finish the article for Joe without ruining Nora's life. Maybe.

"No more beer," MC said slowly.

"I was just about to tell Conrad," Nora said. "But I think he's in the middle of an intense conversation."

MC sought him out in the crowd. He was talking to Jae.

MC and Nora exchanged a look.

"There's more in the basement," MC said. She'd just arrived; she'd deal with her brother soon enough. "I'll grab some."

"Do you need a hand?" Nora looked away for a moment. "Lois won't stop talking to Jim about yoga."

"Uh . . . sure."

And all the careful avoidance she thought they'd been practicing over the last few weeks felt like one long, terrifying wink.

The basement was significantly cooler than the kitchen. It helped MC relax a little as she led them through the finished side, where Conrad's office was, to the dark, cellar-like concrete section, where he and Gabby kept their overflow.

She decided it was time to deploy some strategic small talk.

"It's nice to see you," she said.

"Are you sure?" Nora's voice was wry. "I feel like you're doing everything you can to avoid looking at me."

"Just trying to find the light." MC reached out and caught a string hanging from the lone bulb on the rafter.

But the soft, incandescent glow only made things worse. It brought out the pink flush across Nora's chest. Drew shadows across her eyes.

"I'm glad we're getting a chance to talk in person," MC babbled. "I've been wanting to apologize."

"For what?"

MC bent down to pick up a rack of IPAs. "For overstepping with you the last time we hung out," she said, working her fingers under the cardboard edges. "It wasn't appropriate for me to, you know—" She started to lift the rack, but it was a struggle with sweating palms.

"Make out with me?"

MC fumbled her grip. The rack slipped to the floor, the corner landing on her big toe. A jolt of pain shot up her leg. Tears sprang to her eyes. But the bigger problem was that one of the cans had popped and was currently spraying beer all over Nora's dress.

MC didn't know how to stop the sticky mess from worsening except to take the can and chug it down. Nora watched, a quizzical look on her face.

Then another can popped.

"I got this one," Nora said, picking it up and making short work of it.

When she was done, they stared at each other for a moment.

MC felt lightheaded. "We're going to smell like the inside of a keg," she muttered. Her toe was throbbing.

Nora blinked. Her dress was still dripping. "You're really accident-prone."

"I know." MC walked over to a stack of plastic bins next to the breaker box and started digging around. "I think I can find something to change into here. Are you going to go back to your house?"

"I'd rather not. The weather's pretty bad."

MC cleared her throat. "Well, some of Gabby's old stuff is mixed in with mine." She dug a little deeper. "Here's a dress." She handed Nora a plain black cocktail number, then grabbed an old button-down. "This shirt is fine, right?"

Nora shrugged.

MC pulled her sweater over her head.

When she could see again, she realized Nora had turned around.

"Can you undo the zipper?"

MC panicked. She'd expected her to change upstairs. Now she had to stand behind Nora, palms still sweating, and get a grip on what was essentially a plastic grain of rice.

Nora said, "Do you actually regret it?"

MC finally managed to get the stupid thing between her index finger and her thumb. "Huh?"

"Kissing me."

"Well . . ." MC pulled the zipper down. "Not really, no." Her whole body tingled at the admission, at how close her hands were to Nora's bare skin. "But what about you and Jen?"

Nora shrugged the dress off her shoulders. "We're pretty much done at this point."

MC knew she should avert her eyes. But she couldn't. Nora didn't seem to care. She turned and watched MC watching her, then stepped out of her dress completely.

"Was that my fault?" MC said. "You and Jen ending things?"

"Would you feel guilty if it was?"

MC swallowed. "Yeah, I would."

"Why?"

"Because," MC said carefully, "I don't want to mess up your life."

Nora tugged lightly on the hem of MC's T-shirt and leaned forward another inch, her lips so near to MC's it made MC's mouth ache. "What makes you think you have that kind of power?"

MC held her breath as every thought she'd ever had fled her mind.

"We should get back upstairs," Nora added, finally picking up Gabby's dress and slipping it on. After a readjustment of her clip, she walked back to the rack of beer, the hint of a smile on her face. "But let me do the carrying this time, okay?"

18

To accommodate so many people for Thanksgiving dinner, Conrad and Gabby had pushed together several tables, including their dining table, a folding table, and their dad's old card table, a zigzagging arrangement that stretched from the kitchen to the living room. But the haphazardness was charming; it gave the house a cheery, stuffed feeling that MC remembered from the dinner parties her parents had hosted when she and Conrad were little. Everything had felt so stable back then. Not perfect, but predictable.

She would've enjoyed the nostalgia more if she weren't seated between her mom and Nora.

The spread was impressive. Conrad had cooked a huge turkey and carved it into neat plates of white and dark meat, which were joined by various potluck dishes that ranged from the traditional mashed potatoes to a raisin-gravy vegetable medley that no one touched. The wine and beer were flowing. Conversations had risen to their highest pitch yet. Which was helpful, because they provided cover for MC's dazed silence.

"So," her mom said with a little too much enthusiasm, "I hear things are going very well for Joe."

MC stared down at her plate. "Yep, they are."

"Seems like that literary magazine you did together had a big effect on his career path."

"I guess it did."

MC was trying to figure out how to change the subject from the revelation of Joe's work at Jawbreaker—she was convinced it would tip Nora off to MC's true purpose in Green Hills—when her mom leaned forward and spoke to Nora directly: "Weren't you in the club too?"

"I was." Nora ate a bite of marshmallow topping from her sweet potatoes, turning away from a conversation a little farther down the table about the school's English curriculum, in which Lois was telling Conrad that Shakespeare was overrated.

"Nora was basically a co-editor," MC said in a rush.

"And what do you do now, Nora?" her mom asked. "Do you also write?"

Nora smiled. "No. I'm just a librarian."

And then Conrad was clinking a fork against his wineglass.

"No one panic," he announced, running a hand through his hair and flashing his signature half grin. "I'll make this short. I just wanted to thank you all for being here and pretending to like my cooking." Several people groaned. "Seriously, it means a lot to me, sharing the holiday with you all. Sometimes I roll my eyes at the forced gratitude stuff. But I think that's just because it's embarrassing how much I actually have to be grateful for. Cheers."

Everyone clinked glasses, murmuring in agreement.

"And speaking of gratitude," Gabby said, standing up next. "I want to second everything my smooth-talking husband just said . . . and add a little something extra." She looked over at Conrad. Her face was flushed and eager, but unsteady too. "A piece of timely Thanksgiving news."

MC saw Conrad's eyes widen.

"I'm pregnant!" Gabby said.

The table erupted. MC saw her brother school his face into

a smile. She was probably the only one who could recognize the effort he was making. Even her mom was shrugging in happy surprise, putting a hand on MC's shoulder. "I've always been fascinated by babies," she said.

But MC couldn't get herself to put on a show of good cheer. Her heart had sunk down to her stomach, everything she'd just eaten turning curdled. All she could see was how happy Gabby looked; how Conrad was standing too stiffly beside her, his hands behind his back, like he couldn't unclench them. And of course, she saw Jae, standing up from her seat and leaving the room, while everyone else made their way toward the parents-to-be.

"How far along?" Jim's wife was asking.

"Almost at the end of the first trimester," Gabby said, "but we didn't realize until last week." She laughed. "I was like, wait a minute . . . ?"

MC did her best to tune the conversation out. She needed to regroup. Figure out how she wanted to deal with this new development.

But it was hard to think with her mom right beside her, a living reminder of the damage cheating could do to a family.

Or at least the damage it could do when it stopped being a secret.

"I need to get some air," MC mumbled.

She lurched up from the table, grabbed her jacket from the mound on the bed in the guest room, and went out into the cold.

The afternoon rain had turned to snow. Tiny flakes floated through the night air, glinting in the floodlight that snapped on when MC walked out of the garage. Her breath puffed in front of her as she crunched into the backyard, the grass frozen underfoot. She hadn't come out with a plan, but her feet led her to the old elm tree next to the gardening shed, where she stood under the bare branches and stuffed her hands in her pockets.

Snow melted on her cheeks. She closed her eyes and wished for a version of the past three months where none of this had happened. Not Nora's book, or MC's assignment for Joe. Not reconnecting with Conrad and Gabby.

She wanted everything to feel simple again. Safe.

"Hey."

MC opened her eyes. Nora was crossing the lawn, like it was the reading night after-party all over again.

"You really shouldn't beat yourself up about this," Nora said, coming to stand in front of her. "It's Conrad's bullshit, not yours."

"I know. But he's still my brother. I feel like I'm supposed to talk to him about it."

"Then why haven't you?"

"Part of me feels like it's none of my business. But a bigger part of me is . . . I don't know, scared."

Nora folded her arms across her chest. "Scared of what?"

"Upsetting him."

"He's probably already upset." Nora shrugged. "He deserves to be upset."

MC finally met her eyes. "What would you do? If you were me."

"I'd leave it alone."

"Seriously?" MC laughed. "I think of you as the epitome of painfully honest."

"But we're talking about if I were you, and if I were in your position. And I get that he's your brother. But you haven't been around. You don't know what's really happening, and you haven't had time to earn his trust. So, what do you hope to accomplish?"

"I don't know." MC bowed her head. "I just wish he wasn't doing this. Whatever it is."

Nora glanced back at the house. "Desire is complicated."

"What do you mean?"

"Haven't you ever wanted something you can't have?"

MC looked up. "Yeah."

"And doesn't it make you wonder how much of that is just because it's unattainable?"

"I guess." MC waited until Nora had finally met her gaze again. "But for me, it's more about feeling like what you really want is something you don't deserve. And that's why it's unattainable, right? Even if it was being handed to you on a silver platter, you'd be too scared to go for it, because you know you'd screw it up." Her words made her realize she'd had a little too much to drink. But she couldn't seem to stop herself. "Like, for example, I've spent the last three weeks thinking about you pretty much constantly. But I can't do anything about it."

"MC." Nora sighed. But she didn't say anything else, just hugged herself tighter.

"I'm not exaggerating." MC shook her head, smiling ruefully. "I can hardly sleep anymore. I just lie there, running all our conversations back in my mind, or scrolling through our texts, so I can pick apart everything you said. Get a kick out of your jokes again." Nora put a hand on her forehead, but she was smiling. "That probably sounds weird."

"It doesn't," Nora said quietly.

"And I think back to high school, because how could I not?" She started pacing, back and forth, in front of the tree. "Being here, spending time with you, and with Gabby and my brother, and even with Jae, and Jen, and everyone else who was part of that time in our lives. It's made me realize there's a lot of stuff I'm remembering wrong. Or only remembering partially. But one thing that feels pretty clear is that you were just . . . so out of my league. Like up on this higher plane." Nora was shaking her head now, her lips pressed together. But MC had to keep going; she realized she'd been wanting to say this for weeks. "I mean, you wrote that poem, didn't you? Senior year. 'On the Look.'" It wasn't *Girl Next Door*, but right then, with the past and the present overlapping in such strange ways, MC told herself it might as well have been. She stopped pacing and stepped closer to Nora. "You tried to tell me. But it should've been obvious."

"Why?"

MC took Nora's hand in hers. "Only you could've written something that good."

Nora bit her lip, but she didn't pull away. "I hate poetry."

"Then why'd you do it?"

"Are you seriously going to make me spell it out?"

"Yeah, I am."

Nora's voice was soft when she finally answered. "Because I wanted you so bad."

For a moment, all MC could do was listen to the sound of their breathing, the blood roaring in her ears, the alarm bells going off in her head.

"Nora!" Lois called sharply. "Are you out there?"

Nora stepped back, breaking contact, an icy wind cutting between them.

"Just making sure MC's okay!" Nora yelled. She cleared her throat. "I think she got a little dizzy."

It was true. MC had to put a hand on the trunk of the elm tree to steady herself.

"Come eat dessert!" said Lois. "I made éclairs!"

Nora took MC's elbow, an unreadable look in her eyes, and tugged her back to the house.

19

"To Gabby!" Jim said, hoisting a can of beer over his head.

"To Conrad!" Jerry added, banging his beer against Jim's.

Jim's wife raised her wineglass. "To the kid who's going to have the most annoyingly perfect parents!"

Everyone laughed, leaning back in their chairs, the table an explosion of half-finished plates, mismatched casserole dishes, and countless empty bottles of alcohol. Jim's kids were jumping around on the couch in front of the TV. Jae was long gone. MC nibbled on one of her godawful tahini chocolate-chip cookies as Conrad pulled out his phone and changed the soft jazz to Céline Dion.

"No," she groaned.

But her complaint was drowned out by the dramatic opening of "It's All Coming Back to Me Now."

MC's mom had headed back to her hotel with Lance after dessert. Lois had said her goodbyes next, waving off Nora's offer of a ride home. But the two of them stepped aside to chat at the front door just before Lois left, standing close together, Lois looking irritated—or more irritated than usual—before she finally turned away.

MC, confused and disappointed and extremely self-conscious about how things had gone under the elm tree, worried that Nora would leave soon after.

But she'd stuck around, congratulating Gabby and complimenting Conrad on the turkey. MC had tried to mirror her casual energy, but found it impossible, her thoughts racing over why Nora had wanted them to come back inside after everything MC had said to her—whether the emergence of some partial truth between them signaled the beginning of the end. Or maybe MC was just bad at romantic speeches.

She kept trying to put them back into proximity anyway, but Nora kept letting herself get pulled into other conversations.

As MC ferried dishes from the table to the sink, she felt bitterly certain this was how it was always going to be between them. Talking around their real feelings, speaking in subtext, or speaking directly for only short stretches, after which it was necessary to be silent and apart. It should've been a familiar dynamic, but the existence of Nora's book made it impossible for MC to just let things lie this time. *Girl Next Door* may not have been strictly accurate, but—MC only realized this now—it spoke to her, even just in excerpts, in a way nothing had ever spoken to her before. It made her feel recognized.

Conrad started to sing along with Céline, a hand to his chest, his expression a convincing pantomime of heartbreak. He'd undone the top buttons on his shirt and opened a bottle of whiskey. Gabby went between covering her ears and picking up dirty napkins from the abandoned places at the table. Jim and Jerry, meanwhile, joined Conrad, their deep voices butchering the soprano.

When the theatrics had subsided and everyone was settling back into side conversations, the music normalized. Nora finally said goodbye, brief and awkward, waving at everyone as MC stared at her with open desperation.

And then she was gone.

MC sat with Conrad on the couch for a while, playing with Jim's kids. She helped Gabby cover dishes with plastic wrap and jigsaw them together in the fridge. Jim's daughter started crying uncontrollably at some point, and that was the signal for their family to head home. Half an hour later, Jerry, realizing the energy was gone, made a pointless show of pushing in chairs before grabbing his coat and flashing a peace sign on his way out.

"Big success," Gabby said, stifling a yawn.

"Agreed," said Conrad.

But when she tried to pull him to the bedroom, he said he needed to cool off from the whiskey and ambled to the basement stairs instead.

MC tried not to linger on how disappointed Gabby looked.

Alone at last, she listened to the fridge humming. The clock ticking. She put a hand on her stomach. Too much liquid was sloshing around. She went to the pantry and made herself eat peanut butter, straight from the jar, overwhelmed yet again by the night's events and hoping sleep would clear her head.

She wasn't optimistic. She'd entered a state of disbelief that she'd said all those things to Nora. Her only explanation was that the significance of the spot under the elm tree had possessed her, overriding her judgment, making her feel like they really were back in high school again. She absolutely wasn't supposed to be pursuing Nora in a romantic way. She was in Green Hills to write a story about her—an assignment she was keeping secret not just from Nora herself, but from Conrad and Gabby, and had been for months.

Why did she keep forgetting that?

She needed to talk to Joe first thing in the morning. Get serious about wrapping up the project with minimal damage.

Because if there was one benefit of the night's torturous

rumination on subterfuge, it was that she'd finally started to get an inkling of an idea for how to approach the article, inspired by S. K. Smith herself.

She was screwing the lid back on the jar when there was a faint knock on the door.

At first, she thought she'd imagined it. But then there was another knock, firmer this time.

She walked into the mudroom and peered out the glass panels in the door.

Nora was on the porch in sweats and a raincoat.

"Hey," MC said, opening the door, smiling in surprise.

Nora's expression was grim. "I came back for my cookie plate."

"Oh. I'll grab it for you."

"Don't!" Nora blew out a breath and put a hand on her forehead. "I lied. I mean, I did forget the plate. But I'm back here because you just . . . drive me fucking crazy."

MC frowned. "I said too much, didn't I?"

"No. You said everything I've ever wanted to hear. That's the problem."

Nora stepped through the door, hesitated for a second, and kissed her.

It was like at Delfino's. Unexpected at first, then surprisingly natural. Except now they were alone, and it was dark, and there was no reason to stop. Nora slid her arms around MC's neck. The rainwater from her coat dampened MC's shoulders. MC pulled Nora closer and tugged her shirt up a little, reaching under, her fingers grazing Nora's feverishly hot skin. Nora pushed her tongue deeper into MC's mouth, and MC let her hands roam farther, to the valley of her lower back, the subtle planes of muscle along her shoulder blades.

This, they could do. No talking. No thinking.

At some point, Nora broke the kiss and closed the door behind her. When she turned back to MC, she put her hands on MC's shoulders and pressed down. MC's knees were already weak. She sank onto the bench by the door, and then Nora was climbing into her lap. Rolling her hips slightly. Watching for MC's reaction.

MC ran her palms over Nora's thighs and squeezed. Nora exhaled at the pressure, her breath warm on MC's brow as she rested the tip of her thumb on MC's bottom lip. They kissed again, and MC felt like she was dreaming, like this was all too good to be true.

Eventually she took Nora's hand and led her to the guest room. There, Nora peeled off her raincoat and let it drop to the floor. As they came together again, she made that same low humming sound MC had been trying to recapture in her mind for weeks. The sound of Nora losing control. Giving in to something. Which was why, MC realized, it'd taken such a hold of her. Because for all Nora's self-possession, all her firmness of opinion, all her insistence on doing things on her own terms and no one else's, there was some part of her that could be swept away. And MC was the one who could do it.

"Take your shirt off," Nora said.

"You first."

Nora yanked the flimsy garment over her head. She looked completely at ease in her nakedness. She slowly undid MC's buttons.

"Sorry about the twin bed," MC said.

Nora had started walking back to the edge of it. MC followed. When Nora sat down and spread her legs, MC stepped between them, Nora leaning forward to meet her again. She kissed MC's navel, tracing her tongue around it. MC shuddered as Nora popped the top button of her pants. She'd never moved this quickly before. But she'd never been with someone who'd known her for so long. Even the intervening years of silence had collapsed over the last few months, a buildup amplified by having gone unnoticed.

Before she knew it, they were both on the bed, MC on top of Nora, a knee between her legs. Nora hooked an ankle around MC's calf. MC kissed along Nora's ribs. There was the expected awkwardness of learning someone's body for the first time, but there was also a certain level of comfort, a sense of permission offered a long time ago at last being taken.

When the moment seemed right, MC switched their positions, lying on her back and pulling Nora up, up, up, until she was planting her knees on either side of MC's head.

Nora kept her weight shifted back at first. MC grazed her teeth against the cotton of her underwear. They stayed that way as long as either of them could handle, MC skimming her hands up Nora's sides, feeling her torso flexing, her breathing heavy as she gripped the top of the headboard and finally moved her hips.

"You're so hot," MC said. The infuriating fabric still separated them. Nora whimpered but didn't pick up her pace. Eventually MC couldn't help herself anymore. She curled her arms around Nora's thighs, pinning her, one hand squeezing Nora's leg, the other working below the hem of Nora's underwear to pull it aside. She ran her tongue along the wet mess of her and was rewarded with a gasp, Nora's hands tangling in her hair. It took MC out of herself, in the best way, her focus entirely on what Nora wanted most.

MC circled her tongue for a while, then dipped inside. Nora pulled her hair harder. MC snaked her hands from Nora's hips to her belly, then higher, brushing her thumbs across Nora's breasts. She tried to take her time. But what was happening between them seemed to have its own momentum. She gave in to it, trusting the rhythm, until Nora's thighs tensed up, her torso bending forward.

When her muscles had finally gone slack and her hands had loosened in MC's hair, MC felt a strange surge of warmth in her chest. She closed her eyes. Nora sat back and touched MC's cheek, stroking tenderly along her jaw.

"That feels nice," MC said.

She turned her head to kiss the inside of Nora's thigh. But Nora was already reaching a hand behind her, rubbing slowly between MC's legs. MC laughed, surprised to be switching gears already.

"Tell me what you like," Nora said. Her fingers had started to curl.

"I'm . . . having trouble thinking."

"You need to think about it?" Nora increased her pressure, which made MC's breath get short. "Turn on your stomach."

MC did as she was told, Nora climbing off her for a second so she could rearrange them, straddling MC's back. She felt Nora's hands on her shoulders, Nora's breath on her neck. Nora took her earlobe between her teeth and said, "You make me want to move fast."

"I can tell."

"But I don't need to." Nora worked her thumbs down the sides of MC's spine. "We could take a break. Talk about books."

MC laughed again. "Oh yeah. Extremely sexy."

"I like how smart you are." Nora was leaning over her again, her hair tickling MC's back. "And funny."

"But not intentionally."

"Not always." Nora ran her tongue up the side of MC's neck. "And unexpectedly passionate."

"I'm full of surprises," she managed to say. But as soon as the words had left her mouth, she couldn't help thinking of the one surprise Nora wouldn't be too pleased about.

Nora dropped her knee between MC's legs, draping her body against MC's back. "Is this okay?"

"Yeah," MC said, pushing up onto her elbows a little. Nora ran a hand along MC's waist, bracing herself with the other, moonlight tracing a shadow along the tendon that ran up her arm.

"Can I touch you?" Nora asked.

MC closed her eyes, feeling how wet Nora still was against the back of her thigh. "Nora—"

"What?"

Nora's hand moved lower, but not all the way; MC felt like she was losing her mind.

"Do you just want to say my name?" Nora teased.

MC held one of the pillows in her fists.

"Go on." Nora traced a finger along MC's hip. "Say it."

MC gritted her teeth. "Nora."

"Tell me what you want me to do to you."

"I . . ."

Nora was pressing her hips into MC's, her nipples hard against MC's back, her breath hot against MC's ear, and MC felt so much want, it should've been obvious, all too easy to put into words.

A bead of sweat rolled down her neck. She wanted this, everything, so badly. But she couldn't bring herself to say it. Why couldn't she just say it?

She put her hand on Nora's and guided it all the way down,

rubbing it against herself. Finally, she said, "I don't want you to stop." It was the best she could do.

She felt Nora's arms tightening around her, heard the way her breathing quickened. And that was what she concentrated on, everything turning slick between them, the way they melded together, until she finally finished, an electric jolt to the center of her body.

She collapsed against the damp sheet. Nora left a trail of kisses down her back. She felt overwhelmed, physically and emotionally. She'd hoped these sides of herself could be kept separate.

She cleared her throat and said, "You're not going to leave, are you?"

Nora paused.

"I feel like you're not the type to stick around until morning," MC said. "But I really wish you would."

Nora lay down next to her. MC realized they'd hardly faced each other since she first showed up. She reached out and tucked Nora's hair behind her ear, enchanted by the intricate curve of cartilage, unable to stop herself from tugging her earlobe a little.

"Just this once," Nora said, throwing a leg over MC's hip and closing her eyes.

20

MC woke up the next morning to the smell of frying bacon.

Nora was gone.

Groaning, she sat up, clapped her hands to the sides of her head, and tried to squeeze all the fuzziness and aching between her ears into submission. It didn't work.

She swallowed a few ibuprofen instead and poured herself into the shower.

When she emerged, dressed and a little more alive, she found Gabby in the kitchen, flipping pancakes, looking rumpled in one of Conrad's old hoodies. But her smile was radiant. MC was relieved.

"Hope you're hungry," Gabby said.

"Starving."

MC poured herself a coffee and slumped into one of the stools at the island. The kitchen was mostly put away, but there was still a mess of pots and pans across the counters in various stages of drying, a pile of dirty napkins for the laundry in a corner by the fridge. She focused hard on the napkins, on their festive colors, desperate to think about anything other than the fact that she and Nora Pike had slept together.

"Did you, uh, have any morning sickness?" MC asked.

"A little nausea here and there in October. But I just kept thinking I had a stomach bug." Gabby shook her head. "I still can't believe there's actually a little human getting cooked up in there."

"Me neither." MC laughed. "Or that you changed a tire during the cooking."

"And went out dancing!" She tossed her hair out of her eyes. "Thank god I hardly drink."

"I'm impressed you had the energy to enjoy yourself."

"I just got lucky with this first trimester." She sighed. "Hopefully I stay lucky. It would really suck if I had to give up my whole life after this baby arrives."

"I don't think you will."

"I want to be able to still do all that stuff when I'm mommed up, you know? Change tires. Go out sometimes."

"As long as Joe's in your geographical region, you'll have a willing partner."

"Speaking of willing partners." Gabby stacked the pancakes on a plate and pulled a carton of eggs from the fridge. "I saw some serious looks passing between you and Nora last night. Not to mention a few conspicuous absences."

"Oh." MC blushed, her night with Nora flashing before her. Again. "Yeah."

"That's it? Where are my details?"

"What details?" Conrad said, shuffling into the kitchen in a flannel pajama set. His stubble was unkempt, his eyes were puffy, and his hair was sticking straight up on one side.

"Nothing," MC said.

"MC and Nora are becoming a thing," Gabby said, kissing him on the cheek. She went back to cracking eggs onto the griddle.

"We're not," MC said, not wanting to think about what it

meant that she and Nora had done something so incredibly ill-advised.

"You keep saying that," Conrad teased.

"We just . . . need to talk."

"About what?"

About the novel Nora had secretly written about MC, which now had millions of eager fans across the country scouring the internet for any clues that could lead them to its mysterious author.

About the article MC was secretly writing about Nora, which could blow up both their lives if she did it wrong.

But what she said was: "I just don't think either of us is ready to get involved in a relationship right now."

"It's hardly long distance," Gabby said.

"Not because of that." And because MC couldn't give the real reason, she added, "I went through kind of a rough breakup at the end of the summer."

"What?" Gabby frowned. "How long was the relationship?"

"Almost a year."

"Holy shit!"

"It's not like you think," MC said. "I start slow, keep it casual for a while, and then, when I finally commit . . . I get left."

Gabby whipped her spatula through the air, scandalized. "Why?"

MC remembered Lisa laughing in Grand Army Plaza, her boyfriend's hand roaming across her chest. "I think maybe I'm boring."

"Oh, come on," said Conrad.

"Whatever it is, I'm not trying jump into something right now. Especially with a person from my past."

"Really?" Gabby said. "I think that's the perfect person to jump into something with."

Conrad frowned. "Why?"

"Because it means they get some core part of you. If they knew you a long time ago, and they still want you now, that's deep." She gave him a pointed look.

He turned away, picking up a piece of bacon.

They ate breakfast and talked about the night, what a great time everyone had, how weird Lance was—their mom was coming by before she had to head to the airport, another awkward encounter MC didn't want to think about. Conrad smiled in the right places and even perked up once he was on his second cup of coffee, but MC knew something was off. When Gabby left to shower, MC started washing the dishes and said, "Everything okay?"

"Yeah. Why?"

She tried to keep her voice casual. "It's just big news, that's all. Becoming a dad."

"Hasn't really sunk in yet." He stared at the floor.

"You'll do great."

"Will I?"

"You tend to ace whatever you put your mind to."

"It's putting my mind to it that I'm worried about."

MC pretended to focus on dislodging a chunk of egg from the spatula. "Why would you be worried about that?"

"I don't know." He looked strangely helpless. "I don't feel ready, I guess."

"I think you'll be ready when the time comes." She paused. "If you want to be."

"Yeah. You're right." His voice sounded distant. "I have to run to the liquor store. Mom's insisting on mimosas."

Which was probably true. But MC sensed he was also looking for an excuse to leave. And maybe he needed the fresh air. Maybe pushing him the morning after Gabby's announcement, with Gabby still in the house, was a bad angle of approach.

She thought of Nora's advice about leaving it alone, about needing time to earn his trust.

"I've got the rest of the dishes," she said.

He looked at her with gratitude in his eyes. "You sure?"

"Totally."

After Conrad left, Gabby decided to take a nap. So MC flopped down on the couch and opened her message thread with Joe.

She was still far from thrilled about the prospect of writing the article, but the emergence of a workaround last night kept her from panicking.

She just needed Joe to approve it.

She was starting to type when she heard a voice rising somewhere outside. She turned around and peered out the windows, over the picket fence, to where Nora was standing on her front porch in a silk robe.

Her arms were folded tightly across her chest.

Jen was standing just below, at the foot of the stairs.

MC's heart dropped to her stomach. Her first thought was that Jen and Nora had been inside together. But the picture wasn't quite right—Jen's scarf was snug around her neck, like she'd been in the cold for a while, and Nora was wearing a pair of untied hiking boots, like she'd just stepped out. Jen's truck was parked a little down the driveway.

Jen gestured toward the bare branches overhead. Nora's posture remained stiff, closed off.

MC knew she should stay out of it, whatever it was. But the possibility that Jen was harassing Nora made her antsy. She'd given Conrad space because she was still in the process of earning his trust. But what she and Nora had done last night—secrets aside—made her feel like maybe, for once, she shouldn't be afraid of stepping in.

She pulled on her sneakers and walked out to the gate in the fence.

Jen was still yelling. "Do you honestly think you don't owe me that?"

"I'm done with this conversation," Nora said, watching MC cross the lawn.

MC had to stuff her hands in her jacket pockets to hide that they were shaking. "Everything okay out here?" she called.

"Wow," Jen said, giving MC an up-and-down. "Perfect timing."

"Jen," Nora warned.

"What? Does it make you uncomfortable to have this all out in the open?" Jen snorted. "When she drops you without any explanation, MC, it's because she moved on to someone else and decided to skip the annoying part where she bothers to tell you."

"Enough," Nora said.

Jen raised her hands. "All good. I'm done."

She turned around and walked back to her truck.

MC watched her go, then looked to Nora for explanation.

"Great start to my day," Nora muttered.

An engine revved behind them.

"Maybe you should've stuck around with me," MC said, glancing back at her house. Jen's truck creaked loudly as it backed out. "Can I ask what got her to come to your doorstep like this?"

"A text from Jerry." Nora shifted her hips, silk robe straining a little, as she watched the truck speed off down the empty road. "I guess you and I weren't very subtle at dinner."

MC sighed. "My brother and Gabby may also have been spreading the word."

Nora's gaze snapped back to her. "What word, exactly?"

"Nothing serious. They're just in matchmaker mode."

"Is that what this is all about? Them convincing you to be into me?"

"What? No." MC shook her head. "Can we move the conversation inside, by the way? You look like you're about to freeze."

Nora frowned. "I'd rather put it on hold for now. If you don't mind."

"Actually, I do." MC squared her shoulders; after last night, the stakes felt too high to just set communication aside as usual.

Nora frowned, then turned back toward her door, stepping through without even looking over her shoulder.

MC jogged over and climbed the stairs.

The door led to what MC suspected would be more accurately called a sitting room than a living room. It was crammed with old-fashioned furniture, wingback chairs and tasseled ottomans, Persian rugs, brass lamps. Painstakingly carved bookcases with glass doors held all kind of antiques, from candelabras and tiled boxes to ceremonial knives and porcelain figurines.

"Just your average suburban interior," MC said, checking out a woven tapestry. It depicted a boar hunt.

"It's my parents' stuff."

"From their travels?"

"This is where they store their curiosities. Including me." Nora went into the kitchen, a big tawny cat brushing against her leg. Fuzzbox. He was named for her favorite punk band, some all-female outfit that hurt MC's ears to listen to when she'd looked them up.

"Do you want tea?" Nora asked. "I already had coffee."

"Sure. Thanks."

The kitchen was just as ornate. Even the kettle was hammered tin with a ceramic handle in the shape of a fire-breathing serpent. Nora grabbed it and turned on the burner. Fuzzbox meowed, and Nora scratched between his ears, then set out a dish of dry food.

"When your parents retire," MC said, "will they come back for good?"

"They tend not to share plans with me beyond the next month."

"I can't imagine flying by the seat of my pants for that long."

"Maybe it'd be a nice change for you. Not caring about anything or anyone except yourself."

"I don't know. I don't think so."

Silence stretched between them.

Finally, Nora said, "So, you wanted to talk."

"Yeah." MC rubbed her arms like she was cold. "Last night was really . . ."

"Good?"

"Putting it mildly."

"Okay."

MC tried not to linger on the fact that Nora hadn't echoed the sentiment. "But what I was going to say was—"

"I think the fact that we have history is clouding the issue." Nora leaned back against the kitchen table. "The bottom line is just that we're physically attracted to each other."

"That's . . . definitely a factor."

"And I've decided, as tempting as it is to pursue that more with you, I shouldn't. Because it's just a lot right now."

"Okay." It didn't feel okay, but MC told herself it was only the book that was standing between them—that once they overcame that secret, Nora wouldn't have to talk to her like this. Which was why she added: "It's more than a physical thing for me, by the way."

Nora's jaw twitched. But she didn't say anything.

MC forced herself to go on. "As I said last night, being back home has been a lot different than I expected. I've kind of started to question where I'm at in life, and you're a big part of that—"

"You don't need to give me the details, MC. We slept together, and it was nice, but that doesn't mean we owe each other anything."

MC grimaced, thinking about Jen arguing with Nora about what was owed between them. "Do you actually feel that way?"

Nora shrugged. "We grew up next to each other. We spent time together senior year. That was it. We haven't even kept in touch."

She was right. They'd gone their separate ways, and MC hadn't thought twice about it. She wouldn't even be in Green Hills—in this kitchen—if Nora hadn't written *Girl Next Door*.

As if Nora could hear her line of thinking, she added, "It's not a big deal. We survived without each other."

Which was true. MC had been perfectly happy with her life until September. She wondered if she could go back to that. To New York, to Joe, to walks on Eastern Parkway and long mornings in coffee shops. She'd never been alone, really. Just lonely.

The kettle whistled. Nora took it off the stove, but she made no move to pour. She hadn't even taken out cups.

"I should agree with you," MC said. "Let the past be the past. Not make things messy."

"So do that."

MC tapped her foot; her mind was commanding her to walk back to the door, but she couldn't seem to take the first step. Her voice got small again. "I hate the idea of not seeing you anymore."

Nora shook her head. "Please don't make me do this."

"Do what?"

"Cut you off."

"Like you did with Jen?" Nora's eyes darkened, but MC couldn't stop herself. "Honestly, I think this is bullshit."

"What, exactly?"

"Your whole coldhearted thing."

Nora rolled her eyes. "Just drop it, MC."

"Drop what? A simple observation?" She spread her hands. "Look how much you do for Lois. How you are with those kids at story hour. You go out of your way for Heather. For me. And that's just what I've picked up on from seeing you now and then on the weekends these past few months."

Nora's expression had closed off fully by then, a warning look in her eyes. Twenty-four hours ago, MC would've heeded such a look.

She made her voice as gentle as she could: "Why are you so afraid of letting people into your life?"

As MC watched something break behind Nora's forbidding gaze, it occurred to her that this was actually her own fear too—that she had plenty of relationships, but none of them went deep, because she wouldn't let them. It wasn't just about her dating life, or even her brother. It was about everyone she'd ever met. Even Joe sometimes. And maybe that was why she'd always been so worried about not meeting expectations. Why she always tried to go above and beyond any favor asked of her. Some part of her knew she needed to provide constant reassurance that she was worth keeping around, not because she didn't deserve to be kept around—that feeling was secondary—but because the core exchange of trust at the base of every solid relationship was not something she was brave enough to agree to.

"You have no idea," Nora said, "what you're talking about."

"Then correct me. Like, with evidence."

MC crossed her arms, waiting for the bomb to finally drop between them, her body rigid with dread, but also the most powerful anticipation she'd ever felt. She realized she needed everything to be out between them at last. The truth about Nora's book, about MC's favor to Joe. A picture of the whole house of cards before it finally collapsed. And they could both be mad, and both be relieved, and then move on. Maybe.

"How's this for evidence?" Nora said, looking out the window. "Leave."

"But we're still talking."

"I'm done talking."

"For today?"

"For the foreseeable future."

MC's mouth hung open. "That's not fair."

"Grow up, MC."

MC wiped her sweaty palms on her jeans, suddenly furious. At Nora, at herself—at what cowards they both were, and had always been, each in their own way.

She wanted to make a different choice for once. To be something she'd never been before. To believe that such things came down to willpower rather than character. But when she reached for her voice, the one deep inside her, the one that knew the truth, she realized it still didn't have the words, and maybe never would.

She blew out the breath she'd been holding and walked away.

21

MC hung around the house until Saturday night, hoping Nora might've been bluffing about not speaking to each other ever again. But her texts went unanswered. And Gabby and Conrad were too distracted by their own problems to pay MC much mind.

Right back to where they'd all started.

That night she took a train back to the city, staring out windows, waiting on platforms. Back at her apartment, neither a Rebecca Sloane novel nor a *Matrix* rewatch was enough to spare her from the heavy mood that'd followed her back to the place she'd thought she belonged. Joe wasn't expecting her in Brooklyn until the next day, but she almost texted him about getting some dumplings, or a beer, or even just taking a walk along the frigid sidewalks as drunken couples spilled out of foggy-windowed bars. She kept pulling out her phone, then putting it away again. She wasn't in the mood to be seen.

She took a shower and let herself get a little weepy.

Grow up, MC.

Why couldn't she seem to do that?

Sunday morning, bleary-eyed but feeling a little less dire, she used the one weapon she had against Joe descending on her apartment demanding she rehash every moment of her Thanksgiving: She told him she needed to write. It was just an excuse, at first. She planned to take another crying shower, go out for Chinese, and chip away at a batch of marketing emails for some startup that claimed to have created a software that would allow local governments to mobilize Big Data to solve climate change. But when she settled in at Yang Garden II with her laptop and some wonton soup, she opened the notes document she'd sent to Joe for the A-team meeting instead and read it from start to finish.

They weren't half bad, her little observations of Nora's character, the way she was and wasn't like Nicole Penny. No simple heart of gold, but an unexpected warmth under the prickly conversation. An empathy that came from seeing people clearly, rather than a sentimental sappiness. But the focus on Nora, she realized now, was unfair.

To both of them.

Because this wasn't just Nora's story, and never had been.

She inhaled her soup, jotted a few additional notes, then headed home to finish the marketing emails.

On Monday, she walked up the stairs to the main branch of the Brooklyn Public Library at nine in the morning and shuffled in with the waiting crowd.

Past the Art Deco fortress exterior, on the other side of the tall, gold-embossed gates overlooking Grand Army Plaza, was the usual overheated, vaguely burnt smell of all public libraries in winter. The sun shone through the tall glass windows in the study wings, shafts of illuminated dust teeming over the long tables. She settled in by the religious books, where the people who were not of entirely sound mind were at least dependably quiet, lost in the study of various apocalypses. On her way in, she'd taken a stroll through the fiction section, finding a well-worn copy of *Girl Next Door* face out on the shelves.

Now she laid it down on the table, her computer open but set to the side, a coffee steaming by her right hand. She switched her phone off.

And turned to the first page.

She'd read so many excerpts of Nora's book over the past few months. But her anxiety over consuming it from start to finish—as if sustained attention would be more painful than sporadic glimpses—hadn't allowed her to appreciate the storytelling. She already knew the writing was good. But there was also the larger structure to admire, the alternating sections a masterful build of high drama and humor. It was so utterly Nora, confident on the surface and pensive, even tentative, underneath. MC drank it in greedily, desperate for the connection now that all channels of communication had closed between them.

After she finished it, she read it again. She showed up at the library, day after day, then week after week, sitting in the same chair with the same materials. Sometimes a man would be talking furiously to himself in a British accent. Sometimes a woman with very large holes in the back of her pants would ask MC what her shoe size was, apropos of nothing. Sometimes teenagers would rip through the stacks, throwing their backpacks at each other as a beleaguered woman with a pink mohawk tried to chase them down, high-tops scuffing along the floor. And sometimes someone who looked around MC's age would sit at the other end of her table, canvas jacket zipped all the way up, crying quietly into her hands. At some point, MC pushed a Snickers bar toward the girl, who continued to cry, but dutifully ate the treat.

Even when MC had to break focus and scamper for the bathroom, or step outside to wolf down a PB&J in foil on the stone stairs, *Girl Next Door* lived large in her mind, Nora's fast-paced narrative voice thrumming through her thoughts.

Seth Flanagan had wanted MC to figure out the trigger for publishing it. Why Nora had—at this time and no other time—released a pseudonymous novel that paradoxically relied on so many details from her actual past. And while MC hadn't quite gotten close enough to Nora to find the concrete answer that she'd been given a final extension to investigate, she hoped she'd found something just as interesting, which was her own side of the story. Not the self-deprecating one laced with denial. A little bit of memory comparison, sure—no, they hadn't actually been in math class together; yes, they'd rode the same bus in middle school, though Nora had always sat up front, alone, with wrap-around headphones firmly in place—but mostly what she ended up writing was a reflection on herself as someone else had invented her. The total strangeness of being made fiction, and the even stranger truth that this probably happened all the time, not just in secretly semi-autobiographical books. It was what anyone did when they were fascinated at a distance, making the object of desire both more coherent and less human than anyone really was.

It wasn't as salacious as the usual Jawbreaker feature, but MC hoped that what she'd exposed of herself would make up for what she couldn't uncover about Nora.

The best part was how easy it ended up being to protect their identities after all. She just had to follow Nora's lead.

She finished the draft a week before Christmas—byline: Michaela Carson—and sent it over to Joe.

He replied within the hour.

BRO.

She assumed this was positive. Her assumption was confirmed, several minutes later, when he demanded they gather for a toast that night, the two of them and Sheena and Jerome, to whom he'd forwarded the piece, at their favorite dive bar.

MC felt like she had no choice but to accept. To face her first audience and get used to the fact that she was about to do something totally insane.

When she stepped out of the subway a few hours later, a full-blown snowstorm was underway. Her sneakers sank into the powdery drifts, her socks already soaked from the front end of the commute. But it felt fitting. The frozen toes. The smothering wind. The punishing hike through Bushwick, which looked abandoned that night. When she arrived at the bar, an inconspicuous former storefront, she almost expected the bouncer to turn her away on sight.

He checked her ID and waved her inside.

Joe was over by the bar in a maroon fisherman's sweater, his hair slicked back, his stubble finally trimmed. But the circles under his eyes were dark even in the speakeasy light.

"Haven't seen you in a minute," he said.

"Busy saving your ass."

"I know. I owe you forever." He laughed, but it sounded forced. "Seth is still holding out on the official go-ahead."

"Because I didn't reveal Nora's dastardly marketing schemes?"

"I think his gripes are more about an article that uses fake names for its author and its subject."

"He'll approve it," Sheena said, sidling up to MC and playing with some tinsel on the bar. "You killed it, *Michaela*." She distracted from the awkwardness by giving MC a hug. She was wearing a backless green dress with a black collar, a severe style that showed off her glittering skin. She smelled like peppermint.

"Honestly, Seth should be kissing the ground you walk on," Jerome said, appearing next to Joe and sipping his cosmo.

"Your article's the weirdest, most interesting thing I've read in a minute, MC. Almost made me not care who's really who."

"The fandom will care," Joe said. "But they're just our initial audience."

"To MC," Jerome said, lifting his glass. "Our rescuer from irrelevance."

"And to this whole crew," Sheena added. "You guys are my favorite people in the world."

Joe and MC smiled along with them, clinking drinks. But something was off. It was probably just MC. Even with her mission complete, she felt hollow, like hard work meant nothing if you didn't have the right person to celebrate it with.

She chugged her beer.

"You okay?" Sheena said.

MC blinked. Joe had already turned to talk to Jerome about something else. "Yeah. Fine." She smiled. "Just tired."

Sheena gave her a long look. "Seems like this was a pretty emotional assignment for you."

"It might've gotten a little intense for a minute."

"You're a little intense." She touched one of her gold hoop earrings, dipping her face slightly.

"Only sometimes."

"I hadn't realized that about you. I mean, I might've suspected."

MC sighed. She should've been thrilled at this moment of overt flirtation from someone she'd been vaguely interested in for years, never once thinking she had a shot.

But the only person she seemed to want anymore was Nora.

"Sorry," she muttered, "I need to use the restroom."

As she waited in line with a bunch of other twenty-somethings, her phone buzzed.

All I want for Christmas is youuuu . . .
to be our special guest advisor again tomorrow!!
Last meeting of the semester.
(Kids keep asking about you)

This was the third such string of messages Jae had sent since Thanksgiving break. MC should've already told her she wasn't coming. But she couldn't bring herself to disappoint yet another person—or, in this case, a whole group of people.

She needed to get it over with. To tell Jae she was done with *Explorations*, to tell Joe she needed to distance herself from Jawbreaker after he published her article, at least for a little while. And, since Nora was already finished with her, she needed to be finished with Nora. And with Green Hills, and all the painful confusion that came with it, which had seemed for a few months to be resolving, only to reveal itself as the same tangled mess all over again.

Writing the article had been cathartic. But now that it was done, her heart was raw all over again.

After she relieved herself, her thumbs were hovering over her phone when Jerome pulled her back to the bar. "Joe wants to make a speech," he said with a grin.

"A speech?"

Joe had transferred them all to a high-top table in the corner, already holding a shot glass aloft as Jerome and MC rejoined.

"I just wanted to say some shit," he deadpanned. "But for real. It's been a tough year." His eyes met MC's for a moment. "This isn't an easy industry in the best of times. When traffic is down, I stress myself out trying to figure out trends or whatever. But the reason I got into this line of work isn't to follow the zeitgeist. It's to publish fucking awesome stories." He smiled. "As we close the year out, I think we can all say MC is the one who rose to the occasion this time."

MC's stomach dropped as her friends' faces settled on hers, adoration all around.

"I know we've already toasted her once," Joe added, "but this is personal. MC, you've always been a huge force behind everything I do. You're the person who not only keeps my spirits up, but advises me, guides me, and challenges me. You're loyal as hell, even if you weren't the best kisser at sixteen"—Jerome and Sheena laughed—"and pretty soon the world is going to see what a genius you are, even if you still refuse to take credit in public." His smile widened. "Oh yeah, and Seth just sent the article to legal."

"Let's fucking go!" said Jerome.

They toasted, throwing their shots back. The whiskey tasted expensive. The tinsel was gleaming. Sheena was still watching MC over the lip of her glass.

She'd delivered what her best friend in the world needed most. Met expectations, and possibly exceeded them.

Everyone was happy.

She stared down at her phone.

Grow up, MC.

Maybe there were still a few loose ends that needed tying up in that department.

She ducked away from the table and started to type.

22

The next day, as MC made a circle of desks in Mr. Pryor's classroom, she tried to remember the calculus behind agreeing to run the last *Explorations* meeting of the semester against all her better judgment.

Nothing came.

She knew it had something to do with the whiskey from the night before. An attempt to mitigate the sinking feeling that, even after all her efforts to do the right thing, she'd messed up spectacularly. And if she could just go back once more, talk to Nora again, then maybe, just maybe, she might be able to salvage things between them.

She'd assumed only a few diehards would attend. The holiday break had officially begun at the last bell, a few hours of light left before the next day heralded a dirty-snow Christmas Eve with subzero windchill. But Ben, Sheila, Patrick, Heather, and the rest of the crew shuffled in. Sheila was wearing a knee-length sweater that might've been a dress. Heather was wearing mittens. It seemed the school had already turned off the HVAC.

As they sat down, MC handed out packets of the afternoon's workshop submission, an experimental poem that featured one line per page. As far as she could tell, it was about trees, being depressed, and a dating show MC had never heard of and hadn't had time to look up.

Despite her gloomy mood, the rhythm of the discussion took over faster than ever. Her mind became focused, her muscles uncoiling for the first time since sending her article to Joe. There was just something about getting together and working through something difficult—talking it out, questioning assumptions, eventually remembering that making sense was occasionally overrated. It was this togetherness that MC had always loved, she realized, more than writing, even now.

Especially now.

They took a bathroom break at some point. MC checked her phone. Just one message from Joe.

GOING LIVE THE DAY AFTER XMAS!!!

A wave of bile rose in her throat.

When everyone came back, she tried to keep the workshop talk on track. But it was hard, given how formless the poem was. Or maybe the problem was that it was too formed. Ironically, the piece had been submitted anonymously. While the students had kept their tone cautious and respectful up to that point, now the knives came out. Everyone saw what they wanted to see; everyone wanted to reshape what was there to fit their worldview.

"Pause," MC said, after Patrick had suggested compressing the poem into a single stanza, in the bottom right-hand corner of a single page, with all the lines deleted except the first and last. "I want to backtrack and talk about anonymous submissions."

The room, which had gotten a little testy, a little bored, seemed to snap back to attention. MC tried not to stare directly at Heather.

"Like, should it be allowed?" Sheila said.

MC spread her hands. "Let's start with what it means."

"It means someone wanted to protect themselves," Ben said.

MC shrugged. "It's feeling like the opposite of protected to me. Because if I came out and said I was the one who'd written this, you all probably wouldn't be going to town on it, slicing and dicing it up."

"Did you write it?" Ben asked, wiggling his eyebrows.

"If I say no, then you probably won't believe me, will you?"

"Is it rude to ask the person who wrote it to identify themselves now?" Sheila said. "Like, if they're in the room, they can just tell us why they did it this way."

"But if you ask that, aren't you violating their privacy?" MC said. "Going against their intention?"

Patrick shook his foot and said, "At a certain point, your intentions don't really matter. You put this out for public consumption. Why should you get to withhold your name?"

Heather picked her fingernails, but her posture was tense.

"I can think of some simple reasons," MC said. "Fear of judgment, for starters."

"Okay, but the judgment is happening regardless."

"But it's judgment of the work, not the author."

"It doesn't seem fair," Sheila said. "We all put our names on our stuff. Why should one author have extra power?"

Heather finally spoke. "Maybe it's the only power the author thinks they could have."

"Well," Sheila said, "it's not very brave."

They went back to suggestions for revision. As they talked, MC found herself wondering if Heather really was responsible for the piece, or if it was someone else, someone less obvious.

Jae would know. She was the one managing the submissions inbox while the advisorship was in limbo. But MC didn't want to ask.

The meeting ended. MC got a lot of hugs goodbye, which surprised her. Even Patrick wished her "whatever kind of new year you want to have."

She thanked him, and realized she didn't know.

Conrad had told her to meet him out in the parking lot when she was done. But she still wanted to discuss the anonymous submission with Jae. Not to discover the author, but to give a word of caution about letting students go down that rabbit hole—because sometimes it led to a bestselling novel nine years later and a trail of emotional wreckage in its wake.

As she walked toward the English Department office, she heard low voices arguing. The halls were eerily quiet otherwise. Everyone, including staff, seemed to have fled for their vacations as early as possible. The sky was darkening outside, and the few fluorescents that were still on made it seem like night had already fallen.

MC walked toward the voices, sensing that she was overhearing something that wasn't meant to be overheard, but also worried that Jae was on the receiving end of some disgruntled teacher's rant.

Hers was definitely one of the voices, MC realized as she got closer. But when she reached the door, she was surprised, then not surprised, to find the other one was Conrad's.

"—let it go," Jae was saying. "You're having a baby."

"You think I don't know that?"

"Then take responsibility for it."

"It wasn't planned."

"But it's happening. Jesus, Conrad."

"How is this any more fair to Gabby or some future child?"

"We can put it behind us. We made a mistake . . ."

MC backed away, slowly, on tiptoes.

When she got outside, she texted Conrad that she was ready to go. She still hadn't texted Joe back. But for once, Joe was far from her mind.

Her brother was cheating.

She'd suspected it. More than suspected it. But she hadn't let herself live in the reality of Conrad getting physical with his boss, a woman who wasn't his wife. And now his wife was pregnant with their baby.

A mistake, Jae had called it. MC hoped it really had been singular.

She stood outside the Destroyer of Worlds, shivering in the dusk, until her brother appeared under the floodlight outside the back entrance.

"I thought we said meet in the lobby," he called. "Aren't you freezing?"

"A little."

He unlocked the car, and she got in first, glad not to have to look at him for another few seconds.

When he finally joined her on the driver's side, he sat in silence for a moment, breath frosting in front of him.

"Hello?" he said.

It would be easy to breathe out. To say hi back, to let him turn the car on, and with it the heat. They could focus on warming their hands, and the stiffness would remain inside them both, the unspoken things they believed were their business, their right to put words to or not. MC had done it a million times. Let the moment pass, the tension fade, resigned to the wrongness as an unfixable, maybe even necessary, component of the universe. Better to move on from the certainty of hurt than to linger in it, suffering for nothing.

Or not nothing.

For the truth.

"I lied to you," she said.

"About what?"

"Why I came back to Green Hills. In September." She cleared her throat. "This whole time, actually."

"Can I turn the car on? My hands are about to fall off."

"Go ahead."

He pressed the button, music and heat flooding the car.

She turned the music off. "I'm not writing a novel."

"Could've guessed that."

"But I did write something." She took a breath. "An article, for Joe's website."

"Jawbreaker?"

She nodded. "It's about the fact that Nora Pike secretly wrote a bestselling rom-com under a pseudonym."

She chanced a look at her brother. He was frowning.

"Really?" he said. "She doesn't strike me as the type."

"Well, she is."

"I mean, hey, good for her."

"It's actually not good for her. Or if it is, it's only good because her identity has been protected ever since her book was published earlier this year."

"So how did you figure her out?"

"Joe did. But he wanted me to be the one to come back here to get the story."

"Why?"

"Because I'm the love interest in Nora's book. Or I was the inspiration for it. He thought I could get the scoop without her realizing what I was up to."

"Whoa." He looked intrigued. "Did you?"

"Sort of. I mean, yeah. More or less."

"But she has no idea you're writing about it?"

"No."

"So, you conned her."

"That's one way to put it." She sighed. "Joe needed a big story. He felt like I was the only one who could deliver. So I did my best, for his sake, and now I'm doing my best to have the story come out without exposing her identity to the world."

"Is that . . . possible?"

"In three days, we're going to find out."

"That's super intense."

Conrad pulled out of the parking lot. He seemed like he was mulling things over. But when a minute had passed and he'd said nothing, she added, a little annoyed, "Also, I just heard you fighting with Jae."

Blanching, he pulled off the road, into the parking lot of the Mexican restaurant—El Sombrero—and put the Destroyer of Worlds in park.

"First of all, whatever you heard, you don't understand. And second of all, I don't think you're in a position to be getting on your high horse right now."

"Obviously. Why do you think I started by confessing that I came here and lied to all of you guys for, like, three months?"

"Oh." He blinked. "You did that for me?"

"I did it because I'm sick of us being fake siblings. I get that not everyone will be best friends with their brother. But you deserve the truth from me." She pressed her lips together for a moment. "And I'd like to think I deserve the truth from you."

"Fine." He leaned back in his seat. "I cheated."

"When?"

"October."

MC winced. "How far did you go?"

He blew out a breath. "Let's call it halfway."

"Are you still cheating?"

"No. God. We haven't done anything since I found out about the pregnancy."

"And that conversation I just overheard?"

They'd been maintaining a respectful lack of eye contact. But when MC heard her brother start to cry, she looked over and put a hand on his arm.

"I guess I'm not one hundred percent over it," he whispered. "I'm a fucking asshole."

She agreed, but he didn't need to hear that just then. "What happened with you and Gabby? I thought you guys were rock solid. Wildly in love."

"We were. In the beginning. But it was a crazy time of life. She was just about to start college, I was fresh off eating shit at Harvard . . ."

"What do you mean, eating shit? It was your choice to drop out."

"Yeah, because I knew I was about to fail out anyway."

She blinked. "Oh."

"This is what I mean about you projecting some bullshit fantasy on me."

"I . . . I never would've guessed, Con. I'm sorry."

"It's fine."

"I mean, you really went off about how entitled and pretentious those Harvard kids were."

"Because I was embarrassed I couldn't keep up with them." He snorted. "I don't even know why they accepted me in the first place." He scrubbed at his eyes. "Gabby was so into me, even after I confessed about how I'd messed up at school. She said it was good that I moved back home, that I shouldn't feel bad about transferring to community college. 'What's wrong with being a big fish again?' And she said if I wanted to tell people the truth, I could, but if I wasn't ready, there was no rush. So I went with it, and things felt a little better. But it didn't last. I kept thinking about how I'd failed. How high school had made me think I was something better than I was. I couldn't get over it." He laughed. "That's why I was so psyched when Jae called me over the summer. It was a chance to go back."

MC looked at her brother, whom she'd idolized and envied and resented for so long, never suspecting the self-loathing that'd defined his early twenties. "And then what happened?"

"I don't know. It's complicated. But running the school started to make me feel like my old self, like I was at that peak again—the one I was at when I was eighteen. And she was right there with me." He shook his head. "I think she felt like a failure, too, after her husband left her. We talked about it a lot. Bonded over it, I guess."

MC tapped her knee. "That's pretty hard-core."

"Yeah."

"Which is worst-case scenario."

"I know."

"You have to tell Gabby."

"Even if it's the worst thing I could ever say to her?"

She nodded.

"Well," he said, "I guess you have to tell Nora also. Before the article comes out."

"Yeah." She closed her eyes. "That's why I'm back here."

23

The next morning, MC volunteered to get the mail, walking out along the driveway as slowly as she could. She surveyed the dead plants. The damage to the gravel driveway where it met the road. The state of the oak trees. It was so cold the air felt brittle, but she kept her hands in her pockets and toughed it out. The lights were on in Nora's house. It was hard not to gawk.

She'd been hoping a text might arrive. Or that Nora would be so annoyed that MC was back, she'd find an excuse to come out and say something rude. Anything to get the ball rolling. But MC's phone didn't chime, and the only sound was the wind whistling through the bare branches.

Eventually she went back in. Gabby had gotten a late start on the day and needed help with the ham. MC was assigned the gravy. As far as she could tell, the main thing to do was stir the pot of brown goo on the stove, making sure it didn't burn.

"Have you had any weird cravings?" she said, because Gabby was being unusually quiet.

"Um, sleep?" She laughed, but it sounded forced. "That's about it."

"Building a human is pretty intense."

"Yeah. I thought I'd escaped the z's after the first trimester was so easy, but . . . here I am."

"Maybe it's just holiday stress."

"I guess so."

"I think you're really tough. I mean, for going through all this."

"I don't feel tough. I feel like a drag." Gabby laughed again, but it sounded even more hollow than before. "God, I thought I was going to be this glowing earth mama. But instead, I'm just wiped out and moody all the time."

"Do you want to lie down? I can finish the gravy on my own."

"No, I'm okay. It's nice to have company."

MC tried to smile. "Conrad's still super busy with work, huh?"

"Something about last-minute midyear assessments. And I think he's mad at me."

MC stopped stirring for a moment. "Why would he be mad at you?"

"For making the announcement at Thanksgiving."

"What's wrong with that?"

"I sort of sprung it on him." Gabby twisted a dish towel in her hands. "I tried to consult with him about it beforehand, but he kept being like, 'Uh, I need to think about it.' Except he never thought about it." She sighed. "I figured we couldn't keep it a secret much longer, anyway. And everyone was there, in such a celebratory mood. But he acted like I'd betrayed him."

"He's probably just really nervous."

"I mean, shit, I'm really nervous too. That's why we need to be a team on this." She looked up from the dish towel, her eyes boring into MC's. "The last thing I want is to go through this alone."

MC could only hold Gabby's gaze for a second or two. She was saved by her phone vibrating.

It was Nora.

Lois wants me to invite you to our holiday party tonight.

Gabby leaned over, a hand on her hip, and grinned. MC was relieved to see some of her usual warmth surfacing through the fatigue.

But she was even more relieved that Nora had finally broken her silence.

"Girl," Gabby said, "you have to go."

"But we just told your family I'm coming to dinner."

"I'll say you got sick."

"That suddenly?"

She shrugged. "Food poisoning."

"I feel like Nora doesn't actually want me to be there."

"If that was true, she wouldn't have texted you."

MC texted back.

> Do *you* want to invite me to your holiday party tonight?

Nora replied immediately.

If I didn't, I wouldn't have texted you.

"Ha!" Gabby said, then went to check on the ham.

MC bit her lip.

> Okay, I'll be there.

And I think we should talk.
Even though I'm bad at talking.

> I think so too.
> That we should talk.
> Not that you're bad at talking.

Sorry it took me a while to get over myself.

> Don't be sorry.

> I'm sorry this has been so complicated.
> Party starts at 7. Wear red and green.

> Are you wearing red and green?

> I'm Jewish, MC.

The rest of the afternoon passed in a blur. After the dinner preparation was finished, Conrad wandered upstairs from the basement to help decorate their Christmas tree. Saving it for the last minute was a Calloway thing. Or that's what MC and Conrad liked to pretend. In reality, they'd inherited their parents' discomfort with festivity. By the time Conrad was a teenager, they were lucky to get a tree at all.

But because their celebrations were so brief, they took on a compressed, manic energy that MC had come to love. Conrad put on a felt Santa hat and blasted holiday classics. MC opted for elf slippers and wrapped herself in tinsel. Gabby participated at a respectful distance, complimenting the way the lights were coming together, the even distribution of the ornaments, how happy the two weirdos seemed to be.

By nightfall, one of Gabby's brothers had come by to pick up Gabby and Conrad and the ham. MC said goodbye, then took a shower and got dressed, decking herself out in a big Snoopy Christmas sweater with an old pair of Conrad's black work pants cuffed at the ankle. Her hair was cooperating for once, the semi-tame pile of blond curls tucked carefully behind one ear. She looked like herself. It would have to be enough.

The drive to the library was treacherous. A surprise round of snow had come in with the frigid cold that night, and the Destroyer of Worlds was not, alas, a destroyer of frost. MC blasted the heat and squinted along the dark, winding roads, trying to see past the powerful glow of people's lawn decorations.

When she arrived at the party, Bing Crosby was playing. The lobby had been hung with garlands and golden orbs. Maureen saw her first, wearing a ridiculous sweater of her own—a technicolor Rudolph piece featuring the Red-Nosed Reindeer defecating into a gift box.

Then Lois came over and gave her a candy cane. "Ho ho ho. If you suck it 'til it's sharp, you could stab someone to death."

MC blinked. "I guess so."

"Helen," Lois said, already turning after the head librarian, "I need to set up my karaoke machine..."

MC went over to the drinks table and poured herself an eggnog. She hoped it was alcoholic.

It wasn't.

Nora either hadn't arrived or was hiding somewhere. MC posted up by a bust on a plinth and waited. At least the growing crowd helped her feel less obvious in her loneliness. In the span of twenty minutes, the thirty people in the lobby had swelled to over a hundred. A space had even been cleared near the reference desk for dancing.

She tried to steel herself for the impending confession. For Nora's anger, judgment, and sadness. She reminded herself that they were probably never going to be a thing anyway, and all she could hope for was that Nora might appreciate certain parts of the article in some distant future—the ones where MC had tried to express her admiration for Nora's wit and self-possession, in prose and in real life; the ones where she tried to explain her own deliberately cultivated ignorance as a shield against engaging in honest relationships. The parts where she hoped there was some connection between real life and even the most contrived fiction, in which emotional growth was possible, even if going about it turned out to be a lot more painful and boring than reading about it in stories.

"Wanna shake your tail feather?" Maureen asked.

MC wasn't sure when the children's librarian had appeared next to her. "Oh, uh . . . I'm really bad at dancing."

"That's literally the requirement around here." Maureen looked out at the elders taking their shoes off next to the taped-down dance floor.

"I'm okay," MC said. "Thanks, though."

"Come on, we're the only people here under fifty."

Maureen took MC's hand and pulled her along, MC trying not to spill her eggnog.

At first, she thought she'd just put a few cheesy moves in, then slink off to continue waiting for Nora. But it felt good to be part of a group activity. She bobbed her head, grateful for the low lights. People in red turtlenecks and green chinos swayed their hips and boogied. A few looked like they'd taken lessons, twirling around the dance floor, seasonal pins gleaming, their flesh-toned stockinged feet light and assured. Someone took MC's waist as part of a shimmying chain, and she kicked along, working up a sweat.

She was slowing down a little when Nora finally walked in.

The sight of her brought MC to a full stop.

Nora wore a sleeveless black jumpsuit and a gold chain around her neck, a gold bangle encircling her bicep. Her hair was caught in a high ponytail, like in high school, and the newness and familiarity of her made MC's body feel instantly spring-loaded.

But she looked tense too. Or maybe just hesitant. She kept her hands behind her back as she scanned the crowd.

When her eyes met MC's, MC struggled just to wave, weeks of pining giving way to a riptide of desire.

Which was not the mindset she was going for.

Luckily, Lois got to Nora first, giving MC a moment to gather herself. She left the dance floor to frantically assemble a big plate of cookies. She made a show of studying the display of children's craft ornaments near the computers. When Nora appeared next to her, there was a tectonic shift in her gut. But she tried to play it cool.

"I have something for you," Nora said, looking equally flushed despite having just come in from the cold. She had to shout to be heard over the dance music.

MC cleared her throat. "Like, a present?"

"You could call it that."

"Well, that's really thoughtful of you."

Nora's eyes made a paranoid sweep of the party. "Actually, I'd rather give it to you somewhere private."

MC realized Nora was holding something behind her back.

"Where do you want to go?" MC said, her throat suddenly dry. But Nora was already walking off. MC followed, weaving through the crowd. She headed past the study tables, all the way to the row where the history books were. MC's heart started hammering again. She told herself there was no way Nora was going to put a move on her now, after how clearly she'd shut things down between them last time. And even if, in some impossible alternate universe, she'd changed her mind about all that, MC would stop her. Definitely.

MC caught up to Nora in the stacks. It was dim, quiet. Nora's hands weren't behind her back anymore.

She was holding a small, book-shaped object in patterned paper tight to her chest.

At first it seemed impossible; then it seemed so obvious MC couldn't believe she hadn't anticipated it.

Nora was also trying to come clean.

Being beaten to the punch was unacceptable. MC needed her own wrongs to come out first, because they were so much more damning, and because the only thing that could possibly make them worse was looking like she'd been shamed into admitting them.

Her phone started to buzz. She checked it quickly, saw that Conrad was calling, and cut the call off.

"What I'm about to give you," Nora said slowly, "is something I think you might hate."

Conrad was calling again. MC silenced her phone.

"But what I need you to know"—Nora took a breath—"is the reason why I did it."

"Wait," MC said, finally finding her voice. "Can I just say something first?"

Nora frowned. "I'd rather you not. This is kind of hard for me."

Now Conrad was texting her.

Fuck fuck fuck I fucked it.

"Uh-oh," MC whispered.
"What?"
"Sorry, I need to reply to this real quick."
"Are you serious?"

What happened?

Gabby's gone.
Her family chased me out of the house.

MC looked up. Nora seemed distraught, biting her lower lip, holding the present in a white-knuckle grip. MC was floundering too. Her head was swimming with the scent of Nora's perfume, the nearness of Nora in the stacks. She knew she had to just get the truth out. But she wanted to have time to explain why she'd written the article. Why she still wished she hadn't. How much she felt for Nora now, nine years too late, even if there was no future between them.

But for the first time, her brother needed her.

And she still had one more day.

She looked down at her phone again and typed frantically.

                                         Where are you?

Freezing my balls off behind the deli.

"What's going on?" Nora said.

"Gabby found out about my brother and Jae." MC put a hand on her forehead, like she was checking for a fever. "I think I have to go deal with this."

"Right now?"

MC told herself she wasn't seizing on an excuse, or trying to avoid taking responsibility for her actions; she was allowing a temporary diversion for Conrad's sake, because it was unacceptable to jeopardize his trust the first time he'd offered it to her. "I'm really sorry," she said.

Nora looked miserable. "Please don't go."

"Can't we just talk tomorrow? Or later tonight? This'll take me an hour to deal with, maybe two—"

Nora shook her head, shoved the present into MC's hands, and brushed past her without looking back.

24

One afternoon, when MC and Conrad were kids, they'd gone over to Conrad's friend's house to play video games. This friend lived two miles away. But his house was connected to theirs by a network of unofficial trails that crisscrossed the woods butting up on everyone's properties. MC and Conrad had walked there, and the expectation was that, before dark, they would walk back home.

Maybe the games went later than expected. Maybe MC was slow on her feet—she was only in third grade at the time. But night fell just as they'd started the trek back, and all the familiar paths became hard to keep track of. Everything looked the same in the eerie dim. Conrad kept marching ahead, trying to scout out a house or some other landmark. But it was a spring night, no moon, and the trees were already lush with leaves. MC was terrified. Of sounds real and imagined, of the idea of spending the night outside with no food or shelter. But most of all, she was terrified of getting in trouble.

It wasn't even the prospect of having toys or activities taken away that'd filled her with panic. It was her parents' disappointment. Her dad had never hesitated to give the silent treatment, and while her mother was less icy, she was also less present, content to have an excuse to bury herself deeper in whatever study she was running. MC had wished she could at least rely on her brother to stay by her side, but she was already aware that he retreated into his own world in times of stress.

As she cruised around Green Hills all those years later, Conrad red faced and hunched over in the passenger seat beside her, MC thought back to that night. The fear of disappointing the people you loved, no matter how hard you tried not to, and the consequences of that disappointment.

"What's next?" she said, pulling up to a red light.

"Let's try the Horny Ram."

She put her blinker on. The more popular of the town's two pubs wasn't far, but MC doubted Gabby would be there.

"How long do you want to keep this up?" she asked. They'd been on the hunt for over two hours, and the few other cars MC encountered on the road seemed increasingly fast and erratic.

"Until we find her."

"Maybe this is a sign that she needs space right now."

Conrad shook his head. "If we're apart tonight, we'll be done forever."

"What makes you think that?"

"The way she looked at me before she left." Conrad's voice sounded hollow. He'd given MC the story after she'd picked him up, shaking and wet in the snow. How he'd tried to text Jae about meeting up, then gotten angry when she'd ignored him. That he'd fired off a few messages about how they needed to *deal with what happened* and *decide what comes next*. Gabby had noticed his absorption, and done something she'd never done before.

She asked to see his phone.

It hadn't helped that he'd been weird with Gabby all day, unsettled by the conversation he'd had with MC. He knew what he had to do, but couldn't imagine doing it, and somehow got the idea that tying things off with Jae first would make it all easier.

He hadn't given Gabby the phone in the end, but it was as good—as bad—as a confession. She'd blown up. Right at the dinner table. She'd gotten out of her seat in tears, yelled at him, and locked herself in her old room.

Then her parents and her brothers had gotten involved.

"This is the worst part," MC said, "right now. And even if it takes a while to get better, it will get better."

"I don't know, MC." He started crying again.

"I'm really sorry this is happening."

"It's my fault. I deserve it."

"Yeah, okay. But also, we all make big mistakes. We all feel weak sometimes. Or maybe it's just that we need things that are hard to explain to other people, even people who love us, so we go to crazy lengths to get them."

"She's never going to see it that way."

"We don't know that."

She pulled up at the Horny Ram, which was, unsurprisingly, packed for Christmas Eve. Conrad got out of the car—he insisted on going by himself—and shouldered through the double doors.

MC waited. Her eyes drifted to the patterned wrapping paper by her knee. She'd tucked Nora's gift in the pocket of her door, unopened. Now she picked it up, set it in her lap, and carefully worked the tape off.

A hardcover copy of *Girl Next Door* stared up at her. She knew the loopy script of the title all too well. The cartoon illustration that stood in for her and Nora. When she lifted it up, she saw a note had been tucked under the front cover. She pulled it out.

The first thing you need to know is I WAS NOT IN LOVE WITH YOU IN HIGH SCHOOL.

But I did like you. Maybe more than I've let on.

Most people freak me out. There's just something different about you. Which is weird, because you're always trying really hard to blend in.

Don't read too much into what I wrote. But if it doesn't make you hate me . . . call me. XO

MC leaned back and closed her eyes.

Conrad grunted when he got back in the car. "Let's try Stacey's next."

MC frowned, tucking the book away again. "Stacey Grummond?"

"Yeah. On Bates Road."

"Are they still friends?"

"They go out for drinks now and then."

"Con. I think we need to call it quits for tonight."

"If you're tired," he snapped, "I'll drop you at home and keep going by myself."

"I am tired. But this isn't about me wanting to abandon you on your quest."

"So, what's it about?"

"Accepting that Gabby really doesn't want to see you right now."

Conrad started to cry again. MC rubbed his back.

Then he took out his phone.

"What are you doing?" she said.

He kept typing.

"Let it go, Con."

"Fine." He chucked the phone over his shoulder, where it bounced against the back seat, then disappeared into the abyss.

MC remembered eventually getting back home with him, all those years ago. Finding their way after they'd been lost in the woods for what felt like forever. They'd been expecting their dad to be sitting up in his easy chair, glaring at them the moment they walked through the door. But the chair was empty except for his newspaper. They crept into the living room and realized he'd fallen asleep on the couch. The TV was on. Their mom was still at the office.

As it turned out, it wasn't actually that late.

25

On Christmas morning, MC woke up to a thud.

She'd slept in the guest room with the door open on account of the overactive radiator, tangled in an old quilt. It'd been a fitful sleep. Too many trips to the bathroom. Bad, realistic dreams. Now it was well into morning, and the room was filled with crisp winter sun. Her eyelids fluttered as she tried to adjust to the cutting brightness.

Another thud came, but it was more muffled this time, accompanied by tinkling.

The Christmas tree.

"I thought you were a good person!" Gabby wailed.

MC swung her bare feet to the cold floor and scrambled around for a sweatshirt. When she heard glass shattering, she thought better of it and bounded out in her giant T-shirt, a gift from Joe sophomore year, featuring a certain groundskeeper looking beatific in a halo. It said, HAGRID LOVES YOU.

Gabby was in the living room. She'd washed her makeup off, but she was still wearing her party dress. MC wondered if she'd stayed with her family or gotten a room in a hotel. She looked exhausted, bereft, and incandescent with rage.

"I know you're mad right now," MC said, putting her hands in the air. "But can we talk for a minute?"

Gabby looked at MC like she'd never seen her before. "Did you know?"

MC wanted to say she'd only officially found out a few days ago, not mentioning that she'd suspected something for months. But Conrad was stumbling in just then, and she didn't want to throw her brother under the bus. He looked like he'd already been run over as it was.

Gabby seemed ready to reverse the bus at full speed and pancake him to the asphalt.

"Fuck you both," Gabby said, eerily calm. "I'm just here to get my stuff."

"Gab," Conrad said, his voice cracking, "please don't go. Can I just try to explain—"

"Explain why you fucked your boss?"

"Well, technically—"

Gabby threw a plastic Santa cup filled with peppermint patties at his blond cowlicked head. He managed to duck it. A framed picture on the wall was knocked askew, the two of them laughing together in a convertible on some sun-drenched highway.

"You broke my heart," Gabby said. Her hands were shaking. "I can't even look at you."

"Gabby, I understand if you never forgive me, but—"

"Get out of my fucking sight!"

"I will, and I'll give you as much space as you need, I just want to—"

"Shut *up*, Conrad! I don't want to hear your excuses, or whatever it was she did for you in six months that I couldn't do in nine fucking years." She started to cry.

"This isn't about you versus her," he whispered. "It's about me being a horrible idiot."

"You are a horrible idiot!"

"I agree!"

There was a knock on the front door. Everyone froze.

"Is that the cops?" MC said. The D'Angelos, their neighbors across the street, had a tendency to call the police at the slightest hint of noise.

Gabby raised an eyebrow. "Or is it her?"

Conrad shook his head vigorously.

Three more knocks, short and sharp.

"You know," MC said, "I think they have to say if they're police?"

"Answer it!" Gabby screamed at Conrad.

"I'll do it," MC said.

"No!" Gabby and Conrad shouted at the same time.

Conrad leapt toward the mudroom. MC followed, Gabby right behind her, all of them trying to see through the narrow glass panels in the door.

"Oh," Conrad said, turning the knob. "Uh—"

He stumbled back.

Just as MC realized it was Nora, Nora was right in front of her.

She grabbed MC's wrist. Then she yanked MC out the door, at which point MC stumbled over a planter, lost her balance, and landed on her back in a puff of snow.

The icy cold started creeping through the back of her T-shirt. White flakes twinkled in her eyes. She tried to get up, but Nora pushed her right back down.

"I could kill you," Nora breathed. Her eyes were wide and teary. "I could *kill* you."

Dread surged in MC's gut. Had Nora's editor caught wind of the article and tipped her off? Or had Seth and the A-team decided to publish early?

MC realized it didn't actually matter either way.

She'd missed her chance.

Her voice came out in a whisper: "I'm so sorry."

Conrad appeared at Nora's shoulder. "Back off," he said.

"You back off," Nora snapped.

"Fine," he said, "but can everybody just calm down?"

"I will not calm down!" Gabby cried from the doorway.

"I was so stupid to trust you," Nora said, still staring at MC.

"What is she talking about?" said Gabby.

Gabby was looking at Conrad, who looked to MC. His brow was creased with guilt.

"He knew about this too?" Nora said. She was shaking her head. "Fuck you both."

"Yeah," Gabby said, "fuck you both!"

But Nora only had eyes for MC. "You have *ruined* my life."

"Me?" MC was surprised to hear herself yelling. She got to her feet. "You're the one who decided to write a novel about our senior year where you didn't change a single fucking detail!"

"I never planned to publish it! And I'm not a very imaginative person, okay?" Nora balled her hands into fists. "It was just supposed to be for fun, online. But then an editor offered me a book deal, and I really needed the money for something. I never thought, in a million years . . ." She spread her arms. "Whatever. That's what I wanted to tell you last night, when I thought I needed to apologize. But you don't even deserve it. Because you sure as hell didn't publish my fucking Myers-Briggs results to help someone out. You did it for your pathetic ego."

"My *ego*?" MC's head was spinning. "Are you serious? I did it for Joe. He needed a big story, or he was going to get fired."

"So you destroyed my privacy over Joe Khoury's job at a *gossip website*?"

"I didn't destroy your privacy. I used our fictional names."

Nora shook her head. "How naïve can you be?"

"What do you mean?"

"My *fandom* figured it out, MC."

Her heart sank. "They did?"

"Of course they did! You made it so goddamn easy!"

MC's brain struggled to keep up. Her article was out. Their identities were out? "I thought I covered us."

"Not even close."

"Can someone explain to me what the hell is going on?" Gabby said. Conrad had started inching toward her as Nora and MC went at it.

Nora looked at Gabby and Conrad. "Earlier this year, I published a rom-com under a pen name, which protected my identity—until this morning, when MC and Joe put out an exposé on me for an incredibly dumb website he thinks will save him from obscurity. And yeah, my book was inspired by some real events from high school. Including, among other things, MC's old crush on you, Gabby, which you and Conrad were totally oblivious to, despite how insanely obvious it was."

Gabby and Conrad turned to stare at MC.

MC felt yet another wave of heat rushing to her cheeks.

But Nora wasn't done. "Thanks for sending every crazy homophobic troll to my front door, MC."

MC swallowed. She'd been so sure she was protecting Nora. "I swear I don't know how this happened."

"You don't know anything."

Nora turned and walked away.

MC wanted to call her back, to keep arguing, but she had nothing to say for herself.

She looked to her brother, who had a confused expression on his face. Then to Gabby, who'd put her fingers on her temples and was shaking her head.

"I thought you were working on a novel," she muttered.

She went back into the house and slammed the door.

MC crossed her arms. "Should we wait for her in the car?" she said to Conrad.

He trudged over to the Destroyer of Worlds and got in the driver's seat. She scampered after him and got in the passenger side.

"That's why you never talked to me about girls," he mumbled. He pulled the unwrapped book from the pocket in the door and turned it over, his eyes scanning the copy on the back. "'Back in high school, Nicole Penny had it bad for Michaela Carson. But Michaela was too hopelessly obsessed with Abby Rodriguez—her brother's hot new squeeze—to notice.'"

"She's exaggerating," MC said.

He didn't seem to be listening to her. "Is this why you hardly ever visited us? Because I ended up with Gabby, even though you never bothered to mention you were interested in her?"

"No, that's not it at all." She wrung her hands. "It upset me at the time. But I'm totally over it."

He tossed the book in her lap. "I don't know what to believe anymore."

"Believe me," she said quietly.

"Why? You haven't given me a single reason to trust you. Until yesterday, I guess. And even that was half-assed." He scrubbed his face with both hands. "I can take you to the train station now."

"But—"

"When Gabby leaves, I'll wait for you to run in and grab your stuff."

"I feel like you shouldn't be alone right now."

"Well, MC, you're the last person I want to be with."

Tears welled in her eyes. "Come on, Con. Don't do this."

He got out of the car, tramping off to the woods behind the house.

MC sat, her heart pounding, and watched him go.

Her phone buzzed. Joe was texting again.

DUDE Seth pulled a fast one on me.
I SWEAR I had no idea.
But also.
SHIT IS BLOWING UP!!

She held her breath.

She blocked him.

Then she deleted Instagram, and all her other apps, even as the numbers in their red notification bubbles were climbing so high it was basically a malfunction.

After Gabby stormed out—flashing her middle finger at MC—and got in a car that'd pulled up by their mailbox, MC went back into the house and changed out of her pajamas. She waded through the ruined decorations, trying to tidy up what she could. Trying to be useful, even now, as if it mattered.

She should never have come back here.

On her way out, she righted the Christmas tree, getting pine needles in her hair and sap all over her fingers. She left through the garage, but stopped when she saw a bright, shiny new object in the center of the empty space, a bow on the handlebars.

It had a little tag on the seat. The tag had a note in Conrad's chicken scratch.

> *We heard you ditched your old one in the woods on the side of the road. Try to be less sketchy with the new one! Love, Con, Gab, and Nor Dog (who told us the real story)*

MC sat down in an oil stain and started to cry.

26

There was nothing MC didn't hate about New Year's Eve. The resolutions. The staying up late. The realization that the holidays had come to an end. Champagne made her stomach hurt, and she looked bad in hats and glasses, so there was no way for her to celebrate, except by trying to make out with someone at midnight, which she'd only tried once, at a house party the year after college. It hadn't gone well. Not wanting to be presumptuous by planting a kiss on the girl's lips, she'd leaned in and kissed her neck instead. The girl had looked at MC like she'd been attacked by a real-life vampire. It'd been a torrential downpour that night. Stumbling home, MC had proceeded to trip while trying to avoid an overflowing sewer grate, leaving her with a sprained ankle that'd taken three weeks to heal.

In a sense, her latest plans were an improvement. She'd had it all figured out since returning to the city a week ago, on that terrible Christmas Day. She would spend the night lying on her futon, as she'd been doing nonstop for the past six days, and alternate between staring at the ceiling and rewatching *X-Men*.

The Matrix reminded her too much of Nora.

Unfortunately, *X-Men* depressed her, too, confronting her with the obvious fact that her longtime crush on sweet, caring Rogue was yet another facet of her Gabby fixation. Now Dr. Jean Grey seemed like the real catch. A powerful, guarded, volatile Nora Pike.

"MC?" Laura said, her voice coming through the thin paneling of her bedroom door. "Are you alive in there?"

MC coughed and sat up. "I am?" She looked at her phone. It was only eight p.m. "I am," she added, more firmly.

"Your weird friend is here."

MC sat up, clutching her comforter to her chest. Part of wedding herself to the futon had been about avoiding an all-too-common run-in with Joe on the street. Except now he'd come to her. Which she'd been expecting, but still. "Okay . . . I'll be out in a second."

"Hey," Laura said, sounding annoyed, "she said she'd—"

Joe burst through the door in a wave of expensive cologne. The cold still clung to his shearling-lined biker jacket, little flakes of snow dusting his perfectly defined curls.

"I can't take it anymore," he said, squatting down and putting one butt cheek on the edge of MC's futon. "I need you to stop hating me."

"Is he okay to be in here?" Laura asked, crossing her arms in the doorway. She was wearing a tie-dyed Grateful Dead T-shirt.

"Yeah," MC said, "all good. Thanks, Laura."

Laura shook her head, then walked back down the hall. Joe got up and closed the door.

He said, "It smells like Cool Ranch in here. And not in the good way."

"So?"

"So, you should be out bathing in an infinity pool of free IPA."

"Where is there an infinity pool of free IPA?"

"In the land of literary stardom you are currently scorning."

"Oh. I'm waiting for the theoretical stardom to pass, actually."

"MC," he groaned, "why?"

"Because I got it by sending an army of gay-hating trolls to Nora Pike's doorstep."

"Even if that was happening, which it's not, it wouldn't be your fault."

"Of course it would!"

"Well, let me reassure you that, while some autograph-signing has occurred at the Green Hills Public Library this week—despite shortened holiday hours—there are no violent threats being made."

"How could you possibly know?"

"I called the police department and asked."

"Are you serious?"

He batted his lashes, looking every inch the confident media princeling he was a year ago—no trace of the haggard, furtive air that'd emerged around him in summer and become full-blown in fall. "I don't want any member of the rainbow brigade getting hurt."

"Well, it's only been a week. Who knows what's coming."

"Probably not much. Because if you hadn't blocked your beloved, I could've told you that the main interest to come out of this piece isn't actually S. K. Smith herself, but the real-life romance you delivered to the *GND* fandom."

MC blinked. "That was not my intention."

"Well, people are taking it and running."

Appalling. "Has Nora responded?"

"Not a word."

"Her publisher?"

"Also silent. As exposés go, this is really the best-case scenario. I can see why they're not interfering."

"Or Nora had a mental breakdown and is too fragile to deal with anything more than an email right now."

He took out his phone, typed, then handed it to her.

MC saw a picture of a folding table in front of the Green Hills library, with a line of people on one side. Nora was on the other, Sharpie in hand. It was a story from the *Green Hills Register*. The headline was SMASH-HIT LOCAL AUTHOR DOES SIGNING AT PUBLIC LIBRARY.

MC rubbed her chin. "I guess she's rolling with the punches."

"These aren't punches. *Girl Next Door* is up at number three again on the bestseller list, thank you very much." Joe took out a pack of cigarettes.

"Can you do that in the kitchen?"

He already had one in his mouth. "I'll open the window."

"It's really hard to open this one, because of the bars."

"I'm an expert." He pried at the knob on the gate, but it was stuck. "So, if there was a fire in here, we'd just die?"

"Pretty much."

He inched up the bottom of the window with his fingertips, allowing a sliver of air to flow in, then lit up. "Come to my friend's New Year's Eve party," he said, blowing a puff of smoke out the crack. "I want you to see that this article has measurably improved all of our lives."

"I'd rather not."

"I know the spotlight is nerve-racking for you, but you might actually enjoy it if you leaned into it a little."

She shook her head, trying to ignore the sudden flare of anger she felt toward him—for barging in on her, for guilting her into writing the article in the first place, for showing zero remorse about the consequences. "This wasn't supposed to happen," she muttered.

"Which part?"

"The part where I exposed her, Joe. And, technically, myself."

"You did your best to protect her."

"Apparently my best isn't close to good enough. The sleuths put it together *the day it came out.*" She gritted her teeth. "I thought I was being so careful."

"Nora probably thought she was being careful when she wrote it. And look how obvious the parallels ended up being."

"To us. Because we lived it. This . . . it just doesn't make any sense."

"You're forgetting that the fandom's been on the case for almost a year now. Plus, you've written for Jawbreaker before. Someone probably recognized your style, realized how close these fake names were to the real ones, and just slotted everything else in from there."

"I guess."

"I understand why you took this hard at first, but I'm genuinely surprised by how down you still seem." He ashed his cigarette. "Did you sleep with her or something?"

MC took a breath, unable to admit to it.

Not that she needed to.

Joe sighed. "Did it happen more than once?"

MC shook her head. "She iced me out after the first time."

"I guess the guilty conscience had to step in at some point." He cleared his throat. "You didn't, like, fall in love with her, though. Did you?"

"What? No. Of course not."

"Hm." He shrugged, then opened her closet. "Take a shower. I'm picking out an outfit for you."

"Joe, I'm really not in the mood."

"You're beating yourself up for something Nora had a major part in, and if I can help you pause the excessive self-recrimination, even for an hour, it's worth it."

She wanted to tell him to leave, maybe not come back for a while. But she suspected she was being unfair. Trying to project her guilt onto him so she didn't have to live with it alone.

"What if I have a bad time?" she whined.

"Then you can come back to the Cool Ranch and I will leave you alone until you're ready to be aired out in spring. Promise."

She sighed.

She dragged herself to the shower.

As it turned out, the party wasn't far from her apartment. And it felt good to get cleaned up, to be around people. She was still anxious about having to acknowledge her article. She wanted to forget she'd written it, get back to the way her friendship with Joe had been just a few months ago, when she was free to sit on the sidelines, enjoying everyone else's drama. But she told herself it was just a matter of time. All stories got old. Especially in New York.

They walked into a big, chilly Brooklyn loft with massive glass windows and exposed plumbing. The crowd was spilling out the door and into the stairwell, a cloud of perfume and smoke hanging in the air. Joe said hi to people MC mostly didn't recognize and didn't bother trying to meet.

"Are those my little minions?" said a smooth voice.

MC stared as Seth Flanagan walked up to them in joggers and a T-shirt, every inch the Silicon Valley tech guy.

He flashed a chemically whitened smile. "Happy New Year to all of us."

"May it be better than the vast majority of the last one," Joe muttered. But MC could see a twinkle in her friend's eyes. She had no idea how he could be at ease with someone who'd been so close to firing him. "Nice to end on a high note, at least."

"Isn't it?" Seth grabbed a can of seltzer from a table shaped like a lima bean and cracked it open. "Of course, I have to take a tiny bit of credit."

"For what?" MC asked.

"Dropping in that detail about your class year."

MC blinked, then stared at Joe.

"Class year?" she managed to say.

The color had drained from her best friend's face.

"Didn't you read the final version?" Seth said.

"No." The hairs on the back of MC's neck were standing on end. "I didn't." She'd been too anxious, desperate after her month in that fugue state to just cede control to Joe so she could finally start getting back to something like normal.

"We wanted to situate the readers in the timeline," Seth explained. "And throw a little bone out there for the superfans to gnaw on." He took a slurp of seltzer, then licked the top of the can. "Subtlety isn't my strong suit, but every now and then . . ." He smiled.

MC's mouth was dry. But she forced herself to speak. "Did you get our class year off Joe's résumé or something?"

"What? No. I just asked him."

Joe shrugged, trying to smile, like he'd had no idea that what he shared with Seth would've completely compromised MC's only condition for saving his life.

But before any of them could say anything further, a short, self-possessed woman in a purple tracksuit appeared.

"I was hoping you assholes would be here," she said. There was a touch of silver in her closely cropped hair. "That was some article."

Seth tilted his chin. "The words you're looking for, Lauren, are *thank you*."

"For the bump in sales? We could've gotten that from a

feature in the *Times*. I think I'd rather throw my drink in your faces."

"Minions," Seth said, "this is Lauren Horowitz, S. K. Smith's charming editor."

"I'm not your minion," MC said quietly, even if that was exactly what she'd been. Seth raised an eyebrow. She ignored him and turned to Lauren Horowitz. "And I'm really sorry for the stress I've caused." Lauren Horowitz frowned. "I have to go now." She started to leave, then paused and added, "Happy New Year."

As she made her way toward the door, Joe caught her elbow.

"Can we talk?" he said.

"I'd rather not."

"Come on, MC, please?"

"Make it quick. And preferably somewhere I can actually breathe."

She stomped out of the party and up the stairs, to the smaller knots of revelers on the icy rooftop. She put her hands in her coat to hide that they were shaking.

"How could you?" she said, embarrassed to feel tears pressing against her eyes.

Joe sighed and put his whiskey on the ledge. "I didn't think it would be a big deal."

"Don't lie to me."

"It's not a lie. Entirely." She rolled her eyes. "I didn't know whether it would be a big deal or not, okay? All I knew was that Seth's approval was contingent on a few very minor details being added. To situate the reader, like he said. And the deadline was so close."

He lit a cigarette, hiding his face in the shadow of his cupped hands.

"Do you understand what it's costing you," she said, "to be a *minion* for people like Seth Flanagan?"

"So, it's undignified now and then. In the long run, he'll age out, and I'll never have to deal with that kind of condescension again."

"It's not about condescension, or lack of dignity. It's about who you are, Joe. These people are egomaniacs, and they will turn you into one of them."

He scowled. "What's so wrong with having an ego? You talk about it like it's something dirty. But I want to be proud of what I've accomplished."

"And you're proud of what we did with that article?"

"Yeah, I am. People were *compelled*."

"To ruin a woman's privacy."

He shook his head. "It's so goddamn punishing to pursue a dream here, MC, which you might not realize because you gave up on it three seconds after we arrived."

"Come on, Joe. Open your eyes. These people aren't part of your dream. They're poseurs." She wasn't used to feeling angry. She didn't think she liked it much, but it definitely felt better than being sad. "Or is that what you want to be too?"

She walked away.

"MC!" he called. "Damn it, hang on!"

But she was already in the stairwell, her boots hammering the steps.

27

MC showed up at the Green Hills train station early on New Year's Day. There was a weirdly un-momentous quality to the morning. Conrad picked her up. She didn't expect them to have some big heart-to-heart. For once, that wasn't even what she wanted. They shoveled the back patio together, watched three straight hours of *Arrested Development*, and got Chinese for dinner. Looking at their fortune cookies would've been unbearable. So they threw them out, then fished them from the trash can in a fit of paranoia and stowed them in the back of the pantry for better times. Gabby was still staying at her parents' house.

MC didn't go back to the city the next day, or the day after. She had no plan. All she knew was that she wouldn't survive seeing Joe on the street, or, more likely, having him barge in on her again in her apartment. Conrad tolerated her company without complaint, despite their argument on Christmas. She didn't even need to apologize, which she appreciated.

Work was mercifully slow. She found herself loafing around the house, talking through Conrad's post-break plan to deal with Jae, which involved meeting at a coffee shop to apologize and commit to finishing out the school year as professionally as possible. As for Gabby, all he could do was wait for her to respond to the daily handwritten letters he dropped off in her parents' mailbox, begging her to take him back.

MC wondered if she could figure out a similar approach to

Nora, who seemed to have made it her business to become a ghost, never so much appearing on her porch or at her window. But writing felt like a tainted medium at that point. And anyway, her mailbox was always overflowing now.

MC was experiencing some of the same inundation on the digital end, though she'd decided after New Year's Eve to delegate the management of her inbox to Joe, who'd taken it over with uncharacteristic alacrity.

So she laid low, biding her time.

One week turned into two, then three, MC helping out around the house as Conrad got back in the swing of the second half of the school year. Coffee with Jae had gone as well as could've been hoped for. Both of them were eager to put the affair behind them and move on. But Gabby's absence still hung over the place, haunting them all.

So when MC ran into her at the grocery store one random Thursday evening in late January, she froze up. White-knuckled the handle of her cart.

Gabby looked stunned at first. Then her eyes narrowed.

MC braced herself.

"Oh, just come over here," Gabby muttered. She stared down at a yogurt that contained, for some reason, candy.

"Hi," MC said, bowing her head like a dog that still expected to be sent to the crate. "How are you?"

"Incredibly bad." Gabby's expression was dark, but she looked more put together than MC would've expected. Thick gold hoops dangled from her ears, and she had a big wool scarf on, her peacoat padded out with a chunky sweater over her swollen belly. "You?"

"Same."

"Really?" She gave MC an up-and-down—the sneakers

smeared with dirt and grit, the old cargo pants hanging loose from her waist. She'd shed a few pounds on account of her appetite being spoiled by low-grade depression. And then there were the circles under eyes, the desperate state of her hair. "I thought your article for Joe was a big hit."

"Yeah, well, it kind of ruined our friendship. Along with everything else. So."

"At least it was good."

MC held her breath. "You read it?"

"Of course I did. Right after I read Nora's book." Gabby shrugged. "It's not every day I get to feature in a rom-com *and* a viral exposé."

MC blushed.

"You know, when you came out to me, I thought it was this big moment in our friendship." Gabby crossed her arms. "But I guess you had mixed motivations."

"I'm sorry."

"I was convinced you and Nora were destined to be together. But if you'd been a little more direct with me about your actual feelings, I would've made out with you at least once."

MC looked up in amazement. Gabby's old grin had returned.

"Conrad told me you only overheard him fighting with Jae the day before Christmas Eve," she added. "And that you said right away he should come clean to me. So I guess I can't be too pissed at you for that."

MC bowed her head anyway. "I did think something was going on with him even before then. But I didn't want to push it."

"It's fine. I know you've always respected his privacy."

"I wish I could say that's what it was about. But it was more being scared to talk to him in general."

"It still wasn't your job to police his bullshit."

"No, but—"

"It might've been your job to stay out of Nora's business, though." Gabby raised an eyebrow. "As opposed to coming out here and taking advantage of her."

"I know. I feel terrible about it."

"You should."

MC bit her lip. "Joe told me he was going to lose his job if he didn't have a big story."

"How did you not see that it was his problem, not yours?"

"I just didn't feel like there was a difference. We've always done everything for each other. Especially after we left Green Hills." MC took a breath. "But it was my choice to let go of everything I had here. And that's what I feel the worst about. Cutting my brother off, being weird with you, hanging on to all this shit from high school." Her voice wavered, but she managed to steady it again. "Anyway. I'm extremely sorry."

Gabby seemed to mull this over, squeezing the yogurt cup in her hand. MC was sure she was going to say something about how apologies were ultimately meaningless, how cowardice had a cost, and it could never be repaid.

But instead, she said, "Okay." And rubbed MC's shoulder. "Thank you for that."

"Of course."

Gabby threw the yogurt in her cart and leaned her elbows on the handle, looking like she was about to head off to the next aisle.

MC cleared her throat and said, "By the way, Conrad is missing you pretty bad." She smoothed the front of her ski jacket. "I know he's the last person you want to hear about. And I'd never expect you to feel sympathy for him, because he doesn't deserve it. But he's still my brother. I know all he wants is to see you again. Even just once."

"Yeah, I've gotten that impression from his attempts to be pen pals."

"We didn't have great models of spousal behavior growing up."

"That sounds a lot like an excuse."

"It's just . . . context." She shrugged. "Anyway, it's really nice to see you. Even if the circumstances are bad." A deep breath. "I'm still excited to be an aunt."

Gabby smiled again. "I'm excited for you too."

She started to walk off.

"Tell Conrad he can call me," she said over her shoulder. "I just scheduled the anatomy exam."

When Gabby had turned down the pasta aisle, MC pumped her fist in the air, jogged her cart down the empty dairy section, and hopped on the bottom rack, cruising along like she was ten years old again.

After she'd unloaded the groceries at home, she wandered out into the darkness, up to the picket fence between her house and Nora's. There was a light on in the kitchen.

For once, Nora was at the window, looking down at something. Probably the dishes.

Maybe it wasn't a matter of MC punishing herself forever. Maybe it was just a matter of making herself known, even if it caused discomfort.

She cupped her hands around her mouth and shouted: "Do you know how the Byzantines punished criminals?"

Nora looked up, startled, then flashed her middle finger.

"They hung them upside down and cut them in half!"

Nora opened the window. "That's disgusting!" she said, before closing the window again and walking away.

MC trudged back in the darkness, smiling.

28

The first day of February was bright and freezing. Green Hills looked barren, the ugliness of its gnarled branches and dead leaves comforting in their completeness, a fitting backdrop for MC's mood. The buzz of her reconciliation with Gabby and her brief exchange with Nora had died within hours, leaving her feeling somehow worse than ever in the weeks that followed. Like all the personal growth in the world couldn't outweigh how much of her life she'd torpedoed. It wasn't that she missed her own ignorance, exactly; it was that she had no idea what to do with wisdom except to mope around with it. Even taking a bigger role in *Explorations* as the full-time spring semester advisor had provided no relief.

Which was why she was currently staring out the window, wondering if it was crazy to have started researching a teaching degree, as her students threw around half-hearted critiques of Patrick's cryptic prose poem, which was either an experiment in absurdism or the product of a truly deranged mind.

At four-thirty on the dot, she said, "Any other comments on *An Elegy for Darby's Subaru Forester?*"

"Um, no," said Sheila. "But I have another question."

MC spread her hands. "Fire away."

"You wrote that article about S. K. Smith on Jawbreaker, right?"

Part of her had suspected this was coming, but she had hoped that her students were less online than she was. "I did."

Everyone twitched in their seats, grinning or biting their lips.

"S. K. Smith being the woman you brought here once," Ben said, "to talk to us about magazine design."

MC rubbed her forehead. There was no use denying it. "That would be Nora."

"So . . ." He wiggled his eyebrows. "Are you getting back together?"

"As I said in the article, we were just acquaintances."

"Everyone's shipping you guys," said Patrick.

"Listen, I should never have agreed to write that piece, okay? It was a weird experience, and I'm looking forward to the whole thing blowing over."

Everyone was silent. Then Sheila said, "Is she incredibly pissed at you?"

"Yes," MC said.

"Can she take retribution in any way?" Ben said. "Legally?"

"I don't know. If so, she's welcome to."

Heather scoffed. "I'm sure she'd be relieved to know she has your permission."

"Can we get off this topic?" MC muttered.

Patrick spread his hands, like a lawyer presenting a case. "Before break, you brought up the issue of anonymous submissions. You were in favor of letting authors keep their privacy."

"I was guiding the discussion. I don't think it's as simple as choosing a side."

"You definitely chose a side," Sheila said. "Also, can I record this?"

MC was mortified. "Absolutely not."

"Did you really think," Patrick went on, "you could respect her privacy while publishing an article like that?"

"I was naïve," she grumbled, though what she'd been naïve about was a little more complicated than she cared to explain.

Ben steepled his fingers under his chin. "Do we think there's any way to get her back here?"

"That would be so sick," Sheila said. "By the way, if I can't take video, can I at least use these quotes from you and do a post? A lot of my followers are expecting updates."

"No." MC frowned. "Let's not make this worse. Also, this is a high school literary magazine. It's supposed to be a safe space."

A silence settled over the room.

"What if," Ben said, "we told S. K. Smith you'd sit out if she came to a meeting?"

"She's not going to come," Patrick said. "Whether MC is here or not, S. K. Smith doesn't want attention. She was uncomfortable just being in the room last time, and none of us had any idea who she was."

"Why," MC said, more than a little exasperated, "do you want her to come to another meeting, exactly?"

Sheila frowned. "To talk about being a famous author." She looked to Heather. "You're always at the library. Can you get her to come back?"

Heather shrugged. "I can't make any guarantees."

"But you'll try?"

Heather looked around the room at the dozen eager yet skeptical faces. MC remembered the interest between her and Sheila, the way Nora had played wingwoman on Halloween. "I'll see what I can do," she said, practically cracking her knuckles.

MC wished her luck.

After she'd shrugged on her messenger bag and said goodbye, she found herself skipping the main office, where Conrad had said he'd be done with his school board meeting by five. She walked out the front doors. Across the traffic circle. Past the athletic fields.

Toward the library.

She'd kept away from the building out of respect. But after allowing her students to scheme up ways to invite Nora back to *Explorations*, she felt she owed Nora a heads-up. Reassurance that it was fine to decline, even though she knew Nora needed no such thing. Really, she was just tired of waiting, tired of silence, tired of feeling as brittle as the dead trees looming over the sidewalk.

She was hoping to duck in unnoticed, signal to Nora at the reference desk, and talk privately in a study room or something. But when she arrived at the front stairs, she saw a little group blocking the doors. It consisted of only three people, but they were decked out with huge homemade signs. The signs featured a red circle with a diagonal red line across a blown-up printout of the *Girl Next Door* cover. Underneath the printout was the slogan STOP GROOMING KIDS!

The protestors weren't shouting, but they stared at MC with dead-eyed intensity as she walked up the stairs.

Just as she was about to excuse herself past them, Lois burst through the doors.

"Get a job!" she barked at the protestors. Her glasses were pushed up in her hair and the sleeves of her cardigan were rolled up, like she was more than ready for things to turn physical.

"Get perverts out of our libraries!" a woman shouted back.

MC saw Nora behind Lois, trying to grab her elbow. But Lois was just getting started.

"You people make me sick. I know you're lonely and sad, otherwise you wouldn't be here. But your hate has real consequences for young people in this country!"

"Stop grooming kids!" a man chanted.

The group joined in.

"Stop grooming kids! Stop grooming kids!"

They angled their signs at Lois, waving them in her face.

"Can you give her some room, please?" MC said, walking between the protestors and Lois. She deliberately did not make eye contact with Nora.

One of the protestors bopped Lois with a sign.

Maybe by accident.

Maybe not.

"You think you can intimidate me?" Lois growled, hiking up her slacks.

"You really need to step back," MC said to the protestors, trying to get them away.

"You step back, groomer!"

"I called the police," Maureen said, poking her head out to assess the commotion.

"I don't need the police," Lois snapped.

What happened next was too confusing to feel dramatic. All MC knew was that one of the signs bonked Lois in the head again, and MC had had enough. So she grabbed the handle of the sign and yanked.

The protestors closed in around MC. The tug-of-war intensified. Lois was in the mix somewhere, swearing. MC didn't want to let go of the sign. She knew she should—her peacemaking tendencies practically required her to.

But she didn't.

Someone elbowed her in the eye.

In pain and surprise, she let go of the sign. Lois threw herself at the protestors. Maureen and some library patrons rushed in, including the video game–console guy. Everything became a weird melee.

There was a lone siren, a flash of red and blue.

A single cop car from the Green Hills PD rolled into the parking lot.

A megaphone squeaked on. "Break it up," said a bored voice.

The protestors backed off, yelling about groomers and waving their signs again. MC touched her eye and felt swelling around her cheekbone.

"You're legitimately a hazard to yourself," Nora said. MC had momentarily forgotten she was there. Her hand was on MC's arm. She looked mad, and shaken up, and also like she was about to laugh. "You need to put some ice on that."

"I'm okay," MC said, feeling incredibly relieved that Nora was speaking to her again.

"Come on," Lois said, "let's get you inside." As they walked, Lois patted MC's shoulder. "Good work, by the way."

MC was glad for the warmth. Not just of Lois's gesture, but the literal heat in the library. The confrontation had given her a spike of adrenaline, making her temporarily immune to the winter weather. But now she realized her hands had gone numb. Her back was clammy with cold sweat.

"There's ice in the break room," Nora said, steering MC down a back hallway.

MC tried not to linger on the giant display they passed in front of the circulation desk. It said GET COZY WITH THESE DIVERSE READS and featured *Girl Next Door* front and center.

"I got a life-size cardboard cutout of her," Lois said, pointing at Nora. "But she threw it in the dumpster."

Before Nora had a chance to comment on this, Lois was pulled aside by Maureen.

The break room was small and windowless, with a cooler, a fridge, a sink, and a little table surrounded by folding chairs.

MC sat in one and stared at a bowl of Sweet'N Low packets. Someone had brought in a zucchini loaf. It looked extremely moist.

"I know you hate me," MC said. "But the second you're ready to let me make it up to you, that's all I want to do."

Nora filled a plastic bag with ice from the freezer. "There's no way to make it up to me."

"That you can think of right now."

"This isn't an *actual* rom-com, MC. There's no winning me back." Nora wrapped the plastic bag in a dish towel and handed it to her. "After you're done with this, I need you to leave."

"Some part of you must've known your identity would come out eventually."

Nora had been about to turn for the door but paused. "I never thought the book would get this big."

MC smiled. "It's that good."

"It was published to capitalize on a market trend," she said coolly. "My editor said as much when she offered me the deal."

"Lauren Horowitz, right? She introduced herself to me at a New Year's party. Said she should throw her drink in my face." That earned a smirk. "How did she find you?"

Nora huffed, like MC was forcing her to answer. "She read my fan fiction."

"How long have you been doing that?"

"Since high school."

"Can I ask which fandom?"

"I think you can guess."

MC lowered the ice, remembering their exchange in the stacks, Nora's *Matrix* impression. "Oh my god," she laughed. "Which pairing?"

"Trinity/Niobe."

"You know, I might've read some of it." MC made a mental

note to find Nora's online writing at the next possible opportunity. "What made you try something more realistic?"

Nora turned around again. "I refuse to talk to you about this."

MC practically lunged, blocking the door. "But I've spent so much time thinking about it."

"That's your problem."

"I admit that what I did was wrong. But you're not totally innocent either. You published a book about some of the roughest parts of my life." Nora's expression softened a little. "And I get that in retrospect it was just typical adolescent crap. But it still felt intense to me." MC took a breath, all too aware of how close they were standing, how irresistible Nora looked in her big green sweater with its nylon reinforcement at the shoulders and elbows, like she was ex-Marines or something. "All I'm asking is for you to explain what made you do that."

Nora gritted her teeth. "If I tell you, will you actually leave?"

"Yes."

A pause. "I'd thought about you on and off ever since we graduated." Nora's lashes fluttered for a moment. "And then . . . I saw you."

"Where?"

"At your brother's wedding."

"Why didn't you come?"

"I didn't want to. High school sucked for me, even if it was a little less bad by the end." She sighed. "But then there you all were, right outside my window. Looking the same as ever. I don't know, it affected me." She pursed her lips. "It felt like nothing had changed. Like no time had passed. I'd hit a dry spell with my writing, so I figured I'd do something different for once."

"And people loved it."

"The response was mixed, actually."

"Really?"

"Some of my readers preferred girls getting it on in leather bars after a few rounds of Japanese stick fighting."

"Understandable."

"Yes." She drew herself up. "Now get out."

"Oh, come on," Lois said, barging through the door. "Just forgive her already." MC stumbled to the side.

"Lois," Nora said, "can you not?"

"It was a beautiful article, MC."

"Thank you," MC said, still a little stunned.

"Unpretentious," Lois declared, "yet deeply considered. Even made me laugh a few times." She flapped a hand. "As Nora well knows, I was opposed to her hiding in the shadows ever since I read the first draft of her manuscript."

"Which I never should've let you do," Nora said darkly.

"And I never should've let her in on my taxes. I'd been thinking about downsizing anyway, but something about the word *foreclosure* makes people panic."

MC finally put it together—it was Lois who'd needed the money.

"When I realized that letting Nora help me would get her work out there to a bigger audience, I decided, screw it." Lois shrugged. "Two birds with one book."

"Lois," Nora said, "enough."

"Oh, shush. I've known you since you were a teenager. It always bothered me that the world was missing out on you, and that you were missing out on the world." Nora glared but said nothing. Lois turned to MC. "I could've imagined a more respectful way of going about your work."

MC bowed her head. "Me too."

"I still think it was the best possible tribute anyone could've made to our Nora."

She felt a second surge of gratitude to Lois, not just for her praise, but for her devotion.

Nora, unfortunately, seemed to be feeling the opposite. She looked like she couldn't figure out which one of them to flip off first.

"I should go," MC said, standing up and handing the ice back to Nora. "I just came here to tell you the *Explorations* kids really want you to come to another meeting. But it's more than fair of you to say no."

"You're the last person who should be telling me what's fair."

"Right. Well, I hope the protestors give up after a few days."

"It's none of your business."

MC bowed her head and left the break room. In front of the library, the protestors were still lurking, but the visit from the cop seemed to have inspired them to take a snack break. They drank from steaming thermoses, glaring at MC as she walked back toward the school.

29

"I think she'll work," Laura said a week later, plopping down on one of the couches in the common room and kicking her feet up on the armrest. Despite the freezing rain that fell outside the window, she wasn't wearing socks, her pink toenails cracked and longer than seemed comfortable or even healthy. "It's just four months."

MC leaned her elbow on the bar-style countertop. "If you want to interview other people, I have a guy who's free later today."

Laura frowned. "Guys are gross."

"Just don't want you to feel pressured."

MC had told Laura she wanted to come off the lease right after the confrontation with the protestors. She'd put up a Craigslist ad for short-term subletters and gotten about a dozen replies in the span of an hour. Laura hadn't been pleased with MC's decision, but MC had done her best to make the transition as smooth as possible, vetting her replacements online and coordinating with Laura to set up interviews in person. MC would've preferred to do it all remotely, but Laura insisted that she could only "catch a vibe" when someone was right in front of her. It was a small mercy that Pat and Zeke were working at the bike shop on the day Laura and MC were free to meet Tyla, a British bombshell who'd started a prestigious MFA in fiction back in the fall and had just broken up with her lover. Tyla's word.

Laura gave MC a long look, her red hair shimmering from a rare but thorough brushing she'd performed while MC had made more coffee. "It's him, isn't it?"

"Who?"

"Your weird friend. He's the reason you're leaving."

"Oh, no, not at all."

She'd told Laura there was a family crisis going on at home, and she would need to be in Green Hills for a few weeks more. Maybe even another month. No, she didn't know when she would be coming back. And she didn't want to string Laura and Pat and Zeke along for months, only to end up coming off the lease anyway.

"You guys seemed pretty tense the last time he was here," Laura said.

MC practiced letting go of the urge to downplay. "We're in a rough patch," she admitted. "But moving back home for a while is a bigger decision for me. It's not about Joe."

It was about everything her life had become. The striving she didn't buy into and the comfort of living in Joe's shadow, which now seemed like a continuation of living in Conrad's, but with someone who was nicer to her about it. It wasn't Joe's fault—or her brother's. It was just a status quo she hadn't believed herself capable of moving past. And now that status quo was shattered.

"Well," Laura said, "you've been a chill roommate."

"Thanks. You too."

"By the way, I have a book for you." Laura hopped off the couch and went through the glass doors into her bedroom, which was meant to be the living room but had been taken over as a sleeping space so they could all pay sub-market rent. When she came back out, she handed MC a book with one of those colorful, cutesy illustrations, a trio of figures in front of what looked like the Seattle skyline. "It's a poly rom-com," she said. "They're working for a VR dating startup."

"Oh, cool. Thank you." It was called *Three's Company*. "Did you ever . . ."—MC's voice trailed off. If Laura had read MC's article, or connected it to MC, she would've said something—"get involved in the fandoms around some of these books?"

"No."

MC nodded. "Me neither."

It felt good to remember that the trolls and the superfans were a minority. That most people inhaled a book like *Girl Next Door* and moved on to the next one just as quickly. Even the readers who paid attention to a spectacle like MC's article in Jawbreaker would be distracted by something else soon enough.

MC said goodbye to Laura and bundled herself against the rain. She'd have to come back to put her things in storage in a few weeks. But it might as well have been her final moment in the apartment—everything just as it was, except for the emptiness of her closet. She wondered if she was making a mistake, giving up a relatively inexpensive situation with not-the-worst roommates to float around with Conrad until Gabby maybe, hopefully, decided to move back in someday. They'd started going to couples therapy, so that seemed promising.

MC reminded herself that she had a plan. Or more of a plan than she'd had before. She'd decided to apply to teaching programs for real. Probably at state schools, and ideally for no longer than a year. Her work with *Explorations* felt like the only thing she'd done in a long time that was hers alone, even if it wasn't always perfect, and even if she'd started out doing it as yet another favor. She had no illusions that a real teaching job was as cushy as an impromptu, now-and-then club advisorship. But she liked working with teenagers. A lot more than she liked crafting muscular prose about business capabilities.

She was heading toward the subway entrance on Eastern Parkway, her hood cinched around her face, when she saw Joe sitting in the coffee shop where Lisa used to work. He was with Tyler, his record-long squeeze of four months, their custom high-tops kicking together under the café table. The glass was fogged. But Joe looked happy.

Just after she'd passed, she heard her name. Joe was running after her, no coat, his velour crewneck sweatshirt getting spattered with what MC's weather app had called "wintry mix."

"There you are," he said breathlessly.

"You should get back inside," she said.

He crossed his arms and ducked into the covered entryway of an apartment building. "I hate this," he said.

"I'm not going to ignore you forever." She toed the stone trim. "I just need time."

"Time for what?"

She shrugged. "To figure my shit out."

"With Nora?"

"With everything."

"You don't actually believe it's possible to figure everything out, do you?"

"No. But I feel like there's some baseline stuff you can pin down."

"It's just . . . haven't you already done that?"

"Not even close."

"Okay, fine." He bounced on his heels, one of his curls falling from its sculpted sweep to dangle across his brow. "Can't you do it here, though? With me?"

"I don't think so." The curl was killing her, reminding her of the noodley mop he'd had through most of high school. It was like they were always still kids somehow, no matter what their apartments looked like or how many times they got their hearts broken. "I'm finding a subletter for my place," she added.

His mouth hung open. "For how long?"

"Indefinitely."

He put his hands on his head. "I can't believe this is happening."

"Me neither. But you should go get warm. I'm trying to make a train."

"You're just . . . living at home?"

"For now."

"Bleak," he muttered.

"Don't let me keep you." MC forced herself to smile. "Looks like you and Tyler are going strong."

Joe rolled his eyes. "We're not exclusive or anything."

"Well, I wish you luck."

"Can I at least get a hug?"

"Fine."

They held each other close. Things weren't okay between them. MC was still upset over everything, especially the class year debacle with Seth. But she was also too emotionally exhausted to make a stink over it. And she was thinking about how Gabby had forgiven her, and was trying to forgive Conrad. MC wanted forgiveness in her life. To believe in it, even if she couldn't always give it a hundred percent, or get it a hundred percent.

"Keep in touch, please," he said, resting the side of his head against hers.

"If I unblock you, do you promise not to bombard me?"

"Hm . . . I'll do my best."

"Maybe in a little while you'll come visit."

He drew back, looking scandalized. "Me, in Green Hills?"

"You could come to an *Explorations* meeting. Talk about Jawbreaker. Convince the youth that not all digital media is soulless and transient."

Joe smirked. "Wouldn't I be lying?"

"Not entirely." She shrugged. "It's a nice group."

"To see you, it might just be worth it."

She rubbed his arms. "Go inside, fool. Your hair is getting ruined."

"Okay, fine." He ran off, stopping at the corner to look for her over his shoulder. She waved, and he waved back, and kept running.

30

"I saw you here," MC said, chasing a string of hot mozzarella into her mouth. "With Jae. On my birthday."

"And you just hid from me like a little weasel?" Conrad blew on his slice, the greenish light of the pizzeria making his hair seem gruesomely dyed. The booths were crammed with couples holding hands and smiling moonily, and couples focused on their pizza, pointedly silent. It was Valentine's Day. Paper hearts were strung up in the window, a few cupids hanging from the grease-stained ceiling.

"Pretty sure you were the weasel," MC said, trying not to think about making out with Nora in the booth six feet away from where they sat now.

"We could write a fable together. The little weasel and the big weasel, chasing each other's tails."

"Eventually forming a weasel Ouroboros."

The night had been Conrad's idea, something to distract them from their deserved singleness, or at least just an excuse to get out of the house. As he tried to minimize his after-hours time at school, he was stuck at home by early evening, puttering around the kitchen. Now and then he would cook something over the top to deliver to Gabby, still at her parents' house—lasagna with homemade sauce, brisket and fresh-baked rye—but for himself, he kept to the basics. And since MC remained incompetent in the kitchen, they'd spent six weeks surviving on eggs, peanut butter sandwiches, and frozen burritos.

"Any word from her?" Conrad said, finally taking a delicate bite.

MC shook her head. She'd thought being well-behaved after the encounter with the protestors might earn her a joke text or a passing word on the driveway. But Nora had kept to herself. At least she'd phased out of stealth mode, meaning she got out of her car to check the mailbox when she came home from work—sweeping the deluge of envelopes directly into a garbage bag—and sometimes shook salt over the icy stairs off her porch. Whenever MC caught sight of her, she wanted to run out, say something. Anything. But she didn't want to push her luck.

Conrad said, "You could try what I did."

"Handwritten letters?"

"They don't necessarily have to be handwritten."

"Maybe if we were married, I'd feel like I could pull that off."

"Well, you can't just sit around waiting for her to decide to forgive you for no good reason. Make her something."

"Like what?"

"I don't know. Cookies."

"I'm bad at baking." MC frowned. "I'm bad at everything."

"You're good at talking. Ask her out on a date."

"I blew up her life, Conrad. She's not going to say yes to that."

"But if you ask enough, maybe she'll start to consider it. Women love persistence." She stared at him. "Persistence without creepiness. That's the key."

She moved on to her second slice. "Did you tell Mom that Gabby moved out yet?"

"No. And I don't see why she needs to know."

"It's not like she's going to judge you."

"Honestly, she might."

"She won't. It seems like she's been making more of an effort with us lately. And hey, maybe she'll have good advice."

"After ruining her own marriage?"

"It's just if Gabby doesn't move back in with you when—"

"I'm going to therapy. I'm reading *baby books*. We're on the right track."

MC focused on her pizza. "How's that been? Therapy, I mean."

He took a sip of his beer. "Excruciating."

They ate in silence after that. She'd realized at some point in January that reconnecting with her brother was going to be a long process. Hitting rock bottom together may've built some foundation, but there was still so much unsaid between them, so much time to make up for.

"Whoa," he said, checking his phone and typing furiously.

"What is it?"

He looked up, a flash of old confidence in his smile. "Gab's asking me to take her out for dessert."

"Hey. Nice."

His eyes were already glued to his screen again, thumbs flying. "Do you mind if I drop you back home for the night?"

She sighed.

They packed up their trash and headed out a minute later, Conrad practically skipping down the sidewalk. There'd been more snow in the past two weeks than in all of December and January combined. Dirty berms of asphalt-studded ice were shored up along the concrete, long slush puddles in between. MC had taken to wearing her old snow boots, the ugly brown waterproofing a must whether she was at home or in town. She'd been trying to split her days between the house and the local coffee shop, chipping away at work, wandering around with her thoughts. Sometimes she ran into someone she knew—another old friend from high school, or the parent of a friend—and explained that she was planning a career change to teaching, just spending some time at home to regroup. She'd inevitably feel a stab of disappointment after saying goodbye or continuing on her way. Not because what she'd said wasn't true, but because what she wanted most had little to do with her career, and she had no idea how to explain that to anyone, least of all herself. It seemed impossible that she'd ever managed to be content before Nora. All those girlfriends kept at arm's length. Safety must've seemed very valuable at the time.

Conrad leapt out of the car when they got back, ran straight to the shower, and spent a good twenty minutes getting ready.

After she wished him luck and said goodbye, she was ready to settle into the couch in the living room, flipping channels until she was tired enough to go to bed and be done with the day. But out the picture window, she saw the glint of an unfamiliar car in Nora's driveway. As she walked closer to get a better look, she saw Nora herself come out on the porch, arms crossed.

Wary, MC waited a few minutes, half expecting some new squeeze to saunter out and steer her back inside. But no one came.

Nora stayed where she was.

MC put on her coat and went out to her own porch.

"Hey," she called.

Nora looked over, her face mostly shadowed. "What?"

"Nothing. Just saying hey."

MC saw a curl of steam from Nora's mouth. A sigh, maybe. "Hey."

"Got company tonight?"

"My parents are back."

"Oh." Relief flooded through her. "How's that going?"

Another curl of steam. "Not great."

"If you're looking for an escape, I have some local recommendations." She spread her hands.

"You know how I feel about us hanging out."

"We don't have to hang out. I'm just offering the physical space."

Wind howled through the branches. "It's Valentine's Day."

"Made-up holiday."

Nora rubbed her arms and turned to MC at last. "You know what? I'm that desperate."

MC's heart leapt, but she tried to keep her tone even. "I'll put some hot water on."

Nora dipped back through the door, maybe telling her parents she was leaving, maybe just glaring at them. She came out again in a coat and boots and trudged over, through the gate in the picket fence.

"I think I need something stronger than tea," Nora said.

"Hot chocolate and Baileys?"

A raised eyebrow. "You really have regressed to high school."

"I still make it with mini marshmallows."

MC stepped aside as Nora came through the mudroom, taking her boots off, but not her coat.

"I won't stay long," Nora said. "Just need to get away from them for a second."

"Do you want to talk about why they're driving you crazy?" MC assumed it had something to do with the truth coming out about her book.

But Nora said, "Not really."

And MC figured it was best to let things lie.

She headed to the kitchen and put the kettle on the stove. Nora followed, her arms still crossed.

"So," Nora said, "are you living here full-time now?"

"Pretty much. Gave up my apartment a few weeks ago."

"Why would you do that?"

"My life in the city was driving me crazy."

"Hard being the toast of the town in all your fancy media circles?"

"They were never my circles."

"Joe must be pretty torn up."

"He is. But I think he understands why I need a break."

"I'd say I feel bad for you, but."

"I don't want that. Even if you did feel bad for me."

Nora sat on one of the stools at the island. "Gabby's still gone?"

"Staying with her family for the foreseeable future."

"Conrad's lucky to have you around."

"I'm lucky to have him around too. Not that we have much fun together, to be honest."

"I always wanted a sibling. A sister more than a brother, I guess, but I'd take whatever I could get."

"Joe always says the same thing. I mean, it definitely changes you." MC set out the packets and walked back to the pantry. "But I wasn't exactly thrilled about it when we were growing up."

"He seems like a hard person to know."

"That's one way to put it." She grabbed the bag of marshmallows. "But I think he's changing."

"You believe people can really change?"

"I believe they try to be better. I guess that's not the same thing." She couldn't resist squishing the marshmallows a little. "It's good enough for me."

Nora watched her closely, saying nothing.

"We don't have to talk," MC said. "I can go hang out in my room and you can chill here, watch TV or something."

"That'd be too weird."

"I guess so." MC drummed her fingers on the counter as the kettle started to give a low whistle. Being confined to the kitchen for more awkward conversation didn't feel right. But MC didn't want to lose this moment with Nora either. "There is another possibility." Her heartbeat picked up as she took the kettle off the burner. She wanted to sound casual, but not overly casual. "Remember the old golf course? About half a mile from here?"

"Yeah. Why?"

"It's an easy walk through the trails behind our house. And it's a great spot for sledding."

Nora's eyebrows went up.

"We have nothing to do tonight," MC said quickly. "And it's off-limits during the day, so." She opened a cabinet to reveal Gabby's extensive collection of mugs. "I can put the hot chocolate in thermoses."

Nora seemed to consider this. "Are you asking me on a date?"

"No." MC blushed. "I'm just asking you to go sledding." She was already pouring the hot water. "Unless you'd rather go home."

Silence stretched between them. It went on so long, MC was convinced she was about to be rejected, that she'd have to drink a double serving of instant hot cocoa all alone in her living room, stuffing her face with mini marshmallows as she cried about getting what she deserved.

"I will go sledding with you," Nora said carefully. "But only because my house has been invaded."

MC smiled. "Let me get some gear."

31

They suited up in Conrad's old ski bibs, looking like puffballs in their oversize padding. MC tried to offer Nora a beanie, but she refused, opting for a retro fluorescent ear-warmer band. Their gloves were so big it felt like they were heading out to play hockey. It worked, overall, once they got outside. The air was cold and still, and they were warm and snug. When they started trudging toward the woods, outfits scrunching with every step, MC stole a last look at Nora's parents' car in the driveway, the lights on in the kitchen.

"What's the occasion?" she said, still worried about pushing things too far with Nora, but also freshly curious.

She'd only interacted with Nora's parents a handful of times. The encounter was always unplanned—an accidental simultaneity in their departure or arrival times, quick waves across the fence, vague wishes to take care or enjoy the day. MC's parents hadn't been community-oriented people either, and it worked, the unspoken outsider status of the two couples and their wish for privacy in a small town where privacy was viewed with suspicion. They all had an intensity to them. A drive that wasn't so much about career or money as their own personal goals. Maybe *Girl Next Door* had helped her see it more clearly, but now it seemed obvious to MC—the commonality between the people who'd brought her and Nora into the world, the ways it had shaped them as they grew.

"I sent them an email," Nora said. They were carrying flashlights but didn't really need them, the starry night casting a pale glow through the branches laced overhead. "And it freaked them out."

"What was in the email?"

Nora paused. "I told them I need to move."

"Out of the house?"

"Yeah. And Green Hills."

Which stopped MC in her tracks. "To go where?"

Nora kept walking but slowed her pace. "I don't know yet."

MC shuffled to catch up with her. "I mean, you won't go far, will you?"

"Like I said, I'm not sure."

"Have you told Lois?"

"Yep."

"And what'd she say?"

"She gets it."

"But was she upset?"

"I don't know, MC. If she was, she'll get over it."

MC was stunned. "This isn't about the article, is it?"

Nora laughed. "Of course it is."

"But the attention's going to fade eventually. I'm not saying it hasn't been a massive invasion of privacy, and the protestors are obviously freaky, and I'll say sorry a million more times if you want me to, it's just—"

"I'm not blaming you, okay? I'm still pissed about it, so don't feel like you're off the hook. But as everyone keeps reminding me, my identity would've come out eventually, one way or another. And maybe it's what I needed to force me to . . . move on."

"Move on from what?"

"From this place."

MC didn't know how to respond. She was surprised at how devastated she felt by Nora's news, like they were trading places in some karmic joke, MC stuck back home with all her ghosts, and Nora set free.

"So," MC muttered, "you told your parents they have to deal with the house."

"Either they need to find and manage renters or sell it over the next few months."

"What do you think they'll choose?"

"Selling it. I said I'd help deal with the logistics before I go."

"They wouldn't just hang on to it for a while?"

Nora shook her head. "There's no reason for them to stay tied to this town."

MC didn't know what to do about the caved-in feeling in her chest. "What even made them come here in the first place?"

"The quiet, I think. Or the uneventfulness. They had me when they were still living in the city but decided a kid wasn't compatible with their lifestyle there."

"In your book," MC said, feeling a little flush in her cheeks to mention it out loud, "you said you felt like you were an accident. Or, well, Nicole did."

"They claimed they conceived me on purpose." Nora smiled. "I think they just had really different ideas about what parents owed to their children than, say, Gabby's parents."

"My parents weren't too comfortable in the role either."

"But they were there."

"I'm not saying it's like what you experienced. Just that it was weird to have everyone in their proper places or whatever, but emotionally... you know."

"When I was little, I told myself they were superheroes. Or detectives or spies. They had to be out saving the world."

"What changed?"

"At some point I started to see how relieved they were when I was independent. It could be anything—reading by myself, cooking breakfast. I made it a point to never cry in front of them. And they appreciated it, basically. It's not like they were even proud. They just wanted to be excused."

"Why didn't you rebel? I feel like kids will do anything for their parents' attention."

"I was convinced that if I toed the line, they'd just leave forever. I had to be the version of myself they would accept—the version of myself that was totally okay with being alone—in order to not be alone for real."

"I think I know what you mean." MC cleared her throat. "How do they feel about your book?"

"Oh, they still have no idea about it."

"Really?"

"They don't pay attention to stuff like that."

MC shook her head. "Crazy."

They'd reached the edge of the golf course, the glittering expanse of hills untouched. The stars were revealed in all their glory, the Big Dipper so obvious even MC could pick it out. "Well," she said, "it's your parents' loss."

"What?"

"That they don't know what a genius you are."

"Oh god. You and that word."

"I'm serious."

"I know you are. Crazy person." Nora unslung the plastic sled from her back and positioned it at the top of the nearest incline. "By the way, this is kind of sick."

"Have you never done this before? Me and Con came here all the time."

"Never."

"On snow days, after dark, it'd get so packed."

"As you might've noticed, I wasn't too involved in group activities."

"I wish I'd invited you sooner." She hefted her sled and took a few steps back, then sprinted forward, jumping chest-first onto the rough plastic. The speed was fantastic, just as exciting as she remembered. Cold wind whipped across her cheeks as she jetted toward the bottom, the sound of Nora's sled cutting over the powder behind her. MC whooped as Nora managed to pass her just before they bottomed out.

When their sleds had crunched to a stop, they laughed, then helped each other up.

"It's even better with the Baileys," MC said. She took off her pack and pulled out the thermoses. When she opened the first one, a puff of sweet steam filled the air between them, the melted marshmallows reduced to a foam on the surface of the hot chocolate. She handed the cup to Nora, their gloved hands brushing for a moment. MC's chest ballooned at the slight contact. But then she remembered that Nora was already on her way out, going to places unknown, leaving her past—and MC—behind.

No wonder Nora had been more talkative all of a sudden, more open. There were no strings attached anymore. She was probably thrilled.

"I really like the marshmallows," Nora said.

MC forced a smile. "I seem to remember you going to town on the sweet potato topping at Thanksgiving."

"That's what you remember from Thanksgiving?" Nora took a long drink, hiding most of her expression behind the lip of the cup. MC said nothing, afraid to take the bait too eagerly, not sure what Nora was angling for by flirting after what she'd just confessed.

They did a few more rounds on the same hill, then hiked to another one, where they saw other couples who'd had the same idea. Most of them were busy making out under the trees that dotted the course, but a few were still tearing up the mini slopes. As MC and Nora walked to a spot that seemed set off enough, they drank to the bottom of their thermoses, the overly sweet booziness giving MC something between a buzz and a headache. Luckily, the cold air cut through most of the haze, making her feel clearheaded when she asked Nora if they should do a ride together.

"Double the weight, double the speed," she pointed out, reasonably.

"I think your physics are off." Nora licked her lips. "But we'll have to test it to be sure."

"Do you want to ride front or back?"

"Front."

At the top of the biggest hill they could see, MC set her sled down, leaving her pack aside. She sat in the back with her legs spread, relieved to be in padding that was about eight inches thick when Nora sat between them, keeping a semi-respectful distance all the same.

"So, what's your strategy here?" Nora said.

"When my brother and I used to do this, I would be in front, just leaning back basically." Without hesitating, Nora shimmied closer and nestled herself against MC. MC tried not to think about the pressure between her legs, the smell of Nora's shampoo, how fast her pulse was going. "He would use his heels to get some momentum. Then we'd just tuck in and stay low for the ride."

"Okay. Shove off, captain."

MC dug her boots into the snow and heaved them forward, until the sled tipped over the edge and started to take on a speed of its own. She pulled her legs in tight against Nora's sides and gripped the edges of the sled with her gloves, impressed by how fast they were already going. Her physics were just fine, thank you very much.

Or maybe it was just that this hill was a lot bigger than the others. Halfway down the slope they were whipping through the snow at a worrying clip, and MC could sense that any disruption in their balance would probably send them flying. She tightened her legs against Nora, doing her best to keep the back of the flimsy plastic steady as they hit little bumps along the way.

"We're heading for a tree," Nora announced.

"Trying to veer us a little left."

"Maybe if I—"

Before MC could tell Nora not to attempt anything, Nora had stuck her foot out to adjust course. The heel of her boot caught and sent them spinning like a boomerang. Before MC knew it, they were both tumbling out, a tangle of limbs careening through the snow to a sudden stop.

"Ow," Nora said. She was half on top of MC, their stomachs pressed together, their bodies perpendicular.

"You okay?"

Nora laughed. "That was actually amazing." She got to her knees and dusted off, hovering a little over MC, who was still sprawled on her back, catching her breath. "How do the stars look?"

"Really nice."

Nora lay down next to her, close enough that their shoulders touched.

MC didn't mean to whisper, but when she spoke, her voice sounded small: "I'm so sorry about my stupid article."

"I know you are."

"It was wrong."

Nora sighed. "I'm sorry it took me so long to come clean about the book. I really thought you'd hate me if you ever found out." She pursed her lips. "Isn't that weird? To feel compelled to do this thing that's the opposite of what you actually want to do."

"Not weird at all."

"I'll just have to trust you on that."

"Do you think you can? Trust me, I mean. After everything."

"I don't know." A breath. "But I want to. Stupidly."

"It's kind of relaxing to be stupid. Speaking for myself."

"I'll have to try it." Nora turned onto her side just then, so suddenly it startled MC. But the look on her face kept MC pinned on her back. Nora took off a glove and laid her hand on MC's cheek, bare fingers cold but electric, her face dipping just a little. And just as MC's mouth fell open, the heat of Nora's breath on her lips, Nora said, "Oh my god, what am I doing?" Then drew back, taking her hand away.

She got up and put her glove back on.

"What's up?" MC said, following Nora's lead and getting to her feet.

"What's up?"

"I mean, are you okay?"

"No." Nora forced a laugh. "Everything's extremely confusing and messed up right now."

"Agreed on confusing. But is it so messed up?"

"Of course it is."

"Why?"

"Because you came out here for months—months!—to analyze me for an article. Without telling me."

"And you spent months not telling me you'd written a novel about us."

"Exactly." Nora stomped off. "We screwed up, and we can't take it back."

MC followed. "But I can't think of a single relationship I've ever had, romantic or not, where one or both of us didn't blow it at some point."

"Sounds terrible."

"It's not. Or it is, sometimes, but not always. I don't know, it's just hard."

"Then maybe I'm weak."

"I mean, same." MC took Nora's hand. "But isn't that kind of normal?"

Nora stood still, breathing hard, probably from the intensity of the trek. They were back up at the top of the hill, and the Baileys was sloshing in MC's stomach.

"It's been really nice," MC added, surprised by the desperation in her voice, "to talk to you again."

"Yeah." Nora gave MC's hand a squeeze. "It's been nice to talk to you too."

"And I'm happy with, you know, just talking."

Nora nodded. "Walk me home and talk some more?"

MC let out the breath she'd been holding. "Okay."

Then Nora shook MC's hand, sealing the deal, and laughed.

32

A few weeks later, pulling up to the Green Hills train station in Conrad's leased Prius, MC realized that big changes might be painful, but small changes were the ones that haunted you.

Take the car: a newer, depersonalized twin to Gabby's. Or the fact that MC was the one driving it, after coming to this train station almost seven months ago with every intention of turning back around. And then there was her visitor, the catalyst for all of it, who'd somehow managed to float along, untouched, the entire time.

"Ugh," Joe said when MC rolled down the window. "Fuck. This. Place."

"Hi," she said.

He opened the passenger door and ducked in as if from a rainstorm, hunched and squinting and disheveled. It was a sunny day, unseasonably warm for March. February's snow had almost melted away, leaving only patches of stained ice in the shadier areas of the parking lot.

"Do we really have to go to the meeting?" he said, nibbling at his nails, a habit she thought he'd kicked. "Like, I know you have to go. But I could wait for you somewhere, and then we could just hit up the Horny Ram."

"I think you might enjoy the meeting more than the bar."

"I think I might spontaneously combust."

"Trust me for once." She shot him a look. "You owe me that."

"Oh my god, when are you going to let this go?"

"Maybe when you stop trying to get out of feeling guilty."

As she drove them toward the school, she caught him staring out his window, his expression tight. He'd texted her the night before to ask if he could visit, terse and defensive and a little petulant. But she wasn't dragging him to the meeting as punishment. She wanted him to let go of whatever it was about Green Hills that made him chase coolness so hard he'd almost destroyed their friendship over it.

"How are things with Tyler?" she said evenly, having already guessed the answer but trying to pretend she didn't.

"Let's not play this game." Joe leaned his head back and rolled his neck, staring at her like he'd just been shot in the chest. "I'm dumb, okay?"

"You're not."

"I really am, though."

"No more cool city guys."

"That is my vow." He gestured toward a strip mall. "I'm going to find a hometown hottie. Tonight."

"Jim McDade is taken, by the way."

"Obviously."

"But Jerry Bickley is still single."

"You're not helping." Joe put his face in his hands. "I can just sit and listen at the meeting, right? You were joking before, about the guest speaker thing."

"I think if you just sat and listened, it'd be pretty weird. But you don't need to give a presentation."

"MC, you're killing me."

"I know for a fact they read Jawbreaker. You're basically a celebrity."

"You mean a trashy D-list celebrity chaser."

"Even better."

"I hate teenagers."

"That's very teenage of you."

As MC turned off Main Street, Joe asked for updates on Gabby and Conrad—MC had texted him a little about the drama—and seemed on the fence as to whether Gabby should forgive the cheating. Now she told him about how her brother and Gabby had started seeing each other again, though always out. Conrad was convinced they were on track to get back together for real before the baby arrived. But Joe thought as long as Jae was Conrad's boss, Gabby wasn't going to be locked down again anytime soon.

"And you and Nora?" he added.

"Things are thawing a little bit there too." She pretended to focus on the turn into the school parking lot. "But she's moving."

"To where?"

"She doesn't know yet. She's helping her parents get the house ready to sell."

"As my therapist would say: How does that make you feel?"

"Bummed. I mean, I think it's the right thing for her. Getting out of here finally."

"But you're going to miss her."

She nodded. She expected Joe to add something sardonic to keep her from getting emotional.

But all he said was, "Maybe she'll end up closer than you think."

And at long last, she found herself confiding in him again—telling him about how she and Nora had gotten back into texting and added talking on the phone, Nora's name appearing on MC's screen out of the blue, usually late at night. How their conversations lasted for hours, MC spitballing about applications to teaching programs, the old video games she was playing to kill the lonely hours; Nora fretting over the decision to move Fuzzbox to Lois's for the foreseeable future. How Lauren Horowitz was breathing down her neck about pitching another manuscript, which was, Nora claimed, never going to happen.

By the time they'd parked in the lot by the back entrance to the school, it was like a weight had been lifted between them—even as Joe turned up the collar on his wool coat and glowered at the crucible where all their dramas had been forged.

"Missing your old VW?" she said.

"Oh, just missing everything," he grumbled.

When they reached the doors, Conrad was waiting on the other side to let them in.

"Look who it is," he said, pulling Joe in for a hug. "As handsome as his Instagram."

"God, don't make me blush." MC had forgotten how Joe preened under Conrad's attention. "Congratulations on the impending bundle of joy, by the way."

Conrad coughed. "Oh, yeah, thank you."

"You and Gab'll work things out."

"Thanks, man," Conrad said. "We're trying."

"I'm going to go set up," MC said, heading for the classroom.

"I'm late for a meeting," Conrad added. "Drinks after?"

Joe pressed his hands together. "The Horny Ram is actually my sole reason for being here."

"It's a date." Conrad winked and walked off, still managing a saunter in his khaki chinos.

"You know," Joe said, watching him leave, "it's really a shame—"

"Don't," MC said, eager not to linger on an old nuance in their group dynamic that she'd worked hard to block out. "Come on, we're late."

The students were already in the classroom, the desks arranged in the usual circle. But instead of talking in small groups or passing out packets, they were listening intently.

To Nora.

"I never thought of myself as a writer," she was saying, her gaze flicking to MC and Joe for a moment. She didn't tense up, but it was like the air in the room changed as soon as they walked in. "I wrote online as a hobby, and that's as far as I thought it'd ever go."

"Are you working on anything now?" Sheila asked, looking as close to adoring as MC had ever seen her. She'd propped her chin in her hands. Heather was sitting right next to her, a smug smile on her face.

"Not at the moment," Nora said. "The response to my book was a little too much for me."

MC and Joe had taken their seats quietly, not wanting to interrupt. Now every eye in the room swung toward them. MC had the urge to stand again, excuse herself, run away, and never come back. But Nora headed her off by saying, "And here are the two people I have to thank for that."

"Nora and I," Joe said, leaning back with a smile, "didn't exactly get along in high school."

The kids seemed to be holding their breath.

Then, a second later, Nora smiled back. "I did appreciate his spirit of competition."

"I noted that in your book." He spread his arms. "I'm Joe Khoury, by the way, aka Jake Haddad, aka the cartoonish hipster who's constantly trying to climb the social ladder of White Springs High while pretending I'm not. And in case any of you think graduating will save you from the tortures of high school, we're living proof that the most annoying ghosts never die."

Ben raised his hand, cautiously. Joe blinked and said, "Yes?"

"So, you're the editor at Jawbreaker who commissioned MC's piece?"

"I am," he said, lifting his chin, clearly ready to go on the defensive.

"I really liked the article you guys did last summer on Tina Van Der Beer."

MC was pretty sure that this was the Real Housewife who Jawbreaker had discovered was funding a small island government MC could never quite remember the name of.

"And the shitcoin ring in Venezuela," said Heather. "Did you get legal blowback for that?"

"Oh god," said Joe, folding his arms across his chest. "Where do I start?"

As it turned out, the group had a lot of questions for Joe. How he'd gotten involved in media, who he'd met along the way, who he'd pissed off. Every dirty secret he'd ever uncovered and how it affected his worldview. Was he cynical? Only to the extent that the human species was inherently selfish. Did anyone ever try to get back at him? Yes, but they'd never succeeded.

MC and Nora traded looks as he held court, marveling at the way Joe was somehow coming out on top after his less-than-ideal behavior. Apparently, while it was cool to be a bestselling romcom author, being a shit-stirring raconteur and real-life New York City bad boy was a lot cooler.

Joe rounded out the conversation an hour later with reassurances that he would come back to assist with a magazine-assembly session in April.

"Well," he said when the room had cleared, "that wasn't too bad after all." He threw an arm around MC's shoulders. "Maybe I should trust you more often."

"I'd be careful with that," Nora said.

"Darling Nora. I offer you my apologies, for wrongs past and present, while fully expecting you to reject them."

"How generous of you."

"At least let me buy you a drink. Me and MC are going to the Horny Ram tonight with Con and Gabby. Past time for a reunion, wouldn't you say?"

"I'm not really the reunion-attending type."

"Consider this a private and high-profile gathering at one of Green Hills' most illustrious watering holes."

"When you put it that way," she muttered.

"Also, MC might've mentioned you're about to move, and I think it's basically killing her. Any extra time you can spend with our lovelorn princess would be much appreciated."

MC stared at him, horrified at this breach of trust.

And yet, miracle of miracles, something lit up in Nora's expression.

"I think she'll be just fine," she said. "But what time were you thinking?"

33

Nico Price, onetime theater nerd, turned a bottle of Jack Daniel's over and filled three shot glasses. He'd been in Conrad's grade, a zip-up-hoodie type with a curly ginger mop and soulful brown eyes. Puja Singh had declared a crush on him sophomore year, and rumor had it a blow job had occurred in Mr. Miller's math classroom, during school hours, though nothing more. MC tried not to think about it now, as he moved on to garnishing Gabby's cranberry seltzer with a maraschino cherry.

"Cheers," Nico said, lining up drinks on the bar. The curls were tamer now, but he'd grown a big, bushy beard to go with them, which sort of worked.

"Cheers," Conrad said, handing over his credit card. Joe, MC, and Gabby took their drinks, Joe and MC waiting for Conrad to get his shot in hand before they threw their heads back.

"Ugh," MC said, rubbing her mouth in the crook of her elbow. The whiskey still burned her throat. "That's the only one of those I'm doing tonight."

"We'll see about that," Joe said.

"Can I have a Yuengling, please?" she said to Nico.

He grabbed a pint glass and leaned over to the draft handles. MC caught Joe staring, appraising Nico's black Henley and whatever was underneath it.

When they'd gotten their next round, they gathered at

one of the high-tops by the windows. Conrad was already off searching for a stool with a back as Gabby insisted she didn't need one.

"Only a partial whale at the moment," she said with a grunt, hoisting herself up and smiling at Joe. "I can still dance, if you're wondering."

"I'm going to need some proof."

Her smiled deepened. "Luckily, the Horny Ram always plays the hits."

The bar was packed and loud, but they all leaned close and managed to have a conversation. Or at least, Gabby and Joe did. Conrad was quieter than usual, his eyes glued to Gabby as she dished about her clients and complained about her brothers. MC, meanwhile, kept staring at the door, waiting for Nora to arrive.

"Arm wrestling contest starts in ten!" Nico announced. The crowd cheered and lifted their drinks. MC saw that a few tables were already being moved around by the barbacks. The event, MC recalled from the posters plastered in the entryway, promised everlasting glory and free shots to the winners.

Nora walked through the rearranging just then, fussing with her scarf.

MC leapt out of her seat.

"Hey," she said, meeting Nora before she even reached the table. "Can I get you something?"

"I thought that was Joe's job tonight."

They both looked back at him. He waggled his fingers and stuck out his tongue.

"He's still reliving the glory of this afternoon," MC said. "Best not to interrupt."

"I'll come with you, then," Nora said, her wallet already out. "I should warn you, I can't stay long . . ."

When they got to the bar, Fall Out Boy began to blast from the speakers. Nora pretended to be engrossed in the indecipherable specials on the chalkboard, brow furrowed, lashes low. She'd worn makeup, just some eyeliner and lip gloss. But it made MC's pulse race. As did her tight gray turtleneck.

"Maureen loves this place," Nora said.

MC nodded solemnly. "Do you think it's the buffalo cheese curd tacos?"

"The Five-Alarm Nachos, actually."

"Should we get some for the table?"

"Only if you want this reunion to end in everyone shitting their pants."

"I can think of worse endings."

Nora shook her head, but she was smiling. "Like what, MC?"

"Okay, maybe not. Are you going to compete, by the way?"

"In the pants shitting?"

"No, the arm wrestling."

Nora shook her head and waved to Nico. "Can I get a Yuengling, please?"

"Good choice," MC said, raising her beer.

A few seconds later, Nora finally turned to face her. "Things have gotten a little complicated between us again."

MC looked over her shoulder, like there was someone crowding in behind her, necessitating the half step she took in Nora's direction. "Complicated?"

"Given that there's nowhere any of this can go." Nora changed her position slightly, her leg brushing against MC's.

"That's debatable."

Nora raised an eyebrow. "We got an offer on the house today."

The excitement that'd been surging through MC disappeared. Or maybe just abated for a moment. "I guess I knew that was coming."

"If my parents take it, the closing will be in a few weeks."

"Oh."

"I don't want either of us to get hurt," Nora added. She sounded serious. "So maybe we should just quit while we're ahead. Try to start moving on. In advance."

MC almost agreed with her. They'd been down the road of a fling with an end-date before, even if the reasons for it were a lot more complicated. But the fact that they were here together now—all of them—also made her appreciate the fact that they'd survived the drama. The protestors had protested, the fan mail and hate mail had poured in, books had been signed, and a life-size cardboard cutout of Nora Pike had ended up in a dumpster; Gabby had pushed over a Christmas tree, Conrad had had a cup of candy thrown at his head, and MC and Joe had experienced their first real fight on the rooftop of a boring New York media party. But, in spite of all that, or because of it, they were out at the Horny Ram, potentially on the verge of crippling indigestion but, for the time being, on their feet.

"Arm wrestle me," MC said.

Nora frowned. "What?"

"Beat me in the contest, and I'll consider whether this is something we can move on from."

"You'll consider it?" Nora's smirk had returned. "Is this some humiliation fetish of yours?"

"It's a genuine challenge. And maybe also a little bit of a humiliation fetish."

"I'm not going to sit at one of those tables as a dozen former football players hover over us, shouting and slobbering."

"We'll have our friends to protect us."

Nora chewed her lip. "What if you win?"

"Then I get to keep doing exactly what I've been doing."

"Which is?"

"Just talking to you. Remember?"

Nora huffed. "Fine."

"So, you agree to the challenge?"

"Yeah. Whatever." Her eyes blazed. "If this is how you want to settle it."

They brought the round back to their table and told everyone what they'd agreed to do—minus the stakes, of course. Then they all went over to claim seats. A few judges had appeared on either end of the row of tables. Nico was carrying over the bar's chalkboard to keep score.

Another Fall Out Boy song started to play. Someone turned up the volume.

Nora and MC sat opposite each other and rolled up their sleeves. On MC's side, Conrad and Joe took positions at her shoulders. On Nora's side, Gabby leaned over, the fierceness of her expression or her pregnancy earning her a wide berth.

"Wrestlers," Nico said, "take your positions!"

MC and Nora planted their elbows and grasped hands. The touch was electric—at least for MC. She felt Nora's squeeze all the way down in her gut. She crossed her legs, then uncrossed them when Joe yelled at her about it.

"She's going in confident," he shouted in her ear. "You have to break her will."

"Or she secretly wants to lose," Conrad added with a smirk. "But don't blow your energy at the start."

Joe nodded. "Go for the endurance win. And stop strangling her hand, I'm seeing white knuckles."

Gabby shook her head. "Everyone can hear you, freaks!"

MC was sweating. When she'd made this gambit, she hadn't realized how many people would be watching.

"On my count!" Nico said. "Three!"

She wondered if Nora really did plan on letting her win.

"Two!"

And if that was the case, did that mean she also wanted MC to take things further than talking?

"One!"

Nora rubbed her thumb over the back MC's hand, waking up every cell in MC's body.

"Go!"

Nora's pressure was immediate and sustained, a rush of force that threatened to not only crush MC's hand but dislocate her shoulder.

"Stop her!" Conrad shouted.

Sadly, MC was already almost beaten. Gritting her teeth, she somehow managed to hold out against total defeat, hanging on for dear life. The exertion was kind of exciting. It reminded MC of when she and Nora had worked on the magazine together after school—the unspoken intensity. She pushed past the pain in her arm, fighting to get some leverage back.

"Don't let up!" Joe was barking in her ear. "You're turning it around!"

MC could hardly believe it. She was slowly, painstakingly reversing the direction of their hands, pushing their interlocked palms up to where they'd started.

When she reached the top, she saw the corner of Nora's mouth twitch.

"Finish it!" the crowd was chanting. And though there were five other pairs locked in combat on either side of them, MC felt like the encouragement was for her and Nora alone.

The best part was, Nora had started to smile. When MC got Nora's knuckles to finally graze the table, one of the impromptu judges called it, and Nora sighed, looking bemused.

MC finally let go of her and shook her hand out. The crowd cheered. Joe was hugging her, and Conrad was already calling for shots. When the obligatory drinks were down the hatch, she saw Nora walking off toward the back, shooting a quick look at MC over her shoulder.

For once, MC made no polite excuses. She shouldered her way through the crowd, into the short corridor between the bar and the patio, where she found Nora waiting a few feet from the door. Her hands were folded behind her. Her shoulders were pressed against the cracked wainscoting.

"You look awfully pleased with yourself," Nora said quietly.

"I'm not pleased with myself," MC said, a little wobbly on her feet. But she wasn't about to back down now.

Nora stayed still. Waiting.

MC stepped closer. Placed her hands against the wall on either side of Nora's head, hemming her in. "Just kidding. I'm absolutely thrilled to have defeated you in such a public setting."

Nora laughed, pressing her hips against MC's. "Aren't you going to ask me if I let you win?"

"I already know you didn't."

MC's hands dropped to Nora's hips, then circled around to cup her ass. Nora turned her cheek, seemingly lost in her own pleasure, and MC admired the line of her profile. The way her poker face failed completely when she wanted something bad enough.

"Why are you turned away from me?" MC said, brushing her nose against Nora's ear.

"Because if I let you kiss me, it's over."

"What's over?"

Footsteps and a third voice made them draw back a little.

"Get it, ladies."

It was Jen Turner, her arm around a girl MC didn't recognize.

"Sorry to interrupt," she added. "Nice arm wrestling, by the way." Her gaze went to Nora. "Or I guess I should say nice book." Nora flushed. "Took a bestseller to finally get her attention, huh?"

MC looked to Nora, who said nothing.

Jen raised an eyebrow. "Can we get through?"

MC was more than happy to lean up against Nora again as Jen and her confused-looking date continued on their way.

But when they'd disappeared behind the door, a rush of cold air passing through the hall, Nora backed off and swept her hair up in a bun.

"Love seeing her all the time," MC muttered, trying to hide her disappointment at the moment being ruined. Nora didn't laugh. "Hey. Are you okay?"

"Totally." Nora forced a smile, which MC had never seen her do before, and hooked her elbow in MC's, like they were suddenly just friends. "Think I need another drink, though."

And before MC could get her to slow down, Nora pulled away.

34

"Obviously, the content isn't always age appropriate," MC said, stuffing her hands in her pockets as the lower echelons of Jawbreaker watched her from their swivel chairs. "But ultimately, this is a legitimate journalistic enterprise."

"That's the nicest thing anyone's ever said about us," Joe announced. He was at the back of the conference room, hip propped against a console-cabinet contraption, arms folded across his chest. He was wearing a silk button-down patterned like a Kandinsky print, a reference MC had heard Sheena make just before the meeting had started. She still needed to look it up.

"So, yeah," she said. "I think it's a great fit for high school students."

Joe nodded. "I'm in if you guys are."

"I love the idea of an intern program," said the politics editor.

A newer guy with a severe widow's peak said, "I'd be happy to run the marketing end."

There were murmurs of agreement, though less enthusiasm than MC had hoped. Not everyone was trying to take teenage wannabe journalists under their wing.

"MC will send around the pitch so everyone has info," Joe said, gesturing at the deck on the screen. The final slide read, *Not Every Child Hates You!* Joe's addition, of course. "Shall we move on to fancy chocolate?"

Jerome had just published a feature on a popular new Brooklyn chocolatier that'd built its reputation on handcrafted confections, while actually just melting down Godiva bars and throwing in some fancy add-ons. The chocolatier's main competitor, a century-old family business in Ditmas Park, had sent several overflowing gift towers to the Jawbreaker office in gratitude.

Joe pulled MC aside as everyone filed out of the conference room. She thought he'd have something to say about the meeting, feedback or maybe some excitement of his own—MC had come up with the internship idea as she was wrapping up her applications to teaching programs, because she hoped to have something on her résumé besides just her work with *Explorations*. But when they were alone, he showed her his phone. A selfie had arrived.

From Nico Price.

MC smiled. "World-record turnaround time for hometown romance."

"Please. We're strictly fucking."

"You say that now."

"I guess you'd be the expert."

"Am I, though?" She sighed. "Nora barely texted me all weekend."

Joe looked pensive. "No matter how much of an asshole Jen was, it doesn't seem like Nora to be intimidated."

MC shrugged. "Her writing's a sensitive subject. As you know."

He perused the beautifully wrapped boxes of truffles scattered around Jerome's desk. "Just keep trying her."

"But what if she's realizing that some old flame from Green Hills isn't worth keeping on the hook while she's off kayaking in Myanmar? Or whatever she plans on doing."

"What if she's worried she won't be able to get on the plane if she lets you into her pants again?" Joe finally settled on a chocolate. "I just have a feeling this will get resolved."

"Because it's the most annoying possible outcome?"

He popped the truffle in his mouth. "How is it annoying?"

"Not to me. I just thought you didn't like her."

"My opinions are evolving," he said, still chewing. "And you like her. So."

"So you actually support me now?"

He frowned. "Do you genuinely feel like I don't support you?"

"I guess it's just that we had a bad patch there."

He walked over to the floor-to-ceiling glass, the last salvos of April showers sheeting across the panes, blurring Broadway. MC trailed after him.

"I know I haven't officially apologized," he said. "So, maybe I should just get it over with already." He took a breath and turned to her. "I'm really sorry for putting you in the position that I did. With the article, with Seth, with all of it. For what it's worth"—he lowered his voice—"I'm looking for another job."

MC blinked. She'd already forgiven Joe in her mind, or told herself she'd forgiven him. But now, hearing the words, she realized some small part of her—a core part—had still been hurt. Had been waiting for this, if not exactly daring to hope for it.

"I shouldn't have pushed you like that," he went on, looking out the window again. "It was selfish. I was freaking out, and I knew you'd come through for me. I told myself you're such a great person, you could do something morally iffy and come out golden, you know? And you kind of have." MC frowned. "Okay, fine. Regardless. It was a shitty thing to do. Not best friend behavior at all." He puffed out his cheeks. "The fact that you're still in my life feels like a miracle I shouldn't take for granted. I do plan to earn back your trust somehow."

She leaned her head on his shoulder. "I appreciate that."

"So magnanimous."

"Would you prefer 'apology accepted'?"

"That works." He pulled away slightly, giving her the side-eye. "As long as you mean it."

"I do." She smiled. "Actually, speaking of earning back my trust, there is something you could do for me . . ."

When she left the Jawbreaker office an hour later, her steps were light. Joe had agreed to her plan. She'd been turning it over in her mind for a few weeks, trying to convince herself it was ridiculous, maybe even pointless, then revving herself up about it all over again. But Joe was game, and it gave her a new rush of confidence.

Soho was a mess. Miserable and soaked. Winter had done a number on the concrete, riddling it with potholes. Chunks of asphalt were stuck in the sewer grates. MC headed for the subway with her hood up, her windbreaker not doing much to prevent her button-down from getting soggy. At least there was a hint of warmth in the air, a tentative April balminess that made the scent of a halal griddle by the subway entrance carry for at least a block.

The subway arrived just as MC pushed through the station turnstiles. She hopped in and was carried uptown. Her mom was in the city for a conference. They'd agreed to meet for a late lunch before MC went back to Green Hills. The restaurant her mom had picked was her usual scene: an upscale pub, this time outside Penn Station. MC had made it clear that she preferred

Lance sit this one out, and Dr. Linda Case-Calloway had agreed, without complaint, to the mother-daughter moment.

Her mom was already seated in a capacious booth, willowy shoulders drawn together, gaze fixed out the window, when MC arrived.

"Sorry I'm late," MC said, scooting in across the table.

"You're on time," her mom said, blinking rapidly. "I got here early."

"How was the conference?"

"Useful." She tapped a tall glass of ice water with one hand. MC expected her to continue with the abstracts she was interested in, or observations on the state of the field. But she was quiet. Then: "I wanted to ask you about something—"

"Good afternoon," a waiter said, obsequious in a half apron at MC's side. "Can I get you anything to drink?"

MC ordered a Diet Coke. Her mom said she'd stick with water. MC fidgeted some more. It wasn't like her mom to be nervous.

When the waiter finally swept off again, MC realized she was holding her breath. She didn't even know what she was bracing herself for. These now-and-then lunches were always perfunctory, a way to let her mom know, in broad strokes, how her life was going, the status of her living situation, maybe a detail or two about some interesting thing that'd happened to her since the last time they'd spoken. They were never serious.

At last, her mom blurted, "Conrad told me that he and Gabby are living apart."

MC hadn't realized Conrad had finally fessed up and wasn't sure how much detail he'd included. "For the moment," she said carefully.

A long silence stretched between them.

"Well," her mom said, "what the hell happened?"

"Uh..."

"I'm sorry." Her mom pushed her glasses onto her head and pressed the heels of her hands against her eyes. "I'm just a little shocked by the news."

"Everyone was."

She lowered her hands suddenly. "And I suppose I'm the last to know."

"No. Not necessarily. I mean, he didn't want to worry you."

"Is that really why?"

Of course, MC was about to say, but the waiter was back. "Ready to order, ladies?"

Flustered, MC's mom picked up the giant plastic menu and squinted. She got a Caesar salad with minestrone soup. MC got a cheeseburger and fries.

When the waiter left again, MC popped a straw in her pint glass and took a long sip, letting the fake-sweet rush give her courage. "This is Conrad's situation to explain," she said, "but as for why he didn't tell you sooner . . . I think part of the reason was that he thought you'd judge him."

Her mom's expression suggested total devastation.

"That sounds more intense than I meant it to," MC said, remembering that there were legitimate hazards in truth telling.

"I've been a terrible mother, haven't I?"

"Oh god, Mom, not at all."

"I just wasn't very good at it, right from the beginning. I told myself if I focused on Conrad's academics, his achievements, I would do less damage." She sighed. "Both of you, in your own way, seemed so self-sufficient. Everyone told me how lucky I was, that independence was something I should nurture as much as possible. And your father, well, he was a stoic himself."

MC shook her head. "Aren't you?"

"Hardly. Look at what a mess I made of my marriage."

"Don't say that."

"But I did." She swirled her water like it was a glass of wine. "I was unhappy. And I wanted to be happy."

"Which is understandable."

"But it's also a mess."

MC was at a loss for words. They'd never discussed the divorce directly. Everything had always been about living arrangements, splitting assets—logistics. "Breaking up is super common," she said feebly.

"Yes, well, that doesn't make it pleasant." She frowned. "I just don't want Conrad to jeopardize what he has, what he will have, unless he truly wants something else."

"He wants to stay with Gabby. And I think they'll pull things back together."

Her mom took a deep breath, wistful. "I remember how it was, early in the marriage. The loneliness. The lust."

MC looked around, panicked, searching for any kind of distraction.

"My body was crying out for something different."

"Uh-huh."

"I thought I could ignore it. But when I met Gregor, when I *saw* him, those eyes, those arms . . ."

"I get it."

"I want Conrad—and you—to know that I do care, more than anything, even if I've done such a poor job of showing it. And in this case, I could give him advice."

"Well, I'm sure he'd appreciate if you told him that."

Dr. Linda Case-Calloway sat up straighter. "You're right. I'll do it tonight."

"Yeah, call him."

She shook her head. "I've already tried that for days. He won't pick up. I need to go to him in person, like you did."

"Hang on, don't you have a flight to catch?"

"I'll book another."

"What about Lance?"

"He can extend our stay at the hotel. We've been absolutely loving the sauna."

MC stared out the pub window, traumatized, as her cheeseburger arrived.

Her mom took her phone out without even touching her fork. "I'll tell him to change our travel arrangements."

"Shouldn't you at least text Conrad before showing up at the house?"

"No," she said firmly, "it has to be an ambush."

Her mom texted for so long that MC got out her phone too. She pulled up the thread with Nora.

> Remember that time I saved you from your parents?
> "Save" is a little gratuitous.

MC tried not to get too excited by the prompt reply.

> I would really appreciate if you returned the favor. Where are you?
> In the city, but my mom is about to make us rush out to my brother's so she can "ambush" him about his affair. Lol.

MC tried to think of something that would make Nora take the situation seriously. As she racked her brain, Nora sent another message. A link.

It was a promotional post from their local movie theater, still barely in business. A *Matrix* trilogy marathon running every night of the week.

MC held her breath.

Another notification from Nora popped up at the top of the screen.

Should I get us tickets for tonight?

MC grabbed her soda and sucked it down to the ice.

35

Dr. Linda Case-Calloway used her business credit card to hire a car for the trip back to Green Hills, leaving MC little choice but to ride beside her on the cologne-soaked leather upholstery. Crossing the 59th Street Bridge, MC realized she needed to warn her brother.

What do you mean she's coming right now???
> I mean she freaked out that you haven't been answering your calls and is driving to your doorstep.

In a fit of guilt, MC added:

> I might have insinuated that you waited to tell her about Gabby stuff because you thought she would be mean about it? Haha.

Conrad took a full ten minutes to reply.

What is wrong with you?

She tried to defend herself by saying she thought their mom deserved to know why they didn't include her in anything. They were all adults now. But Conrad wasn't having it.

"What about your dating life?" her mom said, in traffic on the Long Island Expressway. "Anyone special?"

MC stared at her, unsure how to explain *Girl Next Door*, the article for Jawbreaker, or anything about her romantic history up until that point.

"I'm seeing someone," she said slowly. "But it's hard to say how it'll turn out."

"Sounds exciting." Her mom looked cheerful. "Maybe I'll meet her someday."

When the black car rolled up at the movie theater, MC nearly leapt to the curb. "Thanks for the ride," she said, feeling like a thirteen-year-old again. "And good luck with Conrad."

Her mom's expression hardened into its familiar look of reserve. "He's always been unbelievably stubborn."

"Couldn't agree more."

"It runs in the family." One more smile broke through. "It was good to see you."

"You too, Mom."

"Enjoy the movie."

Then she signaled to the driver and sped off.

The theater was big, boxy, and decrepit, perched at the edge of the town's central business district, across the street from the grocery store and a bagel chain MC used to think served the best egg and cheese in the world. The bagel chain was gone now, replaced by a wineshop. But the groceries remained, the giant green sign still visible across the tree-lined street.

She headed inside. Stood in front of the cardboard cutout of the original *Matrix* crew in their signature apparel from the first movie. Black pants and black shirts, lots of nylon and leather.

"Has the ambush started?" Nora said, appearing beside her

in a pair of green overalls, a black long-sleeved T-shirt underneath.

MC attempted to hide her relief at Nora's presence by keeping her eyes on the promotional material. "Any minute now."

Nora smiled. "Poor Conrad."

"He can handle it."

As they walked over to the concession, MC felt a powerful urge to hold Nora's hand. She was pretty sure this was a date. Maybe their first legitimate date ever. But somehow, that made it even more stressful. She thought about Nora getting skittish after seeing Jen at the Horny Ram and kept her hands to herself.

In addition to candy, they agreed to split a popcorn. "And a large Diet Coke, please," MC said, just before they got rung up. She reached for her wallet.

"Make that extra-large," Nora said, pushing MC's hand down. The touch, brief as it was, made MC's stomach flip. "I've had a resurgence in royalties thanks to you being a prying asshole. It's on me."

An escalator carried them to the second floor. The theater itself was almost empty. MC liked to sit in the middle, not too close to the screen, not too far. But Nora went right for the back. They ended up in a corner near the emergency exit.

"Can't even remember the last time I was here," MC said.

"It's got a real rat problem these days."

"Oh."

"Have some popcorn." Nora offered her the tub.

MC became aware that an annoying tapping sound was actually her heel drumming against the floor. She cleared her throat and said, "Did your parents take the offer on the house?"

"They did."

"Wow." MC swallowed. "Good thing you got an early start on packing."

"I know. Feels weird to be almost done already."

"The storage space is big enough?"

"If you can believe it." Nora tore open a bag of sour gummy worms. "I convinced my parents to sell most of the chinoiserie, so that helped."

"You're not going to need a hand-painted armoire where you're going?"

"I hope not."

MC shook her head. "Still can't believe you did it all by yourself." She'd volunteered numerous times to come over, more or less begging to attempt to lift a couch, and maybe picturing some time on that couch in the aftermath of her inevitable failure. But Nora had never taken her up on it.

"Lois and Maureen helped."

"They did?"

"Well, Maureen's boyfriend did."

MC frowned. "So, Maureen's boyfriend can hang out with you, but I can't?"

"Are we not hanging out right now?"

"Okay, but at the bar—"

"It's starting," Nora said.

The lights had just gone down, and the instrumental score filled the theater. The screen rippled green with the opening credits from Warner Brothers. Trinity's voice, soft and serious, piped in over lines of code.

One of the three other audience members whistled from the front row.

MC couldn't focus. The news of Nora's house being sold had sparked a fresh impatience, or a fresh fixation, her gaze drifting to the pucker of Nora's lips on her soda straw, the rise and fall of her chest under her overall straps. By the middle of the movie, when Neo was visiting the oracle only to be told he wasn't The One, MC had worked up the courage to brush her pinky against Nora's thigh.

The touch was tentative. She wasn't sure Nora would even notice. But then, in the glow of the screen, she saw the corner of Nora's mouth move. Just a little.

MC brushed against her again.

Nora's smile deepened as she pretended to concentrate on the movie, a wicked glint in her eyes. MC turned her hand over. Nora's palm, soft and warm, slipped into hers. It was tame—a small squeeze here, the brush of knuckles there. But the longer it went on, the more MC started to fidget in her seat.

At some point, Nora put the empty cup in one of the far cup-holders and set the popcorn in an empty chair.

Then she leaned over and whispered in MC's ear: "Do you think about me when you get yourself off?"

MC's mouth went dry. She swung her gaze to the screen and nodded.

"Do you think about taking my clothes off?" Nora's breath was hot and close, raising the hairs on the back of MC's neck. "Or do I take them off for you?"

"Usually I take them off."

"Slow? Or fast?"

"Slow."

"What do you start with?"

"Shirt."

Nora stifled a laugh. In the movie, Cypher was getting ready to betray Morpheus. The actor, as MC recalled, had played a prominent role in a lesbian gangster film—the Wachowskis' directorial debut and proving ground for some of the stylistic concepts they'd take to dizzying heights in *The Matrix*.

"How often do you do it?" Nora asked, keeping her voice low, skimming the tip of her nose up MC's cheek.

"Every day." MC took a breath. "Sometimes multiple times."

Nora brought MC's hand to her lips and kissed her knuckles. One by one.

Then she separated out MC's index and middle fingers and slipped them in her mouth.

MC's toes curled. The way Nora used her teeth was subtle, maddening. She looked right into MC's eyes as the tip of her tongue traced between MC's fingers. MC wasn't sure she was going to maintain consciousness much longer. But a moment later, Nora pulled up again, slowly, letting MC go with a small, wet pop.

She leaned over the armrest, dipping her face toward Nora's. But Nora put a hand on MC's shoulder, holding her off.

"If you kiss me," she whispered, "it'll be too obvious."

MC settled in her seat again, heart thudding against her ribs, as Nora seemed to go back to watching the movie. But then she put her hand on MC's thigh. Someone in the audience coughed. Nora moved her hand higher, dipping between her legs, rubbing her over her jeans. MC blew a long breath out of her nose, every nerve ending in her body lighting up.

"You feel so hot," Nora said in her ear, rubbing harder. "Do you always get this hot for me?"

"Yeah."

"Do you want me to keep going?"

MC nodded.

Nora undid her top button and pulled down her zipper, slowly working her hand under the fabric, then teasing MC for a second before letting her feel the full length of her fingers.

MC couldn't breathe. The action on the screen felt distant, absurd. She gripped her armrests, incapable of returning any kind of touch while being mastered so thoroughly. Then she asked, "Can I kiss you now?" Because she felt emboldened by the emptiness of the theater, how far away the other people in the audience were.

Nora was still smiling. "No."

She moved her fingers in a circle, watching MC's face. MC closed her eyes, overwhelmed by the pressure of Nora's hand, the weight of Nora's forearm across her stomach. After a while, MC turned to Nora again, wondering if she'd changed her mind about kissing, if she'd gotten her fill of torture yet. But she held back.

"Do you think you can stay quiet when you come?"

MC did not feel capable of answering this.

Nora moved her hand faster. MC's head was spinning. At some point she transferred her death grip on the armrest to Nora's forearm, hanging on for dear life, as Nora brought her to the edge and pushed her over, the theater disappearing, wave after wave breaking through her as she held her breath.

When the pleasure had receded to a bearable level, MC slumped in the seat. Her legs felt like rubber, though she'd been sitting the whole time. But Nora wasn't done. She'd let go of MC and was slowly undoing the buttons on the side of her overalls. Once the waist was loose, she pulled MC's hand in, that same wicked look in her eyes.

Her skin felt even hotter than MC remembered. There was no longer even a pretense of pretending to watch the movie. Nora leaned the side of her head against the top of her seat, watching MC touch her, while MC watched her own hand moving under Nora's clothes. She wasn't wearing a bra. MC leaned in and kissed her neck, still trying to keep the volume at a minimum, rolling a nipple between her fingers.

Nora's pulse was racing under her mouth. "You can go harder," she whispered.

MC went harder. Nora was wearing the same citrus perfume as the night they'd first kissed. It made MC feel insistent. She wanted Nora to know how much had built up in her since they'd last done this, how hard it was to hold back.

Someone got up in the front row. MC and Nora froze, though they were at least fifty feet away. When the person had walked out of the theater, Nora bit MC's ear and said, "I want you inside me."

MC ran her fingertips down the center of Nora's stomach, then over and across her hips. One of Nora's knees had already fallen toward the armrest. "Right now?"

"Right now."

MC slid her hand into her underwear, feeling how ready she was, and pushed two fingers in. Nora looked up at the ceiling, her mouth open a little. MC had never done anything like this before. She couldn't even believe how little she cared about the riskiness of it.

"Deeper," Nora said.

MC went deeper, as deep as she could. Nora had closed her mouth, but her jaw was tense, like she was biting back something. Her forehead was furrowed. Her eyelids had fluttered shut. MC moved slowly, feeling Nora's hips coming up slightly from the seat, seeking contact with the heel of MC's hand. The pressure to give the appearance of stillness made their pace glacial, drawing out every sensation. MC felt like she was about to lose it all over again when Nora finally reached up and put a hand over MC's throat. She closed her eyes, her whole body going stiff. MC watched her in a state of shock.

When Nora had finished, she let go of MC's neck, her hand falling to MC's wrist. Keeping her there for a minute. MC wished Nora would look back at her. But as the credits rolled, her eyes stayed on the screen, heavy lidded.

Eventually *Reloaded* started up, and they left through the emergency exit.

In the brightly lit hall, Nora held tight to MC's arm. MC's heart beat heavily in her chest. Neither of them said a word.

MC told herself not to think about Nora leaving. They'd seized the moment, made use of the time they had left. In Nora's car, Nora kept her hand on MC's leg as she backed out of the parking lot, like she didn't want to lose contact for a second. Or maybe that was just how MC felt.

Nora kept to the speed limit for most of the drive, but hardly braked at the stop signs on their road. Just before she pulled into her driveway, the headlights caught the realtor's sign, hanging from its white post by the mailbox. The SOLD panel was swinging in the spring breeze.

MC finally managed to find her voice. "That was—"

"Do you think the ambush is over?" Nora said, taking her hand off MC's leg, focusing on backing her car into the garage.

"Probably." MC's heart sank. "Are you saying I should go?"

"What?" Nora checked her mirror. "Not necessarily. I mean, if you want to stay out a little longer, I can make tea. Or whatever."

The offer didn't sound entirely genuine, but MC couldn't imagine being apart just yet. "Okay. That sounds good."

They got out of the car. Nora opened the door and stepped

into the kitchen. It was dark. She didn't turn on the lights. MC followed.

In a split second, Nora's hands were all over her again, cupping her face, pulling off her windbreaker, fingernails raking down her back. They were both panting when MC tried to kiss her. But Nora turned away at the last second.

"Okay," MC said, grabbing Nora's wrists, "what is going on with you?"

Some of Nora's hair had spilled out of her ponytail. She pulled away from MC and tucked it behind her ear. "What do you mean?"

"It was kinky, in the theater, to not actually kiss. But now it feels like you're avoiding it."

"Oh." Nora frowned. "I didn't realize."

MC stared. "You look so guilty right now."

"What do you want me to say? I'm leaving in a few weeks and trying not to let this overwhelm me."

"I don't believe you."

Nora looked off, unsteady.

"What happened at the bar?" MC pressed. "I get that Jen was rude, but you acted like I was the one who'd screwed up somehow. And then I didn't hear from you all weekend."

"I just needed space. Why is that such a big deal?"

"Because you didn't actually articulate that, and it hurt my feelings." MC crossed her arms. "Not to mention how confusing it is to then hook up with you, only to have you tell me you're trying to avoid being intimate, even though everything's already ridiculously intimate." MC took a breath, shocked to have put the full extent of her feelings out there without a second thought.

"MC," Nora said. Her smirk was gone, her expression almost pleading.

But MC wasn't going to stop.

"I like being with you so much. I'm so fucking upset that you're leaving."

"But—"

"But what? I'd rather we be honest with each other, even if it's painful." She took Nora's hands again. "I feel like I'm sort of, I don't know, falling—"

"Don't." Nora's eyes had gone wide.

"Don't what?"

"Say whatever you were going to say."

"But you don't know what I'm going to say."

"Of course I do."

"Then why does it matter if I say it?"

"Saying something is powerful." She sounded panicked. "You think you're just trying to get something off your chest, to see if it makes you feel better. But once it's out in the world, it takes on a life of its own."

"I know."

"No," Nora said emphatically, "you don't."

"Then explain it to me."

But Nora had gotten something in her eye. Or that's what MC thought, watching her suddenly put a hand to her face, her forefinger and her thumb rubbing across her closed eyes. At which point MC noticed that Nora was also holding her breath. And that her shoulders had drawn together.

"Oh god," MC said. "Did I—?"

"No." Nora sniffed. "I'm just being a baby."

"You're really not." MC pulled Nora toward her. "It feels like maybe you still don't trust me, though." Nora held her breath, not looking into MC's eyes. "Should I apologize more?"

"No. It's not you." She finally blew out a breath. "It's me."

MC waited, confused.

"This is so stupid," Nora grumbled, scrubbing at her face. "I just can't seem to stop worrying that I . . . manifested something by writing that goddamn book. Something that wouldn't have existed otherwise."

"What do you mean?"

"If I'd never written it, you never would've come back here, never would've started looking at me the way you did." She swallowed. "The way you're looking at me now."

A chill went down MC's spine.

Took a bestseller to finally get her attention, huh?

"So what?" she said, like it was irrelevant that she'd been oblivious, uninterested, fixated on someone else; irrelevant that for nearly a decade, she'd forgotten about Nora.

"So," Nora said softly, "you never would've thought about me."

The woman who'd gotten one look at her at a wedding and written an entire novel.

MC's mouth was suddenly dry. "Doesn't that just make me stupid?"

"You aren't stupid, MC."

"Then . . . trust me to know my own feelings." She gripped Nora's shoulders. "I'm not seventeen anymore. Okay? I want this. Whatever it is. I want *you*."

"But do you see what I'm saying? What if you only want me because I made you want me?"

Silence stretched out between them.

"I mean . . ." MC paused. "You did."

Nora's eyes widened.

"Not like that," MC quickly added. "But you made me see you." She bit her lip. "Thank god."

Nora looked like she wasn't sure what to make of this.

Then a loud, alien warbling broke out across the kitchen.

"What the hell?" MC said, ducking in fear, eyes scanning the ceiling for whatever freak of nature had made its way in.

Nora pitched her voice over the demonic sound: "It's a clock!"

MC saw it hanging over the kitchen table, each number on its face accompanied by a small painting of a different bird.

The noise ceased. MC straightened, still vaguely terrified.

"Eleven," Nora said quietly, "is the kookaburra."

"The kookaburra," MC repeated.

Nora grabbed her shirt and kissed her.

36

On the night of Nora's closing, MC stood at an unfamiliar farmhouse door holding a stack of steaming pizzas. She'd pressed the bell once but hadn't listened for the ring. Now she was worried she hadn't used enough force. To press it again, if it'd already worked without her realizing, was to risk the projection of an unthinkable insistence.

The sun had nearly set. She shifted her weight from leg to leg, forearms scorched, looking at the budding oak tree on the side of the house, a swing set fallen into disrepair beneath it.

She'd finally mustered the courage to try the button again, potential insistence be damned, when the door swung open.

"Yo," Heather said, stepping aside. "Welcome to my crib."

She gestured for MC to take the hall off the mudroom. It led to a kitchen, which was filled with the *Explorations* kids, stacks of printouts, crumpled bags of chips, and some new kind of energy drink MC had seen in bodegas lately.

Sitting up at the bar-style countertop were Joe and Gabby.

"You're late," Joe said, but he was smiling, pointy incisors on full display.

"Are you criticizing the person who brought you dinner?" MC slipped the boxes down next to the sink.

Gabby gave her a side-hug from behind. "Please spare my friend, he struggles with social graces."

Gabby had picked up Joe from the train station a few hours

ago, and the two of them had gone on a short hike along the rail trail. It'd been Joe's idea, a way to get some one-on-one time, a coda to their night in Brooklyn that fall. It must've gone well. Gabby seemed more relaxed than she'd been in months.

Joe seemed more relaxed than he'd been in years.

"Delfino's," Ben hissed, leaping over a chair on his way to the counter.

Heather set out a stack of paper plates and napkins and threw back the box tops, filling the air with cheesy goodness. MC let the kids serve themselves first.

It'd been Sheila's idea to gather the whole group to assemble the magazine. MC had thought it sounded great. So far, it didn't seem like a whole lot had gotten done. But the spirit was good. Even Patrick was there, taking up what looked like permanent residence at the dinner table, hair gathered in a high bun as he tapped around on his laptop. At the moment, he was trying to show everyone—anyone—his cover mockups. The deadline with the printer was the next morning. MC suspected it was going to be a late night.

The doorbell rang again as she was serving herself two slices, Joe telling the kids about the strategic value of blank space, Gabby asking if anyone had finalized the table of contents yet.

When Heather came back, Nora was trailing behind her.

She'd told MC she wasn't coming—she wanted a few hours to herself after handing over her keys. MC figured she must've changed her mind.

"Hey," Sheila said, eyes wide, "can I get you a slice of pizza?"

Nora smiled. "I can grab it, but thanks."

"Are you going to look at the draft?" Patrick asked. He sounded downright eager.

"If you want me to . . ."

Nora's eyes met MC's, but the next second, she was being dragged over to the table and hustled into Patrick's chair, which he'd vacated so she'd have a prime view of his screen. MC tried to hide her anticipation, focusing on her pizza instead. But even after three weeks of nonstop time together, it still gave her a thrill to realize Nora was anywhere near her.

"Wow," Gabby whispered, lightly punching MC's shoulder.

MC's mouth was stuffed with cheese. "What?"

Gabby shook her head, smiling. "You said things were casual."

"They are."

"That's how Conrad looked at me when I walked down the aisle, girl."

MC almost choked. "Her closing was today."

"So?"

"So now she's going to travel for a while before she figures out the next place she wants to live." Though it hadn't escaped MC's notice that no tickets had been purchased, and no plans had been made, except an occasional mention of the fact that she could always stay with Lois for a while until she had a better handle on her itinerary—and besides, Helen still hadn't found anyone to fill her position at the reference desk anyway.

MC knew it couldn't last forever. But the absence of concrete details made it easy not to dwell.

"Speaking of places to live," Gabby said, "what's the latest on your teaching programs?"

MC swallowed, not wanting to think about the fact that she'd just thanked Jae for an effusive letter of recommendation. "I should start hearing back in a month or so."

"And if you get accepted somewhere in the city?"

"I was kind of thinking I might spend my first year out here and commute. Help you guys with the baby." She frowned. "Did Conrad not run that by you yet?"

"He did. But are you seriously trying to drown in diapers while getting a graduate degree?"

"I need more grown-up cred." She shrugged. "I told Conrad I can find my own place, though. If you end up moving back in."

Gabby sighed. "I want to see how the first few months go. If I stay with my parents, my mom can be on hand, and everyone's promised me they'll be civil when Conrad's around. I just don't want to risk putting the baby in a toxic environment, you know?"

"Of course. Conrad will be ready when you're ready, even if it takes a while."

"Hey," Nora said, walking into the kitchen alcove where Gabby and MC had posted up. She looked to Gabby first. "How've you been?"

MC saw that Joe had taken Nora's spot over at the table, gesturing all over the place.

"Okay," Gabby said, brightening. "I mean, I feel like a walrus, but that might just be the Snack Barn milkshakes I've been treating myself to every day."

"They're definitely giving you a glow." Nora cleared her throat and flicked her gaze to MC. "Can I talk to you?"

Gabby winked at MC.

MC followed Nora out onto the back patio, a blue stone expanse off the kitchen. MC closed the sliding glass door behind them. There was a short set of stairs in the corner leading down to a neat garden, circular beds of spring flowers in bloom. Nora walked until they were out of sight of any windows, then stopped, pausing with her back to MC.

"I have to tell you something," she said.

Nora's serious tone made MC nervous. She tried to crack a joke: "You find me insanely hot?"

"That's . . . not it."

MC waited, her suspicion that Nora had finally figured out her departure plans becoming more and more of a certainty.

Nora turned around and took a breath. "They're making *Girl Next Door* into a movie."

"Oh." MC breathed a sigh of relief, rubbing the back of her neck. "Weird."

"Yeah."

"Or not weird, given how successful it is. Just weird because it's us. Kind of."

Nora bit her lip. "I've been asked to help write the script."

MC paused, wondering where this was going. "That's awesome."

"A few months ago, I would've turned it down. No question. But with my identity being out there anyway, and some issues I've been having with figuring out where I want to go from here . . . I'm going to accept the offer."

MC nodded. "Congratulations."

"Thanks." Nora tucked her hair behind her ear. "They think I should move to LA."

"Right. LA. Movies." MC's heart sank again, but she forced a smile. "At least it's closer than Myanmar."

Nora frowned. "What?"

"Nothing. It'll just be easier to visit you on the West Coast versus somewhere on the other side of the world." MC cleared her throat. "If you want me to visit."

Nora took a deep breath, consciously dropping her shoulders from her ears. "Actually, the bigger thing I wanted to ask you is . . . I was wondering if you wanted to move with me?"

MC stared.

The idea of going with Nora, anywhere, in any capacity, hadn't even crossed her mind.

"When?" she asked.

"I would fly out in a week. But you could come later. When you're ready."

As soon as MC's mind had started to fill with possibilities, she realized what they all meant. "The teaching programs I applied to are local."

"I know."

"And the baby's due next month."

"I know."

"I guess technically I might be able to defer with some schools. Or see about transferring? But my brother..."

"It's pretty much the opposite of what you were planning on. And there's a lot to work out in terms of logistics." Nora's eyes were wide. "But I wanted to ask you anyway. Just in case."

MC watched her closely, trying and failing to avoid thinking about the past three weeks—the past nine months. "You know I want to be with you," she said softly. "But I can't leave here again so soon. Not after how long I've been gone."

Nora nodded. "That makes sense."

"I would really like to visit you, though. In your fancy Hollywood apartment."

Nora rolled her eyes. "I'm not going to live in Hollywood."

"You know what I mean."

"I do." Nora rested her shoe on a gargoyle. "Visits would be good."

"I'm sorry it's not as good as living in the same place."

"Don't be sorry. I'm the one who needs a fresh start. To try something different for once in my life." She sounded like she was trying to convince herself. "It was just a crazy idea, I guess. That we could both get to do what we need to do and still be together."

"I keep having the same type of thoughts." MC took Nora's hands in hers. "But maybe a long break won't be so hard for us. Having had some practice." Her heart sank at the expression on Nora's face, so she added, "I really appreciate you inviting me to come with you."

Nora blew out a breath. "Don't mention it."

"And who knows what'll happen in the long run?"

"You could decide that teaching is boring." Nora planted her hands on her hips and straightened, like she was gearing up to spit. "The baby could be a nightmare."

MC laughed. "I can't even imagine you in California."

"Me neither." Nora sighed. "That's kind of the appeal."

"You'll have to take up surfing."

"You just want to see me in a wet suit."

MC raised an eyebrow. "We've got ocean here. There's still time."

"Do you think I can find an all-black surfboard?"

"With, like, knives for fins? Sure." She paused. "Before you go, there actually is something I wanted to give you."

Nora narrowed her eyes. "You're not planning some horrible surprise going-away party, are you?"

MC smiled. "It's something much worse than that."

37

MC watched as Conrad pulled a massive ring of keys from his coat pocket and opened the door that led to the high school's performing arts wing. It was on the other side of the building from the English Department, part of the sprawling, single-story façade along the asphalt circle where the buses gathered. But while the rest of the structure was low and mostly brick, this area had outer walls of plate-glass and a raised roof. MC remembered lingering outside the doors on spring nights just like this one, waiting to go see her brother sweep everyone away with his charm and vocal range during school plays.

But tonight, there were no crowds, no cars, no people at all. The benches in the entryway were unoccupied, a few stray pieces of trash tucked in corners. When Conrad, MC, Joe, and Nora walked in, there was even a hush to the air, like they'd entered a church.

"You kids have fun," Conrad said, tossing Joe the key ring. "Lock up behind you when you leave."

"Wouldn't want anyone sneaking in here to steal the flying monkey costumes," Joe said.

Conrad was already jogging back to the Destroyer of Worlds. He and Gabby were going out for a night on the South Shore, which Joe had promptly labeled a babymoon, much to Conrad's annoyance. Nora had brought her car, too, so the three of them could make their exit later.

"Showtime," Joe said, taking MC's hand and tossing his backpack over one shoulder.

"What should I do?" Nora said, looking just as confused as she had when MC had first sprung the details for meeting up here on her. She'd made the official invitation at Nora's going-away drinks at the library earlier that night, pulling her aside from a debate Lois and Maureen were having about the political milieu of *Horton Hears a Who!*

"Take a seat," MC said, throwing open the auditorium doors and hitting the house lights. "I know you like the back row, but I'd recommend front and center."

Nora shook her head, still perplexed, but took MC's advice. Joe, meanwhile, jogged up to the booth in the back and got to work powering up the stage lights and audio, like Nico had showed them. They'd only gotten to do one practice run onstage. MC hoped it would be enough.

"Holy shit," Nora said.

MC looked back at her. Nora had put her face in her hands, but when she raised it again, she was smiling.

She'd figured it out. Obviously.

Once Joe had set everything up in the back, he joined MC onstage. They disappeared behind the curtains with his backpack to get changed into the same getup they'd worn junior year. Loose black pants, snug black T-shirts, no shoes or socks. Joe took out his makeup bag to do some quick eyeliner for them both, adding some glittery blue shadow to make it pop. He insisted on a little blush but relented on the lipstick. They'd studied an old video of their performance to get all these details right. Now, as they looked at each other, the lights already hot onstage just a few feet away, it really felt like they'd traveled back in time. Joe had more stubble now, a better haircut. MC stood a little straighter. Cracked her knuckles.

"Ready?" he said.

"As ready as I'll ever be."

He grabbed her hands and grinned. "Love you."

"Love you too."

They headed out onto the stage and took their positions at opposite ends. Dipped their chins, gathering themselves as Joe queued the music on his phone. When the track came on, full of reverb on the giant speakers, the beat led them in like a ticking clock.

Joe, of course, had been the one to get obsessed with Massive Attack. It fit the brooding vibe he'd been going for junior year. Hardly anyone at their school had heard of them. When it came time to choose a song for the talent show performance, "Teardrop" seemed almost too perfect—fresh and retro all at once. Most importantly, the beat was slow enough that, as complete amateurs, Joe and MC could actually dance to it.

Now she realized how spot-on Joe's taste had been. As the steady heartbeat rhythm of the song filled the theater, they moved through complementary gestures of cheesy agony, until the heavy entrance of piano chords began to draw them together.

At first, MC tried not to think about Nora watching her. In high school, that had been her mantra—forget that anyone is watching—which only made her that much more self-conscious. Now she tried to change tactics. To feel Nora's eyes on her in the darkness. She swept her arms toward Joe, twisting through one of Jim McDade's mom's elaborate pirouettes.

They swirled together, broke apart. Not every step was perfect, as MC had hoped, but they always managed to find the rhythm again, the repetitive bass line and gentle vocals leaving room for stray movements.

Halfway through the piece, MC could feel herself loosening up. It was kind of fun, dancing around with her best friend on an empty stage, an old hit bringing back memories of how seriously they'd taken themselves as teenagers. They still took themselves seriously, of course. But back then they'd cared about expressing it. Getting into writing, or dance, or any of the arts had seemed cool in and of itself—but so much of the appeal, MC realized now, was just in having an outlet. A shape for all the insane feelings churning through their bodies.

No wonder it made them cringe to look back on it. What they thought was so well-masked had been naked the whole time, obvious to anyone who bothered to look.

That was the thing about getting older. Things didn't get easier, but they got easier to hide.

Except it was stifling, the effort of maintaining all that armor. The opposite of how MC felt now, dipping Joe in her arms, then letting him dip her in turn. Like they were free again.

The music pared back as it came to a close, the piano dropping, then the percussion, and finally the bass. MC and Joe finished with their backs pressed together. They held the pose for a few seconds after the track cut out, just as Jim's mom had instructed them to.

Then they stepped apart for a bow.

A full decade ago, in this very auditorium, they'd been met with a cavernous silence. Hundreds of suburban teenagers staring blankly back at them, confused by five straight minutes of UK trip hop and interpretive dance. It still hurt to remember the muffled laughter that broke out just before the clapping finally started. Even if that clapping eventually built to an applause, MC and Joe had known that their performance wasn't being cheered.

It was just the weirdness of it—the delight of something random, inexplicable, freakish. They'd curled up in Joe's bedroom later that night and watched back-to-back movies just to stop themselves from crying. As it turned out, neither of them was strong enough to handle scrutiny, like real artists would.

Nora gave them a standing ovation.

Joe pulled MC against his side and rubbed her shoulder. The clapping gave way to a wolf whistle, the smile back on Nora's face once again. MC sighed.

Then she and Joe hopped off the stage.

"Were we low-key dance prodigies or what?" Joe said, shaking his hips.

"Honestly," Nora said, "it's even better than I remembered."

"S. K. Smith approves."

MC wiped a hand across her forehead. She was still sweating from the lights, the movement, the nerves. But the way Nora was looking at her in that moment made it all worth it.

"Wish I could stick around and bask in the adoration," Joe said, thumbs flying across his phone, "but Nico's almost here."

"You're leaving?" MC said, not exactly disappointed, but missing him already all the same.

"He wants to see my eye shadow. In private."

"Leave us the keys," Nora said. "We'll lock up."

Joe handed them over, then gave MC a final hug. "Dream team," he said.

"Always."

He let go and winked at Nora. "Be good, girlies."

Then he sauntered up the aisle, leaving MC and Nora alone.

They stared at each other.

"Just so you know," MC blurted, "this was not about me trying to get you to change your mind."

"I know."

"I had just remembered you asking about a reprise or whatever."

"I know, MC."

"And I thought—not that it was a going-away present, exactly. More of a parting gesture."

"It was perfect."

MC blew out a breath. "Okay, good."

"I wouldn't mind learning some of those moves myself." Nora hoisted herself onto the stage.

MC scrambled after her. "Which ones?"

"The ones where you guys were rubbing up on each other."

MC laughed.

"I actually hate dancing," Nora added. "I just like watching you do it."

"I'm surprised."

"Why?"

"I don't know, you're so body confident."

Nora squinted up into the stage lights and said, "That doesn't apply to dance." When her eyelids fell, MC saw her gaze linger on MC's mouth.

MC cleared her throat. "Can I ask you a question?"

Nora raised an eyebrow. "I don't know, can you?"

"I'd like to take you to the airport tomorrow."

She stiffened.

"It would mean a lot to me," MC said in a rush, "saying goodbye for real."

"You do know I plan to continue talking to you when I'm gone."

"I know."

Nora pursed her lips. "Is it embarrassing that I'm worried I might lose my will? If you're there."

"Not at all." MC kissed her. "I promise to shove you on the plane." Another kiss. "And if you use your jiujitsu on me or whatever, I'll just bike you cross-country."

Nora kissed her back. "You," she said, "are a kookaburra."

38

A month after Nora had left, MC and Conrad stood in the doorway of MC's old room. Where the guest bed had been, there was now a crib, puffy clouds on the sheets. A mobile with baby stuffed animals hung over it. The dresser had been replaced with a changing table, its drawers stuffed with several sizes of diapers. Baby lotion, a pack of wet wipes, and a neat stack of burp cloths waited patiently on top.

The rug had been changed out, too, the beaten-down navy shag that'd been there since MC's adolescence rolled up and chucked in the basement. Now the floor looked bright and cheerful with a patterned, all-wool spread that Conrad had spent a small fortune on. He'd gotten the matching curtains, too, which had been a lot harder to hang than MC had anticipated.

"Do you think she'll like it?" he said, nibbling his lower lip.

"Definitely."

"It's not too basic?"

"It's . . . for a baby."

"You know what I mean."

"I think it looks happy."

"Does Gabby want happy?"

"I feel like every parent wants happy for their kid."

He gritted his teeth. "We still need to do the rocking chair."

The box was out in the garage. When Conrad turned on the overhead light, MC was amazed by the size of it. It was like he'd ordered a new fridge. "That better not be as heavy as it looks," she said.

"It's not."

It was. They had to cut the box on the spot and lug the chair to the room in pieces—base, arms, backrest. This was no ordinary rocking chair, but an electric recliner swivel-glider.

"You went all out," MC huffed, trying to help Conrad get the base in just the right spot. Apparently, placing it in the corner would've been too straightforward. Conrad claimed they had to factor in the degree of recline vis-à-vis the proximity of the walls, as well as how to keep the stupid thing level on account of it resting partly on the high-pile carpet and partly on the wood floor.

"Gabby's doing the hard part," he said. "I'm just trying to help with a few details."

"I think she would've been fine with, like, a beanbag chair."

"A beanbag chair?" His face darkened. "We have no idea what condition she'll be in after she gives birth. C-sections take six weeks or longer to recover from. Even if it's a vaginal delivery, she'll almost certainly have hemorrhoids."

"Okay, thank you, I get it."

He folded his arms across his chest. "Bringing a child into this world is intense, MC."

"Fine, but bringing a child into this baby paradise shouldn't be."

"It's not paradise," he grumbled, plopping down on the half-finished chair and almost tipping himself out of it. The swivel had a much greater range of motion than MC would've guessed.

She tried to soften her voice. "Of course it is."

The due date was only a few weeks away, but the stress of Gabby's insistence on staying with her parents had turned

Conrad moody. MC wasn't in the best place herself. The brave rush she'd felt in sending Nora off to LA had fizzled within the span of a few hours, leaving her tearful in the car when she'd gotten back home, and sleepless in the nights that followed. To top it all off, the anniversary of their dad's death had been the day before, giving the house an air of solemnity that bordered on haunting.

Now Conrad was throwing himself into the nursery, like MC had been throwing herself into *Explorations*, and communication had gone by the wayside. As usual.

"I know what I did was bad," he said. "But I don't understand how she's still so pissed at me."

"It's probably going to take years for her to really move on."

He scratched his stubble. "So, we'll screw this baby up with our problems the second they're out of the womb."

"Isn't that what everyone does?" He shot her a look. "This kid is going to be able to survive your BS, I promise."

"How do you know?"

"Because as BS goes, it's not that bad."

"You just said it'll take *years* for Gabby to move on."

"But the baby's not going to know about any of it."

"What about when they get older? Will we tell them about it then? Or never say anything?" He got up. "What if somehow they figure it out?" He spun the mobile. "They just . . . hate me forever?"

"You don't owe them every detail of your relationship."

"This is kind of a big one."

"It is right now. But hopefully in the long run it won't be."

He shook his head. "This isn't how I wanted to do things."

"What do you mean?"

"I mean my life. This isn't how I wanted to do it."

MC nodded. "I'm sure most people feel that way at a certain point."

"That's basically what Mom said to me."

"Really?"

"She said everyone makes mistakes, and those mistakes have real consequences for other people, and that's why I'm right to feel freaked out about becoming a parent."

MC laughed. "She's so intense."

"She's right, though."

"I'm sure that wasn't the only thing she said to you."

"She said I have to accept it. That everything I do won't always be good, and it won't always be enough, but I have to go on. I have to keep trying."

MC paused, thinking about Nora. Their calls had dwindled over the weeks since she'd left. Even their texts had turned superficial—a joke about the writers' room, a picture of the crappy, rock-strewn beach along the Green Hills rail trail. Suddenly their lives had nothing in common, and MC was starting to wonder if it was worth continuing to hold out, to buy tickets to visit in some last-ditch effort, or if it was better to just leave well enough alone.

Conrad, of course, had already been through the existential questions with her a hundred times.

"I think," she said finally, "you're going to do better than you expect."

He smirked. "What makes you say that?"

"Instinct."

"But haven't you gone through life being annoyed at me, like, the whole time?"

"Yeah. But being annoyed by someone doesn't mean you don't think they're great. It doesn't mean you don't love them."

Conrad stared at her. "Fair enough."

"And I'm sure Mom knows what she's talking about and all. But she's leaving out the good stuff. The normal, nondramatic stuff—the stuff where sometimes you do a great job and that also has real consequences. Like how you were mad at me about lying to you, but still let me move back in with you, for months, and never complained. Even though I blocked you out for a long time before that."

"This is your house too. It's been good for me, having you around. Especially since you don't think I was a hundred percent evil for what I did to Gabby."

"It was pretty rough, but you're making up for it. Plus, you ended up writing most of my grad school applications for me, so thanks for that."

He smiled. "Have you told Nora about St. John's?"

MC had been accepted into a teaching program in Queens. She had, in fact, texted Nora about it, and Nora had replied to the news with congratulatory emojis and a string of hearts. But that was it. MC was reasonably confident she was happy for her, just like she was probably happy for herself, going their separate ways toward self-actualization, or whatever they were supposed to be striving for. It still hurt.

"I told her," MC said.

"And?"

"That's it. I don't know." She collapsed in the electric swivel rocker-glider thing and almost went flying. "I'm starting to think whatever we had was temporary."

"Didn't seem temporary when it was happening."

"And then it ended anyway." She got up and wandered over to her window, which looked out on the driveway. She stared at the rucked-up gravel, spring weeds running rampant, and thought about the way growing things broke apart solid things all the time. "Yesterday I was thinking about how Dad was just, like, building some cabinets when he died. The same boring old job he had to do all the time. He was probably thinking about nothing, or what he wanted for lunch. And meanwhile there were all these loose ends, all this stuff that, deep down, he wanted to fix, or change, or whatever—and all of a sudden, it was just . . . over." She sniffed. "It just feels like there's so much in life you don't get to choose."

Conrad came over to stand next to her. Looked out the window too. Then he threw his arm across her shoulders in a sporty way, like he was back on the basketball team, and she was somehow also on it. "Dad dying," he said, "has nothing to do with you and Nor Dog getting back together." He shook her a little. "But nice try."

She leaned her head against his shoulder. "It sounded so good, though."

"You're better with words than you give yourself credit for. But as your big bro, I'm not easily fooled."

"I just really miss her." MC was appalled to feel tears gathering at the corners of her eyes.

"I know."

"Do you think she's done with me?"

"No idea." He rubbed her shoulder. "But if she is, she'll be missing out."

39

"And who can say what foul combination spurred that intestinal distress? The pepperoni, the half-baked cookie, the two Red Bulls I chugged to impress?" Ben's cheeks were pink under his patchy attempt at a beard. "But one thing remained clear to me, 'pon my final attempt to flush: All bad things pass, at times the worst all in a rush."

The senior common area erupted in cheers. Everyone at the fifteen café-style tables got to their feet, thumping their hands together, howling for more from the Bathroom Bard of Green Hills High. "The Dump I Did Take," as it turned out, was the Poem of the Year in this edition of *Explorations*. MC had a feeling there would be more recitations at the after-party. Luckily, the theoretical grown-ups in attendance—MC, Joe, Gabby, and Conrad—were not invited.

But it was nice to be at the official portion of the evening. Sheila had gone all out, turning the small area, with its black-and-white-checked floor, into a coffeehouse. There were electric candles on the tables, and little cups of espresso and hot chocolate for sale at a makeshift bar in the back. The presentation area was on the other end, with a faux-stone wall for backdrop and a mic stand placed in the center of three overlapping rugs. MC had made a few remarks to start the night off, complimenting the students on their intellectual intensity and telling them she'd been honored to work with them; she hoped everyone who'd gathered to hear their stories and poems—a crowd of nearly sixty—knew what a feat it was to not only write, but take feedback, revise, and present that writing to an audience of listeners known and unknown.

From there they'd followed the table of contents. Each student took a turn up at the mic, with a few other interludes from various members about the art and photography featured in the pages of the magazine. Ben, as the most popular presenter, had been in the final slot. Now, as he stepped into the arms of his comrades, MC wondered if she should get back up and make some closing speech. She'd dressed up a bit for the occasion, just like the students, in dark jeans and a little black jacket, her curls gathered in a neat ponytail. She'd finally gotten a haircut the week before. Not for the occasion, but on the off chance that a new look might help her move on from mourning Nora. Unfortunately, the look had no effect on her depression. It did, however, remove a shocking amount of dead ends, and reconnected her with yet another old high school friend, who'd recently come out of cosmetology training.

Before MC could head back up to the mic, Heather beat her to it.

"Most of you have probably already figured this out," she said, her sequined button-down sparkling in the low lights, "but we had some help this year from a few alumni." People whistled. "To thank them, we'd like to invite them to share their work from when they were students, which can be found in this rare edition of *Explorations*."

To MC, Joe, and Gabby's horror, Heather held up a copy of their old magazine, grinning wickedly.

"Where did they get that?" Joe whispered.

Gabby was already glaring at Conrad, who was literally rubbing his hands together.

The crowd was cheering again.

"I'm not going first," Joe said, crossing his arms and leaning back in his chair.

MC was about to sacrifice herself when Gabby got up, drawing a fresh wave of applause.

"Just so you know," she said, grabbing the mic like she did this all the time, "I may have been the only person in our whole grade who had a sense of irony." She opened the magazine and searched for her piece. "Let's just pretend that's what this is."

With one hand on her belly, the other on the magazine, she launched into a caper about a posse of hyperintelligent turkey vultures. The hideous, oversize birds had been infamous nuisances in the school parking lot back in their day. From the peals of laughter the story got now, it seemed they were still well-known. Gabby's story was so absurd it bordered on genius at times. It was a side of Gabby that MC had completely forgotten about. When she looked over at her brother, smiling and shaking his head as one of the lead turkey vultures prepared to remove his own feathers in a political demonstration, she realized he'd forgotten about it too.

"Was there anything worse than the sight of its puckered flesh?" Gabby said with great feeling. "But even in his ugliness, Roxanne loved him, and sheltered him under her wings."

Gabby, like Ben, received a standing ovation.

Unfortunately for MC and Joe, there was little irony or absurdism to hide behind in their own work. Joe recited a poem cycle in the style of Shakespeare's Dark Lady sonnets, while MC read a short story about a tense relationship between two sisters living, for some reason, in Idaho—a thinly veiled attempt to cast judgment on her brother. At least the students were gracious with their applause.

She was about to encourage the audience to stay for drinks, as they had the commons for another hour before they needed to clean up. But before she could get the announcement out, she saw people's heads turning toward the back of the room.

"Hi, everyone," Ms. Kim said. She was standing alone at the bar. "Reading night has always been my favorite tradition here—don't tell the basketball team—and this is probably the best one I've seen in my time at Green Hills High." Most people were smiling. But Gabby had gone rigid in her seat, Conrad staring down into his lap and jiggling his knee.

"Anyway, I wanted to congratulate all of you, current students and alumni, on your accomplishment. I feel honored to get to share it with you, as this will be one of my final weeks here."

Murmurs rippled through the crowd. Conrad finally looked up but didn't seem surprised.

"I've been offered a teaching position in the city," she said. "As much as it pains me to say goodbye to all of you, I think administration isn't exactly my calling. The district is still determining your next principal, but in the meantime, I wanted to say that this year, while difficult at times, has also been extremely rewarding. I'll miss all of you." She smiled, though it looked forced. "Who's ready to party?"

Someone started a slow clap, which built into a decent roar, everyone getting to their feet. MC couldn't help sneaking glances at Conrad and Gabby, who were pointedly not looking at each other.

People started to get up in a flurry of scraping chairs. In the blink of an eye, a line formed at the bar. Knots of students gathered around tables or up at the mic, talking and laughing, paging through copies of the magazine. The electric candlelight was entrancing, twinkling off glasses and the big windows overlooking the garden beds. But MC felt unexpectedly detached from it all, an emptiness in her chest as Joe told her he was getting up for an espresso. She knew she should go with him. Stretch her legs, shake off the funk. But some powerful inertia had taken hold of her, pinning her to her seat.

"Hey!" Heather announced. MC looked up to find her standing on a chair at the neighboring table. "Hang on!" The chatter faded. "We still have one last reader."

Everyone shifted, looking around, until it became clear that the final author was coming in through the back entryway.

There was a scattered applause as she walked, back straight, jaw tight, toward the mic.

MC stared.

Nora's hair was swept back in a clip, eyeliner dark, cheeks drained of color. When she stepped up on the carpets, she stared out at the crowd with a look of complete terror.

She cleared her throat. "Can someone pass me the old magazine?"

Joe brought her his copy, and MC noticed that Lois, Helen, and Maureen had squeezed into one of the entryways near the stage. Maureen was filming on her phone. Helen looked vaguely confused. Lois was beaming.

MC tried not to gape.

The silence deepened as Nora cleared her throat once more. A few other people had taken their phones out to record whatever was about to go down. But Nora didn't shy away from the attention.

"This," she said, "is called 'On the Look You Give (Before Turning Away).'"

The whole room—Joe and Gabby and Conrad, Jae and Lois and Helen and Maureen, Heather and Sheila and Patrick and Ben—seemed to take a breath with her.

But MC was still frozen.

"It's weird," Nora said. "String lights in a dark room . . . make me think of you."

She coughed. The mic buzzed with feedback. Everyone winced until it stopped.

"The tacky charm," she went on. "The warm glow. I would like to lie with you, in a dark room like that, under string lights."

She took a shaky breath before continuing.

"See the parts of you that catch color. Blue wrist. Green brow."

She looked up from the page, at MC, then back down.

"I would kiss you first—this is a dream, right?—give in to red wanting. Wrap my legs in yours and squeeze, the soft edges of our arms running parallel." She pressed her lips together. "My breath in your ear would sound like yellow, your nose would be tipped yellow . . . in the lights."

One last, deep breath, and every eye in the room was moving between Nora and MC.

"Sometimes I am so sure you want this, too, because of a look you give, before turning away. And you wouldn't even think I'd write poems—I don't, except for ones about you. It's just the way my hands itch when that look passes, my only consolation the perfect line of your neck."

A drop of sweat rolled down her temple.

"That's it. Thanks."

Nora stepped away from the mic.

Heather got up first, whistling and thundering her hands together. Sheila, Ben, and Patrick were right behind her, along with Joe and Gabby, shouting Nora's name as they clapped. Conrad shook MC's shoulders. Lois and Maureen snapped their fingers. And suddenly everyone in the room was going wild, the way they had when MC had read the poem herself ten years ago. For a second it felt like the echo went both ways, the past and the present switching places.

MC was the last to rise, her cheeks burning, her heart hammering against her ribs. Nora kept her chin tucked despite all the admiration. The edges of her ears had gone crimson.

Conrad stood up to offer Nora his seat, sparing her any more attention by issuing a command in his best vice-principal voice: "Students and staff of Green Hills High, you may resume partying!"

And they did.

Eventually, MC turned to Nora, freshly shocked to find her sitting there. But when she'd recovered, she reached under the table. Put her hand in Nora's lap.

"I don't even know where to start," she said softly.

Nora stared back at her with that stern, focused look of hers. "Do you want to get some air?"

MC stood up and pulled Nora to her feet, then led them out of the crowded commons, away from the stares, into the dim of the hall. They walked deeper into the school, flanked by lockers, taking one turn, then another. In the silence, with so many lights off, MC could really believe the place hadn't changed in a decade. That every last one of them—she and Nora, and Joe and Gabby and Conrad, and even Jen Turner and Nico Price and Jim McDade and Jerry Bickley—had never left. Linoleum floor. The scent of lemon antiseptic. The whir of air ducts and the intermittent red of emergency lights. All of it gave off a strange, homey feeling. Comforting and stifling all at once.

Nora finally stopped and leaned back against the lockers.

"You were really good up there," MC said.

Nora grimaced. "You were right."

"About what?"

"It's hard to recite sensual poetry."

MC wanted to reach out and touch her, hold her close and kiss her, but she kept herself in check. "I still can't believe you're here."

"Me neither. Turns out I really don't like writing scripts."

Silence stretched between them.

MC struggled to make herself speak. "Did you . . . quit?"

"I shifted into an advisory role. Technically."

"Whoa."

"Don't worry, everyone was relieved about it."

"Is that why I hardly heard from you? Because you weren't happy?"

Nora nodded.

MC couldn't help laughing. "You could've just told me that!"

"It took me a while to admit it to myself. You were next on the list."

"I thought we're supposed to be good at this kind of thing now."

"Can't we just appreciate that the cycle of foolishness is getting shorter?"

"Fine." MC pursed her lips. "So . . . what happens next?"

Nora pulled her in at last. MC felt a rush in her chest, desire and something more complicated. Nora ran her hands from MC's waist up to her shoulders, then over her neck to her jaw.

"I don't know," Nora said. "You've made me into a crazy person."

MC felt feverish under her touch, a month of brooding like kindling in her gut. "Same."

"I don't want to be apart from you anymore."

"Sounds good to me." The lockers made a rattling sound as MC pressed against her, needing Nora as close as possible. "But are you sure I wouldn't be wrecking your self-growth and stuff?"

"I have no idea."

"Where are you staying?"

"Lois's attic. You?"

"I'm still crashing at Conrad's. Figured I'd commute to school."

"Look at us, moving up in the world." Nora's hips moved a little, the lockers rattling again. She tilted her face, brought their mouths close, but hesitated at the last second, narrowing her eyes. "I think people are going to put videos of me reading that poem to you on the internet."

MC leaned forward, kissing Nora's neck. "Probably."

"Also, the *Girl Next Door* script is definitely going into production. They've already found a distributor."

"That's cool." MC brushed her lips against Nora's, then lightly caught Nora's lower lip between her teeth. "Who's going to play us?"

Nora sealed their mouths together, kissed her hard. "I don't really care," she said. "Do you?"

ACKNOWLEDGMENTS

First and foremost, thanks to you, reader, for picking this up.

Thanks to my family, whose love and support are why *Girl Next Door* exists at all. From encouraging me to write when I was a kid to watching my own kids so I could get writing done, you kept the faith. I couldn't be more grateful. To my dad for setting me on the path. To Mom for only wanting me to do this insofar as it makes me happy—and letting me define happiness even when my judgment was questionable. To Rich for reminding me that persistence can be heroic. To Ave for everything, but especially for being real. What I know about humor, I know from you. To Morgan for being the secret genius reader of my work for nearly ten years. I don't think anyone has ever been so lucky to get such a sister-in-law.

To Orawan for space to work in peace, and for new friendship. To my whole New Haven community; I knew it would be home from the second I arrived.

To Brian for values. I hope you got a kick out of this.

To Erika for being the best of the best and a beta reader extraordinaire. To Andrea for bringing invaluable rom-com expertise and making brilliant suggestions about Joe. To Kate for the final sendoff, and a phenomenal catch. Also to Alwa: there would be no MC without the worm inside. To Janet, Mary, and the old Headless crew for lessons on how much fun a literary magazine can be. And to the teachers and students of Clarion West's class of 2018 for a serious education in craft.

To Cristina for thoughts on Gabby, and gainful employment.

To Jaya, real-life next-door neighbor and best friend since kindergarten. I don't know how we got through high school, but I know I was wearing a dragon sweatshirt and you were wearing velour sweatpants. The bird clock's for you.

To public libraries and the amazing, important people who work there. Unsurprisingly, being a page was my first job as a teenager, and remains the best. Much of this book was written or revised in public libraries.

To Katy Nishimoto for being the first advocate for this book.

To Ashley Herring Blake for providing such a lovely early blurb.

To Rebecca Podos, most excellent agent. Getting an email from you was one of the coolest moments of my life. You're a consummate professional in several capacities, and I'm so excited for your next book. Also to Jamie Carr, for the first years.

To Sophia Kaufman, editor of my dreams. Literally! I was napping when Becca left me a voicemail that you'd read my manuscript and wanted to talk. I feel unbelievably lucky to have been noticed by such a smart, subtle, and rigorous mind. This book improved in countless and immeasurable ways under your guidance. And to the entire Harper Perennial team—copyeditor Carol Burrell, proofreader Katie Shepherd, production editorial manager Stacey Fischkelta, designer Jamie Kerner, marketing director Lisa Erickson, publicists Heather Drucker and Nicole Sklitsis, production supervisor Michael Fierro, and cover designer Oliva McGiff—thank you!

Lastly, to Caitlin—this whole thing is for you, and because of you. Where would I be if you hadn't struck up a conversation with me when I was wearing a fake mustache? I still can't believe you spent the next decade enduring and sacrificing so I could pursue something this insane, but even if you hadn't, I'd still feel like the luckiest person on the planet just to know you. I love you and the girls so much.

ABOUT THE AUTHOR

Rachel Meredith has been writing something or other her entire life. Born in New York City, raised on Long Island, and now a New Havener, she spends her days as a copy editor and proofreader, where she's able to put her English degree to use on all sorts of grammatical minutiae. When she's not lost in a book, she's hanging out with her wife and their two wonderful daughters.